Praise for *Sapphire Trails*

"In *Sapphire Trails*, the electricity is high, the energy potent, and the plot charged with excitement, suspense, and intrigue! Once again, author Marilyn Jax creatively and meticulously weaves two plot lines with so many twists, turns, and surprises, it leaves the reader glued to the page from start to finish. Marilyn Jax keeps penning these five-star novels."

— **Fran Lewis, author, New York reviewer, educator**

"Delightfully suspenseful story. *Sapphire Trails* by Marilyn Jax is one of those books that readers will speed through yet wish for more after the ending. All the scenes are active, and there are enough sequels between the scenes to (barely) give readers a chance to catch their breath before diving into another nail-biting scene."

— **Judge, Writer's Digest Book Awards**

"Unlike many mysteries on the market, Jax has written one whose correct solution is difficult to guess before the case is actually solved. It isn't until the final pages that the solution becomes clear, providing exactly the kind of entertainment expected of a good mystery."

— *US Review of Books*

"A truly riveting read that captures the reader's total attention from beginning to end. *Sapphire Trails* clearly identifies Marilyn Jax as an experienced and singularly gifted novelist who will leave her readers eagerly looking toward her next literary effort. A solid entertainment from first page to last, *Sapphire Trails* is highly recommended for personal reading lists and community library collections."

— *Midwest Book Review*

Praise for *Road to Omalos*

"Jax expertly weaves this gripping narrative from the opening paragraph. Meticulously drawn details entice and enthrall, consistently employing the five senses to bring her literary vision vividly to life. Vibrantly depicted characters often struggle with conscience as they vacillate between virtue and obligation, in an array of interlacing subplots that serve to enhance this spellbinding tale."

—*US Review of Books*

"Marilyn Jax has done it again! The suspense, interplay, and conflict between the characters will keep the reader on edge right up to the brilliant, unexpected, and explosive ending. A Greek thriller!"

—Dr. Thomas Rumreich, forensic odontologist

Praise for *The Find*

"*The Find* is a gripping suspenseful murder mystery from beginning to end. Modern criminology is joined with Aztec history to solve a murder decades old and to give flesh and narrative to a skeleton found beneath the rubble. Throughout the novel, there is much to uncover. Written in a crisp style, *The Find* is quite a find!"

—Michael Berenbaum, author, lecturer

"From the Caribbean to Miami to London and back, the plot has more twists than even the most addicted mystery buff can handle. Just when you think you've solved the case, a new suspect takes you in another direction. Marilyn Jax has written a thriller that will keep you guessing to the very end."

—Ron Meshbesher, past president of the National Association of Criminal Defense Lawyers

ALSO BY MARILYN JAX

The Find

Road to Omalos

Sapphire Trails

. . . and watch for *The Ploy*

NEVER IN INK

a novel

NEVER IN INK

a novel

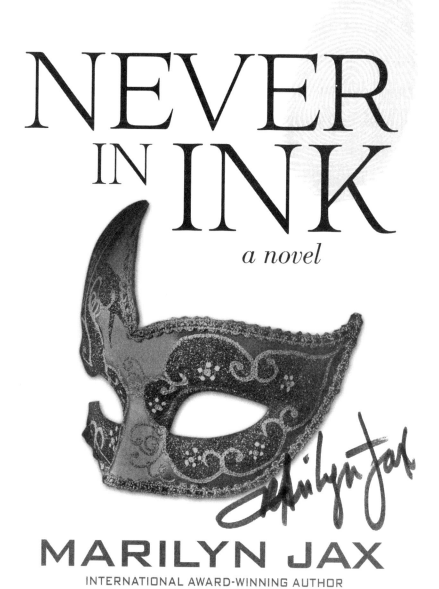

MARILYN JAX

INTERNATIONAL AWARD-WINNING AUTHOR

ISBN 13: 978-1-59298-921-8

Library of Congress Catalog Number: 2014910731

Printed in the United States of America

First Printing: 2014

18 17 16 15 14   5 4 3 2 1

Also available electronically.

Author photograph by Patrick Broderick.
Cover and interior design by James Monroe Design, LLC.

Beaver's Pond Press, Inc.
7108 Ohms Lane
Edina, MN 55439-2129
(952) 829-8818
www.BeaversPondPress.com

BEAVER'S
POND
PRESS

To order, visit www.BeaversPondBooks.com or call (800) 901-3480.
Reseller discounts available.

Dedicated to my adored Aunt Marjorie.

Together we share gripping conversations, trade stories, swap recipes, learn family secrets, enjoy picnics in the glorious sunshine, and recall fond memories of summers on the farm.

I love you with all my heart.

ACKNOWLEDGMENTS

I extend a heartfelt thank-you to all my readers. Without you, writing would be far less satisfying. To those who closely follow my main characters, Claire Caswell and Gaston "Guy" Lombard, they thank you as well for being interested in their development in each new tale in the Caswell & Lombard series. They look forward to keeping you intrigued in *Never in Ink* just as much as in all past novels and those yet to come.

Daniel, you've lived through the crafting of yet another novel. Thank you for always being there, and for your ever-present support and love. I return those gifts to you tenfold.

To my incredible family, friends, and fans who faithfully wait—sometimes impatiently—for each new book, your encouragement keeps me going. My heart is brimming with gratitude for each and every one of you.

And to my exceptional managing editor, Hanna Kjeldbjerg; my exceedingly talented designer, James Monroe; my marvelous editor, Wendy Weckwerth; my brilliant proofreader, Angela Wiechmann; and the staff at Beaver's Pond Press. Once again, I could not have done it without all of you. Thank you.

Finally, *Never in Ink* is a tribute to the unforgettable times I have spent in Europe. The warmth and hospitality of the peoples of Italy, Switzerland, and France will always occupy a special place among my most treasured memories.

PROLOGUE

1975
Turin, Italy

ANTONIO ROBERTO DINETTO raced after his seven-year-old sister, Esmeralda. She giggled and screamed for close to fifteen minutes as she managed to stay four giant steps ahead of her big brother. Antonio was two years older, but not as quick on his feet.

Nearly out of breath, Esmeralda called out, "Catch me! Catch me if you can!"

Just then, Mamma DiNetto poked her head out of the wood dwelling's front door and yelled out in Italian, "Come to dinner. Both of you."

Antonio and Esmeralda reluctantly obeyed. Playtime was over for another day. They rushed inside, washed their hands, and dropped into chairs on one side of the unadorned rectangular table. Carlo, who at sixteen was the oldest of the three siblings, had already situated himself on a seat across from the other two. As usual, and for no particular reason at all, whenever the trio of children exchanged glances at the dinner table, gales of laughter spontaneously erupted. This evening was no exception. A rather strange phenomenon, but it was commonplace in the home.

Tata Fabio and Mamma Bianca displayed stern expressions. Each sat firmly planted, one on each end of the simple table, as if they were anchors stabilizing a rocky boat of energetic children.

Mamma Bianca gestured to the siblings to fold their hands and bow their heads, and they did so without hesitation, each forcing a lively grin back inside with great difficulty. She uttered an Italian prayer of thanksgiving—the same prayer she recited before every family meal, all of which were long, leisurely affairs.

A medium-sized bowl of risotto, cooked in chicken broth and butter, made its way around the table, allowing all a meager portion. A plate with warm slices of bread followed minutes later. The second course, an inadequate chunk of ham cut into ultrathin slices, made the rounds about half an hour later. It proved barely enough for each family member to have a scanty taste.

As usual, the amount of food barely sated the stomachs of the growing children, and Antonio suspected his parents could have eaten a bit more as well. But they all made do with what they had. It was enough.

Tata Fabio worked hard. His family was his world, and his reputation was vital. What others thought meant everything to Fabio DiNetto. His children dressed in clean clothes at all times. And they were taught manners and respect—and knew how and when to use both.

Antonio glanced at his father and then toward his mother. Life was not easy for either of them, and their faces showed it—more lately than ever before. Even at nine years old, he knew they looked older than their actual years and too fatigued. The closer he studied his parents, the more he realized something seemed terribly wrong. They appeared tense and agitated. Yes, something was definitely in the air. He was sure of it. But what? He sensed he would soon find out, and he waited in restless anticipation.

Tata Fabio gazed at each of his children, one at a time, without uttering a word. The expression on his face was one the children hadn't seen before. He cleared his throat jarringly, and all talking and silliness abruptly ended. A deafening silence filled the room. Antonio heard loud, repeated beating sounds and soon realized it was the hard thumping of his own heart. As the seconds passed, the atmosphere reminded him of a balloon being pumped with so much air it was about to burst. He couldn't stand it much longer.

Finally, their tata spoke.

"We are moving," he said. The children darted their eyes quickly and unblinkingly to each other. "We are moving to America. To the United States of America." Tata hesitated before continuing. "Our relatives from southern Italy moved there after the war ended. Your mamma and I were teenagers when the last bombing happened in 1945. We stayed in Turin to watch over your grandparents until they died. The war was hard on them, and their lives ended too early. Your mamma and I married in our late twenties. Carlo, you were born four years after we married, then we waited several years before you, Antonio, and you, Esmeralda, were added to our family." He nodded at each child as he spoke his or her name.

"After the war ended, the automobile industry boomed here in Turin, and we saw hundreds of thousands migrate from the rural areas of southern Italy in search of jobs. Seemingly overnight, the market flooded with workers. I was sixteen, but I remember it well. The streets were overcrowded with people wherever I looked.

"But now, it's the 1970s, and things have changed once again, and this time not for the better. The thriving automobile industry has been thrown into a decline. Jobs have all but disappeared."

He paused. "I have decided to move our family to give us a fresh start. Italy has been our home, and we will always love our land. But it is time to make a new home." He looked away, refusing to meet the eyes of the stunned children. He had made up his mind. That was obvious. "We are the last of the family to make the journey toward a better future. It is our turn. The rest of our entire extended family is there now—and happy. They are waiting for us. They have started a chocolates business that is thriving. We have been invited to join them."

At first, none of the children spoke. The shock of their tata's statements reverberated in their minds.

It was Esmeralda who broke the silence. "*But why*?" she sobbed. "I don't want to leave my friends. I don't want to go." Her voice quivered as she moved from hostility to devastation.

"We are going for new opportunities," Tata Fabio said. "We are starving here. I can no longer support my family as I need to."

Antonio glanced at his mamma. Her eyes refused to allow welling tears to flow, and she maintained a rigid pose. "It is best, children. You will all go to new schools and meet new friends. You will have better opportunities for education there."

Carlo spoke. "I will not go. Italy is what I know. I will stay here."

"No. You will come with us," Tata DiNetto said. "We will go together as a family. There will be no further discussion. We leave two weeks from today. Travel arrangements have already been made by our family in America."

Antonio stared at his parents, trying desperately to gather from their nearly expressionless faces if this was what they really wanted for the family. Finally, he decided to ask the question directly. "Is this what you *want*?"

"It's what we must do, son," Fabio said.

"I don't like it," Antonio said. "Not at all." He threw his hands into the air and twisted his face into an ugly look of disgust. "As if what I want, or what my brother and sister want, matters at all." His face reddened, and he bolted from the table without being excused. He ran to the front door, yanked it open, and raced outside into the cooler air. Hot, salty tears rolled down his cheeks, and he wiped them away with the sleeve of his shirt. His world was falling apart, and he had no say in it—and no control over it. He was being forced to leave everything he knew, to relocate to a foreign country, where he didn't speak the language, didn't know the customs, had no friends, and would probably hate the food. He loved pasta. Olive oil. Parmigiano-Reggiano cheese. Balsamic vinegar. And Italian chocolates. How could he possibly give them up?

Suddenly, a wave of foreboding settled upon him like a falling mist. He couldn't shake it. This was a mistake. His family must not move to America. Something terrible was going to happen if they did. He just knew it.

He ran back inside. "Tata!" he yelled. "We have to talk about this!"

Mamma Bianca held her index finger to her lips. "Quiet, Antonio. Your tata has gone to bed. He is tired. You must not disturb him. He will not change his mind." She reached out to put her arms around her middle child and hold him close, but he pulled away and dashed from the room.

He fell into bed and cried himself to sleep.

THE NEXT morning, Tata Fabio found the lifeless body of his oldest son, Carlo, hanging from a rafter in the shed adjacent to their dwelling.

1

Office of Caswell & Lombard, Private Investigation
Miami Beach, Florida

"SOMETHING BIG IS about to go down," Sergeant Massey said. His face displayed dogged determination as he perched on the edge of his chair. "Something *huge*. My top detectives have watched a man for some time now, and they inform me he's prepping to make a major move. The man is dirty, but his business appears as clean as new-fallen snow—as far as we can tell, that is. Much too clean for a man of his character. Bottom line? We think his business is a front, but we don't know for what at this point." He paused. "That's where the two of you come in."

Private investigators Claire Caswell and Gaston "Guy" Lombard exchanged quick glances, then simultaneously returned their undivided attention to the Miami-Dade police sergeant.

"Okay. You've definitely piqued our curiosity," Claire said, leaning in closer. "Go on, please."

"Well, several days ago, out of nowhere, my officers became aware of a sudden swirl of activity surrounding the subject's establishment. That's clearly out of the ordinary, mind you, since days and weeks usually pass with no activity whatsoever at the business. My officers are sure that some kind of plan is definitely afoot. We just don't know what it is." He stopped talking and looked directly at Claire. "We need you and Lombard to shadow the subject, watch his every move for the next ten days or so, and determine what he's up to. I've convinced the department to hire your firm. Find out what you can. We've spent too much time and effort on this one to let it slip through our fingers. What do you say? I'm hoping it's yes."

"I'm confused," Claire said. She grabbed a legal pad and pen from the corner of her desk. "Why can't the department's officers and detectives handle it? Why do you need us?"

Guy, Claire's business and life partner, listened with growing interest. "Tell us more," he invited. "There has to be more to the story."

"The man we've had under surveillance is an Italian American in his late forties who resides in Miami-Dade County," the sergeant offered. "He was born in Italy, and he travels back to his home country frequently. He's suave and debonair. Cunning and sinister. Also, a ladies' man par excellence." He paused. "Always surrounds himself with women. Attractive women. And he's a manipulator to the nth degree, one of the best we've seen. Seems he can get anyone to do anything he asks."

"And?" Claire persisted, drawing out the word.

"And he lives like a self-appointed king in a large mansion on

Star Island. While the residence is in a public neighborhood, there's a guardhouse at the entrance to the area that gives the illusion of a *private* community. I'm sure you know the place."

"We do. It's one of the highest-buck neighborhoods in Miami Beach," Guy said.

"The subject owns two Ferraris—one new and the other an early model. Both very valuable. Also owns a Rolls-Royce. And as I said earlier, he travels out of the country often. A couple weeks ago, we received an untraceable anonymous tip whispered into a disposable cell phone—possibly from an enemy of his, we'll never really know—urging us to trail the man like bloodhounds. The subject was already on our watch list, and the cryptic call only raised our concern to new heights. We've learned over the years that tips of this nature often pan out.

"We know DiNetto is into something criminal. We can smell it. Our cop instincts are sending up massive red flags. He's up to no good. And whatever it is, we need to stop it in its tracks."

"Still not hearing *proof* of any illegal activities," Claire said.

"Hold on," Massey said, fidgeting in his seat. "The name of the man we're watching is Anthony DiNetto—or according to his Italian birth name, Antonio DiNetto." He passed several photographs of the man to Claire and Guy. "DiNetto boasts loudly about being in the music production business here in Miami. Claims to own a company called Magnifico Notte Music Production, Inc., in downtown Miami. *Magnifico notte* translates to 'magnificent night' or 'splendid night' in Italian. We've staked out the business for months on end, and guess what? No one—including DiNetto himself—steps foot inside the place. We peeked through the windows and saw only a single phone sitting on one desk and a file cabinet on a sidewall. That's it. No visible recording equipment. Some business, huh? Then last week, at close to midnight, a trio of men appeared out of the shadows and walked directly into the front door of the business—DiNetto and two others. One of my officers grabbed a couple shots with his cell phone, but it was dark and difficult to capture clear images of the others accompanying DiNetto. But one of the other men definitely resembles a big muckamuck in the Florida casino business." The sergeant stopped to crack his knuckles. It was a longtime habit that always annoyed Claire. "We have no proof that anything illegal went on at that meeting, but it sure as hell does not pass the smell test."

She and Guy gazed at the photos.

"How long were they inside?" Guy asked, continuing to study the pictures.

"For a while. My officer estimated close to two hours. Then the three walked out in unison, jumped into a shared cab, and sped off. Strange activity, considering the business appears to be phony. We believe the meeting had nothing to do with DiNetto's business. We think it might have been a meeting about finances—perhaps a loan to DiNetto to fund some scam."

"Does the business file income tax returns?" Claire asked.

"It does," the sergeant said. "We checked that out right away. Claims to make a fair income each year. And the corporation always pays its annual taxes—and on time. So neither the Florida Department of Revenue nor the IRS complains. We could have busted the pretend business right away, but instead we decided to wait and watch, to see what we could learn. We want the real story."

"Okay. And how exactly can our firm help, Sergeant Massey?" Claire asked.

"I'm getting to that," he said. "You see, we just learned that DiNetto is planning to leave the country in three days. We want the two of you to follow him—to watch and record his every move and activity. You'll stay in the background and find out what he's hiding."

"When you say he plans to leave the country, where exactly is he traveling?" Guy asked.

"First to Italy, with a side trip to Switzerland, and then on to France. He'll be gone a total of eleven days, including travel," the sergeant said. "And get this—the man's actually made arrangements with FedEx to fly his new Ferrari over the pond to drive while he's there—his F12berlinetta. It's quite the vehicle. It has a Grigio Silverstone exterior and a Rosso red leather interior with matching red seatbelts and full electric seat ventilation to heat and cool the two front seats. We've done our homework. It's got a V12 engine and privacy rear windows. The price tag comes in at over half a million dollars."

"You're kidding, right?" Claire asked, looking astonished. "He's flying his half-a-million-dollar Ferrari over to Europe using FedEx?"

"FedEx does that?" Guy asked.

"No, I'm not kidding, and yes, FedEx does it," the sergeant said. "DiNetto's a man with a lot of money, and he's not afraid to spend it."

"You expect us to keep up with a Ferrari while driving a *rental* car?" Claire asked. She chuckled softly at the preposterous notion.

"Well, yes. We want you to tail him in a Fiat—a Fiat 500 Abarth, to be exact. It has a top speed of 129 miles per hour, and hopefully you'll never need to go faster than that. We'll arrange for a black one. It's a common color in the sea of small European cars, so you should blend in and hopefully go undetected. A small car will make it easier to park and maneuver around and through the always-congested traffic."

"Europe. Here we go again," Guy said. He looked at Claire with uncertain eyes, and she knew he was reflecting back on the case that took them to Crete.

"You said he leaves in three days?" Claire asked. "That's not much time to get ready."

"You shouldn't need to take much with you—probably just a duffel bag between you and a backpack each." He hesitated for a brief moment. "As you know, DiNetto is out of our jurisdiction the second he leaves Miami-Dade County. We've worked too long and hard on this one to just let it go because he leaves our sight," the sergeant said. "He needs to be watched closely, and you're just the two to do it." He bored his eyes into Claire's. "Can I count on you both? The entire Miami-Dade Police Department is depending on it." He paused, cracking his knuckles again. "And me in particular. I'm up for captain."

Claire's professional relationship with Sergeant Massey had been strained over the years. In her role as a senior investigator for the State of Florida, she'd occasionally needed to work with him on cases. Based on his past actions and comments, it had always been clear to Claire that he didn't favor women in law enforcement, and that bothered her considerably. She was a talented and savvy investigator who had earned her sterling reputation the hard way— one difficult case at a time. And the sergeant's continual oblique remarks that women should stay home and have babies stuck in her craw. But somehow, after he'd witnessed her abilities firsthand over the years, the relationship between Sergeant Massey and Claire Caswell had evolved. It certainly changed after she and Gaston Lombard—the legendary former Miami-Dade state attorney with his steel-clad reputation for being tough as nails and masterful at putting thugs behind bars—had merged their collective talents to form Caswell & Lombard, Private Investigation. Things between Claire and Sergeant Massey were less uncomfortable these days. And now they even referred work to each other, when appropriate, and called on each other for professional opinions on cases or to obtain other information from time to time.

So the fact that the sergeant had driven over to their private investigation office to ask his question in person, rather than merely picking up a telephone and making a call, spoke volumes. Claire held her chin with the thumb and index finger of her right hand and eyed the sergeant carefully, trying to surmise the particular importance of this case. Massey was a seasoned Miami-Dade police sergeant and a rough character. Over the years, he'd seen it all. Nothing rattled his nerves, and he never showed as much as a trace of emotion. He remained stoic, through and through. Today, however, sitting across from the investigators, a few beads of sweat drizzled down his forehead, and he cracked his knuckles even more than usual. His eyes darted everywhere in the room, except toward Claire.

She had her answer.

"Can we get back to you shortly?" Claire asked. "I want to talk this over with Guy before we give you our answer."

"Time is short," the sergeant warned. "Don't delay. We need to make the travel and other arrangements at once if you take the case. Get back to me soon. Today." He paused to crack his knuckles yet again. "And hang on to the photos for now."

"You'll have our answer within the hour," Guy said.

GUY AND Claire discussed the sergeant's request over cups of coffee.

"Europe again. After the case in Greece, I don't know if I'm up for it," Guy said. "I have to be honest with you."

Since the moment Sergeant Massey had mentioned Italy, Switzerland, and France, pangs of anguish had plagued Guy. Being beaten severely while working a case that had taken the sleuths to Greece and the island of Crete had left a bitter taste in his mouth. Healing had taken time, but it had happened . . . for the most part.

His remaining facial scars were the only permanent reminders of the physical injuries he sustained. But the psychological damage had been more difficult to leave behind, and those invisible internal scars were newly healed and still fragile. Solving a case in Montana more recently had helped him decide to look to the future, rather than remain stuck in the past. Personal counseling after the incident was also integral in his healing process. But now they were contemplating taking on another case that had the potential to yank those dark, horrific memories squarely back into his life—a case that might cause that still-raw pain, stowed so carefully away just beneath the surface, to gush back in a profound way. He didn't want to chance it.

"Claire, I'm not willing to take the case," he said. "And I won't talk about it further. End of discussion."

Claire looked at the man she loved. They had worked cases together back when she was a Florida state enforcement investigator and he was a Miami-Dade state attorney. She had loved him at first sight. And the feeling had been mutual. Dating had quickly turned into a torrid romance, and the two had shared a high-rise condominium in Aventura—a city in northeastern Miami-Dade County—for the past several years.

Starting a private investigation firm together had been risky, but it was something they'd both wanted. The business had mushroomed in a just short time, and now the investigators were in high demand throughout all of Miami, the state of Florida, and anywhere else their services were needed. The firm's reputation was solid, and it grew with each successful investigation. Right now they were needed in Europe, but she didn't know how to handle Guy's trepidation. She understood his concerns, but felt compelled to take the case.

"Let's think it over," Claire said. "It's a great opportunity for us.

And we're being asked only to follow the man and watch his actions. How difficult can that be? It would look great on our résumés too—a high-profile case referred to us by the Miami-Dade Police Department. And we'll get to see Italy, Switzerland, and France. We've always wanted to visit those countries."

"Claire, I get it. You want us to take the case. But what about me?" Guy asked. "I say no!"

Claire sipped her coffee. "Okay. Okay. I'll call the sergeant and say no, but I think we're making a mistake. Sometimes facing your fears head on is the only way to deal with them."

"You're not convincing me," Guy said. "Give it up, will you?"

She picked up the phone and dialed the number.

"Sergeant Massey?" she said. "I'm calling you back regarding that job offer. We've discussed it, and I'm afraid we must decline."

He sighed on the other end of the line. "I'm disappointed. I won't deny it," the sergeant said.

"I am as well," Claire said. "Thank you for thinking of us."

"If you change your minds by tomorrow morning . . . "

THE FOLLOWING day Claire got up early. She fixed a cup of steaming peppermint tea and carried it onto the balcony. As the sun started to show its glorious face, blinds began to open in apartments and condos across the way. A new Miami day was underway. It already felt hot and steamy. She sat down on an outdoor chair and sipped the tea. She badly wanted to accept the sergeant's plea for their assistance, but the firm had two partners, so it had to be a mutual decision. If Guy was dead set against it, so be it. They had agreed from the outset to only take cases they both felt strongly about, and this was clearly not one of those, at least for Guy.

The condo balcony offered a bird's-eye view of the yachts and smaller boats making their way up and down the Intracoastal Waterway. Claire's eyes followed the water vessels as they cruised under slow throttle. She never tired of the showy exhibition. Minutes drifted by.

Guy poked his head onto the balcony. "There you are. Care for some breakfast?"

"Morning, honey. Yeah, I'll be right in." She finished her tea and stepped inside. "Something smells good."

"Scrambled eggs, cinnamon toast, juice, and coffee await the lady," he said, using his aristocratic voice. "Please have a seat, and you will be served." He gestured to the kitchen table.

"Oh, you're being a silly thing this morning," Claire said, chuckling. She gave him a kiss on the cheek. His highborn act—which he used only on rare occasions—always amused her.

"How did you sleep, m'lady?" Guy asked.

"Not well. I kept thinking about the case we turned down. How about you?"

"Not great either." Guy's tone turned serious. "I want you to call Sergeant Massey back and tell him we've changed our minds. Tell him we'll take the case. It's the right thing to do."

Claire tried to speak, but words wouldn't come—at first, anyway.

"Are you sure?" she finally blurted out with abundant excitement in her eyes. "I don't want you to feel pressured in any way. We'll take the case only if it's something you really want to do. We have plenty of other files to keep us busy."

"I'm sure," Guy affirmed. "Call him as soon as we finish breakfast, and break the news."

Claire smiled. "I do love you."

AT 8:00 a.m. sharp, she made the call.

"We'll take the case," Claire told him. "We've given it more thought. It will be our absolute pleasure to assist the Miami-Dade Police Department, sir."

"Excellent. Then it's settled," the sergeant said. He didn't seem surprised. "We'll make all the arrangements on this end for the two of you to coincide with DiNetto's itinerary. Tomorrow, I'll drop off your airline tickets for each leg of the trip, an address with directions to where you'll pick up the Fiat when you land, a copy of the full itinerary, two global cell phones, two credit cards for all expenses, and plenty of euros. I'll also make sure there's a sealed envelope waiting for you when you pick up the rental car. It will contain other information you'll need to shadow DiNetto, including additional photos of him, known haunts, et cetera. Watch everything the man does, and call me with periodic updates while you're away. I want you to uncover the tiniest details of his life. Find his secrets."

"I understand."

"Keep a low profile over there," Sergeant Massey warned. "No police should be involved. You're Americans, and this is an American citizen you're following. It's a US investigation. Italy doesn't need to be involved. Nor does Switzerland or France. Remember that. Oh, and one more thing," Sergeant Massey continued. "Remember that DiNetto is a ladies' man. He tends to surround himself with female company, and women love being around him. They claim he's irresistible. Watch out, Ms. Caswell. Don't get too close and fall into his web. Keep a safe distance."

"Of course," Claire said. "I understand completely."

"I'll drop by your office tomorrow, then." Through the phone she heard him crack his knuckles loudly. "And Ms. Caswell, you and Mr. Lombard should be prepared for anything on this investigation. Anything at all. None of us can predict what might come up over there. You'll have to go with the flow and improvise as necessary. Do whatever needs to be done to get results. Don't worry about the cost. Use the credit cards I'll give you. And bring along plenty of disguises. You'll probably use them all."

"THE PLAN is hatching," Claire said, turning her attention back to Guy. "We're all set. Let's get our files in order so we're ready to leave." She pushed her chair back, stood up, and walked over to Guy. "But first I want to thank you for being courageous. You're my rock."

2

"THERE'S SOMETHING ELSE," Claire said. She dropped her body back into the chair. "I think we should hire an assistant for our firm. It's really overdue. And I'd like to do it before we leave. That way, if anything crops up with our cases while we're away, our assistant can either let us know or—better yet—handle the matter for us."

"Whoa. Slow down. This is sudden," Guy said. A furrow dented his brow. "I've never thought about adding someone else to the mix."

"Actually, I've been thinking about it for a while," Claire said. "We can afford an assistant now, and if the person is skilled in computer forensics and technology, he or she could actually be a great asset."

Guy pondered her words. "I guess I *would* feel more comfortable leaving for a time if someone was manning the fort." He paused. "Yeah, I think I like the idea. Maybe even a lot." He nodded slightly.

"My thoughts exactly. I'll contact the law school at the University of Miami to see if any students come to mind when I describe what we're looking for. Perhaps a bright student who excels in the study of criminal law? I'm thinking it should be a part-time job, at least for now. The person could answer the phones and conduct online research when we need information. And whenever things are slow, the assistant could use the time to study. Sound like a plan?"

"It does. But we leave in three days," Guy said. "Can we get it done before we leave?"

"I hope so," Claire said. "I'll make the call."

MINUTES LATER, Claire reported back. "The dean of students suggested three candidates. They're all *brilliant*, according to her, and are seeking part-time employment. She agreed to send them over this afternoon, scattered between 1:00 and 4:00 p.m. That way we can interview all three and make an informed decision."

THAT AFTERNOON the sleuths interviewed the students. The first two were highly impressive and articulate, but it was the third interviewee who sped to the top of the list in the estimation of both Claire and Guy. Jin Ikeda left the other worthy candidates in a trail of dust. There was something about him. Something special. He seemed the perfect fit. They offered the job to the twenty-four-year-old on the spot.

JIN WAS raised in an American family of Japanese descent. His parents were medical doctors associated with the Mount Sinai hospital in Miami Beach. He had a willowy frame, and he wore round, rimless eyeglasses that, with the help of perfectly placed brows, intensified his dark, polished eyes. For the interview he'd dressed impeccably in an ice-blue cotton shirt, charcoal-gray slacks, and a Burberry burgundy-striped tie. He pulled his straight raven hair back into a short ponytail.

Along with an instantly likable personality, the law student was bilingual in English and Japanese. He showed a native speaker's command of the English language as he answered Claire's and Guy's questions, and he came across as sincere, polite, intelligent, discerning, quick-witted, and eager to be selected for the position. His computer skills were admirable, and it seemed he was a bit of a natural sleuth. He responded without hesitation to their queries and asked good follow-up questions. He was in his second year of law school, with the goal of becoming the leading US legal expert in the field of computer forensics investigation. No small goal, to be sure. His inner drive was unmistakable, and his abilities appeared keen.

The investigators filled him in on the activities of the firm, detailing precisely what they would expect of him. Hours and wages were discussed and agreed upon, and Guy handed Jin a key to the office, making sure to explain how the alarm system worked. The firm's new employee was assigned the extra desk and computer at the back of the office.

"Welcome to our firm, Jin," Claire said. She smiled broadly.

"Welcome, Jin," Guy parroted.

Jin grinned from ear to ear. "This is a match made in heaven," he said. "You'll see. I love to work. I love to hunt things down on the computer. And I'll enjoy watching the two of you in action too." Although he tried to maintain a poker face, the corners of his mouth refused to cooperate. He was elated to be hired and couldn't contain his exuberance.

TWO DAYS later, Claire and Guy took a taxi to the airport and boarded a 777 heading to Milan, Italy.

During the flight, Claire fell fast asleep and found herself dreaming about Italy—the land brimming with sumptuous pastas, delectable wines, fast cars, crowded streets, clothing designers, arts and culture, all things Michelangelo, the Vatican, gondolas, history, tales of Marco Polo, and of course legends of the Cosa Nostra.

Guy glanced over at the woman he liked to call "my beauty" and smiled contently, knowing she loved him. Fortune had dealt Guy Lombard a winning hand when Claire Caswell had walked into his life several years ago, and he never took the gift of their relationship for granted. He was a lucky one, and he knew it. Reaching over, he gently grasped her hand without waking her. He closed his eyes and drifted off.

Soon the flight attendant woke them to take a beverage order and announce a meal was about to be served.

The investigators would soon venture into an undefined situation for which there was no real means to prepare. Their assignment was simply to follow an Italian American man who resided in Miami and was returning to Italy for a visit—something he did on a fairly regular basis. The Miami-Dade police knew little about him. But their collective instincts and experience calculated that something was terribly amiss with the man, that he was involved in unidentified nefarious activities, and that things were about to come to a head. As the investigators picked at the food sitting on the trays before them, a bit of apprehension clouded their whispered conversation. Claire was on high alert, but she didn't know why.

After the meal, Guy pulled the *Financial Times* from his briefcase and dove in. Claire turned on her Kindle. She had downloaded travel books for Italy, Switzerland, and France before they left, and it was time to get acquainted with some of the customs of the countries and their languages.

"*Ho bisogno di fare pratica con il mio italiano,*" Claire muttered under her breath.

"What?" Guy asked, puzzled.

She turned to him and smiled. "I said, 'I need to practice my Italian' in Italian." She returned to her reading.

The flight wore on.

Before long, Claire let her e-reader slip to her lap. She turned it off and closed her eyes. Long flights such as this made her extremely sleepy. In her dream state, she and Guy strolled along the damp cobblestone streets and wide sidewalks of Italy, window shopping, studying the architecture, noticing art everywhere, sampling food and coffees at the ubiquitous cafés, and thoroughly enjoying the country so new to them. Claire enjoyed the images and sensations that swirled through her mind, thoroughly captivating her.

After a time, remaining deep in sleep, she jolted violently. She attempted to scream "Help!" several times, but could produce only muffled groans. She wriggled fitfully in her seat.

Guy awakened, watched her struggle, and touched her arm gently. "Claire, you're dreaming. Wake up. We're on a plane, traveling to Italy. You're fine, honey. I'm here with you."

Claire opened her eyes only slightly. "It was horrible."

"You were dreaming again, honey. What was it this time?"

"A man chased me. His steps were heavy . . . and he was fast. I tried to get away. I tried so hard. I ran for a long time, until my legs started to collapse under my body. That's when he caught up, lunged at me, and grabbed me." She swallowed with difficulty. "He pulled me into a dark alley. I was trapped." She stopped to gather her thoughts before continuing, clearly exhausted and disturbed by the vision. "He started to . . . he started to . . . " Tears welled in her clear green eyes that usually danced with life. "I fought back. I fought hard. I screamed for help. I hit him. I tried to kick him. And I just kept screaming."

"Well, it was one of those vivid dreams you have," Guy said. "But it was only a dream." As he continued to look at her, grave concern crept over him. Through the years, he'd learned her dreams were often premonitions of things to come. And this dream terrified him. "We need to stick together while we're in Europe. You know— you watch my back and I'll watch yours." He attempted to give her a reassuring smile, but inwardly he vowed never to let her out of his sight—not even for a short time.

Later, as he dozed again, Claire reached into her backpack and pulled out two peanut-butter-and-chocolate candies. She unwrapped them and popped them both into her mouth at once, allowing the pieces to melt slowly as she savored the delightful blend of flavors. She ordered a cup of hot tea and drank the steaming beverage while deep in thought. The dream had bothered her immensely. More than she let on. She stared straight ahead, reliving it time after time, taking in all the details and setting them firmly in her memory. Now that she knew what might lie ahead, she would be ready.

She turned on her Kindle and looked up the Italian phrase meaning, "Call the police."

"*Chiamate la polizia,*" she said softly, repeating it over and over until she had memorized it. "*Chiamate la polizia.*"

A chill came over her, and she retrieved the blanket from the seat pouch ahead of her. She pulled it over her shivering frame and leaned close to Guy to share his warmth.

Day one
Milan, Italy

LANDING IN Italy was a welcome conclusion to the long flight. Claire yearned to stretch her legs. The Milan Malpensa Airport buzzed with the movement and chatter of travelers, and Italian was spoken almost ubiquitously throughout the crowds. People spoke quickly, and passionately, many using hand gestures to get their points across.

Guy pulled their wheeled duffle bag, and the investigators each slung a large backpack over one shoulder. They hailed a taxi and handed the driver a piece of paper indicating the address of the rental car company. Adrenaline flowed through their veins as the cab made its way through the congested streets of Milan. Claire had never seen so many bicycles, motorcycles, mopeds, cars, and buses all packing the streets at the same time in a fierce competition for limited travel space. It was sheer mayhem. And there were so many near misses that Claire closed her eyes for a second or two, needing a brief retreat from the chaos.

Designer boutiques lined the streets of certain sections of Milan—the fashion capital of Italy—and Claire craned her neck to take them all in. She didn't want to miss a thing. She even noticed a sign indicating "Lombard: Milan" and pointed it out to Guy.

"Relatives?" she inquired with a smile.

"Cute, Claire. Real cute. Actually, it's just reminding us we're in the Lombardy section of Italy." He returned a quick grin.

The energy of the city was undeniable. The taxi driver turned his head from side to side as he drove, constantly checking out every female walking along either side of the street. Each time he turned his attention back to the road in front of him, he would slam on the brakes, nearly rear-ending the vehicle just ahead.

Claire looked at Guy and rolled her eyes.

Guy nervously eyed the driver, wanting to arrive safely at their destination and questioning whether that could happen under the current circumstances.

Despite the somewhat terrifying ride, the investigators enjoyed a good look at the city as the taxi careened through the streets. Museums, fashion outlet malls, cafés, bars, street markets, and intriguing little shops were everywhere. And people. So many people. People milling around—chatting on the sidewalks in front of restaurants or waiting in lines outside their entrances—seemed commonplace. Claire rolled her window partway down and inhaled the smells of the city. "Aah!" Aromas from the pizzerias and other Italian eateries filled the air.

Suddenly, the driver jammed the brake pedal to the floor as he plowed the taxi into a bicycle just ahead. The crashing sound was dreadful, and the bicycle crumbled as if made of paper. The young man riding the ten-speed flew into the air and landed on the street between two other automobiles. The car behind their taxi applied its brakes, but couldn't stop in time. It slammed into the rear end of the cab, propelling Claire and Guy into the backs of the front seats. Confusion abounded. Blood trickled from Claire's forehead, and Guy's head throbbed from smashing into the driver's seat headrest.

"*Shit!*" Guy screamed at the driver. "*Didn't you see the bloody bicycle?*"

Silence. Only silence. The driver didn't answer.

"He's not going to answer you," Claire said. "Look at him. He's dead."

A single bullet had penetrated the driver's head, traveling in one temple and out the other.

Claire felt dizzy, and everything suddenly went black.

3

WITHIN MINUTES, PEDESTRIANS, police cars, and two ambulances crowded the street. Sirens blared harshly, and lights were flashing, marking the accident scene. Medics tended to the critically injured bicyclist, carefully lifting him onto a stretcher and loading him into an emergency vehicle. Onlookers made way for the ambulance as it navigated through the congestion. Other emergency workers pulled open the front doors of the taxi and removed the driver's lifeless body.

"*She's unconscious!*" Guy hollered from the backseat. "*Help her! Please!*" He pointed to Claire. His unhealthy pallor and overwhelmed tone drew the attention of one of the emergency workers.

The medic pushed into the rear of the taxi and took Claire's pulse. While muttering under his breath in Italian, he applied pressure to her forehead using a sterile cloth.

"I can't understand you," Guy pleaded. "Is she okay?"

A well-dressed man standing near the wrecked taxi said, "I will translate. She's lost a lot of blood, I'm afraid, but the wound is actually very small."

Guy looked up at the man and thanked him.

The man listened to the medics' conversation. "They are transporting her to the hospital. You are to ride along." The stranger handed Guy a business card. "If you need anything, please let me know."

Guy shoved the card into his pants pocket, nodded, and thanked the man a second time. Then Guy gave the officer standing next to him his name, Claire's name, and a contact phone number before grabbing their duffel and backpacks from the backseat and following the stretcher carrying Claire to the remaining ambulance. He jumped into the vehicle through its open rear doors and sat down next to her. He took her hand in his and kissed it gently.

"I'm so sorry," he said. Tears filled his eyes. He reached for a blanket from a nearby stack and carefully placed it over Claire. "She'll be cold."

The ride to the hospital was slow as the ambulance made its way through the tangle of traffic. Guy waited desperately for Claire to open her eyes, but she didn't. He needed to see those beautiful green eyes looking back at him. How could this happen? Why?

When they arrived at the emergency room, the stretcher carrying Claire was quickly rolled inside to an awaiting room. She was examined closely to determine the extent of her injuries.

"Come," a nurse said to Guy in polished English. "We need to look at that bump on your forehead too." She led him to an adjacent bed in the same room and motioned for him to lie down.

A doctor appeared and examined the protuberance cautiously. He spoke English as well.

"Your lady friend will be fine. Her body is merely resting after the sudden impact to her system. But you, sir, have sustained a concussion. You will need to relax in bed for some time. Here." He stopped talking and looked Guy squarely in the eyes. "You will both live, sir. But you will both be required to stay a few hours—to be observed."

"Just what we didn't need," Guy mumbled, adjusting the pillow under his head.

"This is always the case, it seems," the doctor replied. "You have no other choice but to rest for a time."

Just then, a policeman entered the room. "I would like to ask you a few questions, Mr. Lombard, if I might," he offered in English. He turned to the doctor for a nod of approval.

"Make it quick," the doctor said. "The man needs to sleep. Two or three minutes only." He left the room.

The policeman informed Guy that sadly the bicyclist had died en route to the hospital.

Guy grimaced.

"Tell me everything you remember about the accident," the policeman directed.

"There isn't much to tell," Guy said. "The driver had several near misses before the crash occurred. He was easily distracted and couldn't seem to keep his eyes on the road."

"The accident was not the fault of the driver," the officer said. "It would appear someone intentionally targeted him—with a single bullet from a rifle that ended his life. Why, I ask myself. Was the gunman after the driver? Or was it the two of you he wanted to harm or kill?"

Guy opened his eyes wide. "The thought hadn't crossed my mind."

"Why are the two of you in Italy?" the policeman asked. "I assume you are Americans."

Guy swallowed hard. Twice.

Just then, the doctor reappeared. "This will be enough

questioning for the time being. My patient will get worse unless he rests. *Arrivederci,* officer."

The policeman set his business card on the bedside table next to Guy. "I will expect a call from you when you are able to talk, Mr. Lombard. Please do not make me wait too long."

Guy turned his head and closed his eyes. The words the officer had uttered tormented his thoughts: *Or was it the two of you he wanted to harm or kill?* Guy wanted desperately to talk the whole incident over with Claire, but he would have to wait for the opportunity. For now, she was alive. And he was alive. They had both survived the crash. He fell asleep.

TWO OR three hours passed before Guy struggled to open his eyes. But they wouldn't cooperate. He had a horrific headache. What was that sound? What were those words? Whose voice did he hear in the far distance? He forced his eyes open to slits and blinked. The image looking down at him was quite blurry.

"Oh," he groaned. "My head. It hurts."

A voice came from the other side of his bed. "Take these pills, Mr. Lombard. They will help."

Guy was pulled up to a sitting position. A nurse handed him two capsules and a small paper cup half filled with water. He dutifully placed the pain-killers into his mouth and drank the cool liquid. He opened his eyes a crack wider and tried his best to focus. Before long, he saw Claire's sweet face looking at him.

"Welcome back, honey. You've been sleeping a long time," she said. A small bandage covered the cut on her forehead.

"Are you okay, my beauty?" Guy asked, furrowing his brow. "I was worried."

"I'm fine. Actually, it's you I'm worried about. The doctor said you'll need to take it easy for a couple days. And they're keeping you here under observation for another twenty-four hours."

"Out of the question," he said. "We don't have time for this. I need to tell you something. It's important." The tone of his voice signaled urgency, but as he finished his sentence, his eyes dropped closed, and he fell fast asleep again.

Whatever it is, it will have to wait, Claire thought. Rest is the most important thing now. She leaned over and tenderly kissed his bruised forehead. When she did, she noticed the scars that still remained from the case they investigated in Crete. The new bruising demanded a place alongside the earlier marks. Her eyes misted. "You've been through a lot," she said softly.

Claire started to get up, but a sudden bout of dizziness overtook her. She dropped back down on the chair next to Guy's bed and grabbed the bedrail for support, holding on tightly as she closed her eyes. The sudden impact of the accident remained fresh in her mind—the sound of the taxi smashing into the bicycle, the scream of its rider, the crunch of metal hitting metal as the car behind them slammed into theirs, sailing forward and hitting her head on the seat in front of her.

"You good?" a voice sounded in the room, interrupting her thoughts. It was a nurse. "Maybe lay down." She pointed to the bed next to Guy's. She helped Claire out of the chair and into the adjacent bed, then covered her with a blanket. "You both need rest. More rest."

Claire didn't argue. She knew the nurse was right.

TWO HOURS passed. Claire and Guy awoke at the same time. They turned to face each other and stared without talking. The incident had been bad, but it could have been worse. This realization haunted both investigators.

Claire's mind raced as she studied Guy's eyes. What were the odds something like this would happen shortly after they arrived in Italy? Who would have wanted to shoot *their* taxi driver? Who was the driver? Did he have something to hide? What was he into? Was he a criminal? How could they have been so unfortunate as to be passengers in that particular cab? What had the man done to warrant being murdered? And the poor younger man on the bicycle. She'd asked a nurse about him when she first opened her eyes. The nurse had only shaken her head from side to side. He had died too. Two people had lost their lives—one was murdered and the other was horrific collateral damage as a direct result of the murder. She and Guy had lived through it all. As she sifted through the circumstances and details of the tragic incident, it hit her: What if she and Guy, not the driver, had been the intended targets of the shooting? Or what if the plan was to shoot the driver so the resulting crash would injure or kill both her and Guy?

"Guy, we need to talk," she said. "I think I know—"

"Not here," he said quietly, cutting her short. "We'll talk later. When we're alone."

He'd been watching her face, and he knew she'd figured it out.

"Shh," he warned, putting his index finger to his lips. He motioned around the room with his eyes.

Claire nodded almost imperceptibly.

"Let's get out of here," he whispered.

"But they want to observe—"

"I'm leaving now. And you're coming with me." Guy was adamant in his demand. "Something tells me we're not safe here." His tone remained low and solemn.

"Sure you're up to it?" Her voice was low too.

Just then, in the corner of her eye, she noticed the shadow of a person hovering just behind the curtain surrounding their beds. But when she turned toward the silhouette, it had vanished.

"I agree. Let's get out of here!" she muttered.

The investigators quickly gathered their belongings, including the duffel and backpacks, and furtively stepped from the room, making certain not to attract attention. They hid behind a pillar until the coast was clear, scanned for the closest exit, and darted to the door.

Just as they stepped outside into the fresh air, they heard the shout of a nurse, "Where you going?"

"Run!" Claire shrieked.

The two never looked back. They ran until the hospital was far behind them and only then stopped to catch their breath.

"Someone was definitely eavesdropping on our conversation in there," Guy said, panting. A grave expression penetrated his face.

"I know. I saw a figure behind the curtain," Claire said. "Wonder who it was?"

"I don't know," Guy said. "But I don't like this one bit. I'm not sure we should have taken the case. If the shooter's goal was to kill us the second we arrived in Italy, our problems may have just begun."

"Let's not jump to conclusions. Not yet, anyway. We don't know for sure that someone tried to hurt us—or kill us. The bullet may well have been intended for the driver. But I agree we need to be on our guard. And we need to be *extremely* cautious." She looked at Guy. "Are you feeling better? No more headache?"

"I'm okay. How are you?"

"Good. I think."

Her words sounded convincing, but her inner voice, the one she always listened to, was screaming: *Two people lost their lives today. But you and Guy were the intended targets!*

4

CLAIRE AND GUY braved another taxi to get to the car rental location, where a black Fiat awaited them. A man dressed in blue jeans and a white T-shirt handed them a sealed envelope and two ignition keys. He also gave them several folded maps and two bottles of water. He spoke no English whatsoever, and he moved with haste. He seemed to know exactly what to do and wasted no time doing it.

Precious hours had been lost due to the accident. It was time to find their hotel, check in, and search for the man they were hired to follow.

Claire pushed gently on her temples.

"Headache?" Guy asked.

"Yeah. A bad one," she said.

"Me too," Guy admitted.

"Well, I guess we shouldn't be surprised, should we?" She grabbed a container of aspirin from her backpack, shook two tablets into her hand, cracked open a bottle of water, gulped, and felt them slide down her throat. She handed two to Guy, and he did the same.

The investigators said *grazie* to the man, settled into the Fiat, entered the address of the hotel into the GPS, and drove off. This was new territory for them, and they would need to rely heavily on the satellite navigation guidance. As Guy drove, Claire mentally inventoried the items she had packed in the duffel and backpacks for the trip.

In addition to the compact high-powered binoculars she'd remembered to include, there were black jeans, blue jeans, tops in a panoply of colors, thin sweaters, socks, undergarments, and shoes. Plus, they had the shoes, clothing, and jackets each wore on the plane. She had packed light, as Sergeant Massey had recommended. She had filled one backpack with everything the two might need whenever disguises were required.

She smiled as she thought about the wigs she'd included. For her, she brought a red wig in a short, wispy cut and a brunette one in a long, straight style with bangs. She also had some hairpieces to clip on. And for Guy, she'd packed a thick, curly salt-and-pepper wig and one styled in a pale blond crew cut. She chuckled. Neither of them looked anything like themselves when they pulled one of them on. It was amazing how a change of hair—both color and cut—could alter one's appearance so dramatically.

She'd tossed in many pairs of nonprescription eyeglasses in various shapes and sizes, both regular and sunglasses, and a variety of scarves, caps, and berets. She also included a clear zip-top bag in the duffel filled with makeup—red, orange, coral, pink, and even dark purple lipsticks; different tones of blush; many shades of eye shadows and brow pencils; and other items that could change her look quickly and considerably, when and if needed. The kit even extended to some cosmetic fake teeth—both uppers and lowers—that would rearrange the jawline, smile, and outward impression significantly, plus some stick-on eyebrows, mustaches, and goatees for Guy. Because Guy's facial scars were a distinguishing feature a wig couldn't cover and glasses couldn't camouflage, there was also a tube of concealer to hide them.

She imagined all the different looks she could create for herself and Guy with only a moment's notice. She knew the real goal of a disguise was to blend into the crowd—to conceal one's true identity by altering one's appearance, to become absolutely unrecognizable.

This was Claire's bailiwick. Each new investigation thrilled her. This case was unusual, and it seemed quite simple on its face. Follow a man, observe his comings and goings, keep a record, and get paid handsomely for doing so. And accomplish these tasks in Italy, Switzerland, and France. Could it get better or easier than this? For a few fleeting moments, she found herself anticipating the challenge. Then reality hit. What was she thinking? Her nagging inner voice, the one that never misled her, returned to shout a reminder: *Two people lost their lives today. But you and Guy were the intended targets!* She swallowed hard, hit with the realization that this case promised to be anything but easy. They had to remain vigilant at all times.

Claire continued to take in the sites of the city as they sped along its streets. Everything about Milan was delicious—the people, the streets, and the Old World charm—and she tried to absorb it all.

As they approached a red traffic light and came to a stop, Claire looked out the passenger window. The driver in the car next to them was staring directly at her. When her eyes met his, he immediately turned his head to look straight ahead. He wore a dark cap, had piercing pitch-black eyes, and appeared unshaven. Normally a glance from a stranger would not have bothered Claire, but this one did. His sinister gaze sent shivers down her spine. The light changed, and Guy sped off. Claire didn't have a chance to memorize the license plate on the man's car, but she did make special note of its model and color. If she needed to recognize it again, she could.

She mentioned the incident to Guy, who shot her a concerned frown. Soon enough they were far away from the strange car and closing in on the hotel.

Okay, that was twice today, Claire thought. First the terrible taxi incident, and now the stranger who leered. Someone might not want the two sleuths poking around in Italy. Was it DiNetto? How would DiNetto know they were in Europe to tail him? And if not DiNetto, then *whom*?

They arrived at the Hotel Principe di Savoia, and Guy found a spot near the entrance to park the car. He grabbed the duffel, each lugged a backpack, and they walked into the lobby. It was a stunning hotel with décor reminiscent of an opulent past—thoroughly charming. A glorious fresh flower arrangement sat on a round, elaborately carved antique table in the entrance area, dark polished wood was visible everywhere, and the check-in counter was a thick slab of marble. Claire and Guy checked in and were given a luxurious suite on the fourth floor. They passed a lounge, a restaurant, a concierge station, an exquisite clothing boutique, and an upscale men's shop on the way to the elevators.

When Claire and Guy walked into their room, they were taken aback. It was the most elegant space they'd ever seen. A gold silk shantung coverlet topped the bed. And its six oversized, cushy pillows looked so inviting that Claire had to hold herself back from jumping into it on the spot. A massive, ornate mahogany desk sat in one corner of the room, and a plush fabric sofa and coordinating chairs adorned the living space. Heavy brocade draperies decorated its many windows, and the room afforded the duo a pleasing view of the city.

"Okay. It's settled. I'm never going back," Claire said.

Guy smiled. "Nice. DiNetto knows how to live, doesn't he?"

Claire walked into the sitting room and noticed a tray sitting on the coffee table. An ample arrangement of fresh fruit, a bottle of Amarone wine, crackers and Brie, and a small container of assorted nuts welcomed them. She called to Guy, and within a minute the two were enjoying the generous gift. As she sipped from a glass of the rich, dry red wine, Claire noticed a note card inserted into the fruit bowl. She reached for it and read it aloud: "To welcome you to Milano. Have an interesting stay, and always be careful."

"Hmm, the hotel treats its patrons very well," she said. "But 'Have an interesting stay, and always be careful'? Odd choice of words." She looked at Guy. "We'll have to remember to thank the front desk."

"Yeah," Guy said between bites. The food tasted good, and he was obviously starving.

Thoughts spun through Claire's mind. Why was everything stacking up so strangely since they left Miami? Her dream on the plane, the accident, the strange man in the car, and now this rather oddly worded "welcome" note.

"Actually, I think I'll call the front desk now to thank them. That way, we won't forget." She picked up the phone and dialed the operator.

"Yes, *signora*," a male voice responded. "How can I be of assistance?"

"We wanted to thank the hotel for having a lovely welcome tray waiting for us in our room. We're really enjoying it," Claire said.

"*Signora*?" the man's voice said. "Pardon?"

"The wonderful tray of fruits, wine, and cheese," she said. "We'd like to say thank you."

"*Signora*, this is not from the hotel. We unfortunately do not offer this type of greeting for our guests . . . even those staying in the luxury suites."

"But," Claire said, "the Amarone—"

"*Signora*, I apologize, I have another call I must take. Please enjoy. Whoever sent it up to your room must be a fond friend. Amarone is a *fine* wine. Very pricey." He chuckled. "This *is* the country of love, wine, and food. It is all around us." With another half-suppressed laugh, he hung up.

Claire turned to Guy. "This is *not* from the hotel," she said, gesturing toward the tray. "So who would have sent it?"

"I have no idea. But I'm enjoying it, nonetheless," he said. He spread another cracker with Brie and popped it into his mouth. He took another sip of the wine. "This is some of the best wine I think I've ever tasted. Maybe Sergeant Massey arranged for it?"

"Not a chance," she said. Who else knew they were in Italy? Her body quivered. "I don't like this, Guy. Someone wants us to know they're aware we're here. This isn't good. The tray wasn't a *welcome*; it was a *warning*."

Guy bolted from his chair. "I almost forgot. I need to call the officer who spoke to me at the hospital." He reached into his pocket for the policeman's business card, but it wasn't there. "I was so sure I put it in my pocket," he mumbled. "Oh well. I guess he'll find me if he needs to." He also discovered he no longer had the card from the man who translated for him at the scene of the accident. He remained certain he'd put both in his pocket, but perhaps he'd forgotten them on the hospital stand in his rush to leave. His headache had been fierce at the time, so anything was possible.

Claire and Guy unpacked. As they did, she brought up the stranger in the car next to them at the stoplight.

"It was probably nothing," Guy said introspectively. "Maybe just an Italian man noticing your light-colored hair and that pretty face." He tried to get her to smile.

"You're probably right," Claire said. She shrugged her shoulders. "I'm tired, but I think we should get going. Our time in Milan is limited, and we need to locate DiNetto as soon as possible—and start shadowing him. Sergeant Massey will expect information soon. He's an impatient man."

"That leaves us no time to deal with jet lag," Guy said. "Well, let's have a cup of strong coffee downstairs before we leave, at least. I think we can both use one."

"No argument here," Claire replied.

Within minutes, the investigators were sitting on comfortable chairs in the lounge, drinking hot coffees.

"We'll need to keep our eyes peeled for DiNetto," Claire said in a hushed tone. "He's staying at this hotel, and we need to find him." She pulled his photos from her backpack, held them low, and studied them. Then Guy took another look.

"He's distinguished-looking," Claire said. "He'll be hard to miss."

"And we'll want to keep our distance if we spot him," Guy said. "Attract no attention whatsoever. Meld into the background."

"You're sounding like me," Claire said. "More and more, your investigative skills are coming to the surface. I like that." She praised him with a smile.

Suddenly, a commotion in the hotel's lobby—which was adjacent to the lounge—drew the sleuths' attention. Claire got up and walked a few feet in the direction of the noise, looking to determine the cause. A small herd of people clustered in the entrance area, encircling a man—a man everyone seemed to know or recognize. He was clearly a person of prominence. A man of distinction. Someone the crowd appeared exceedingly happy to see.

Claire moved closer to the throng. She kept a safe distance as she tried desperately to get a look at the man. She leaned forward and moved her head to one side. Just then, the Italian man standing next to Claire moved and bumped her slightly, upsetting her balance and sending her sprawling to the floor.

"*Scusi, signora,*" the man said, reaching down to help her up. "*Scusi!*" The man was clearly upset he had triggered her fall.

"I'm fine. No problem. Really," Claire said, smiling to reassure him. "I'm okay."

Much to her chagrin, the crowd had started to disperse, and the man she had craned her neck to see was gone.

Claire returned to Guy and explained what happened. He seemed distracted.

"Did you hurt yourself?" he asked, not even looking in her direction.

"Nah. Just my pride," she said. "But I wish I could have grabbed a glimpse of the man garnering all the attention. I was hoping it might be—"

"Well, you're in luck," Guy said. "Take a look at the man sitting at the far end of the bar. He's the man you tried to see in the lobby. And you'll be pleased to know, it's Anthony DiNetto. My eyes haven't left him since he walked into the room."

The hotel bar was crowded now, and Claire let her gaze fall on DiNetto. She eyed the man with curiosity. He sat on a bar stool drinking what appeared to be some kind of clear alcohol. Two men stood to his right, another sat on the stool at his left, and a group of women gathered behind him. The men were conversing, and as she watched, the three leaned in closer to hear what DiNetto had to say.

DiNetto's demeanor oozed both power and authority. He dressed in a black cashmere pullover sweater and black wool slacks. His hair was dyed pitch black and slicked straight back. Claire caught a good look at his face when he turned to the man sitting next to him. She was surprised his face appeared pleasant and almost baby-like in person. He presented himself as a well-manicured, elegant man, and his sizable watch and heavy neck chain were simple in design.

"My guess is, the man hasn't done much honest work in his life," Claire said. "Physical or otherwise." She continued to eyeball him, somewhat taken in by what she was seeing. "He looks better in person than in his photos."

Guy turned to look at Claire, as if to access her thoughts. "Remember Sergeant Massey's warning. Don't get too close to the man."

"Rest assured, that will never happen," she said. "He's as slick as they come."

Minutes passed, and the investigators never moved their eyes from DiNetto.

Unexpectedly, he rose to his feet, turned, and walked in Claire and Guy's direction.

"*Shit!*" Guy whispered. "Try to act normal."

"Go with me on this," Claire said, talking under her breath without moving her mouth.

At that moment, she dropped her open backpack onto the floor. A tube of her coral lipstick started to roll along the carpet. She got up and walked to retrieve it, looking downward the entire time. Just as she reached for it, a larger hand beat her to it. When she looked up, she saw Guy's face. He handed her the lipstick, and they both returned to their seats.

"Nice play," Guy said. "Quick thinking."

"And great playing along," she said with a wink.

They observed DiNetto strutting from the room.

Moving without attracting attention, they followed after him.

5

DINETTO STROLLED INTO the lobby and stopped at the concierge desk, where he engaged the hotel employee in what appeared to be serious conversation.

Guy held up an index finger to Claire and motioned for her to stay put. He slowly passed behind DiNetto and listened. He heard the concierge talking about restaurant and theater reservations. The investigator stopped only feet away, with his back to the two men, and stooped low, presumably to tie a shoelace. When he noticed DiNetto walking toward the elevators, Guy made his move.

The concierge was about to go on break, but the investigator stopped him.

"Excuse me, sir. I'm wondering if you could assist me in scheduling dinner plans for this evening and perhaps get us some theater tickets as well."

"Certainly, sir. What type of food are you interested in?"

"Well, I'm not sure. Something special. It's our first time in Milan, and I'd like it to be spectacular."

As Guy prolonged the conversation, Claire took his cue and walked to his side. She glanced down at the notes the concierge had just written after talking with DiNetto. She needed three things: the name of the restaurant, the time of the reservation, and the theater information he was arranging for DiNetto.

"What about Conti Café?" she asked. "I'm told it's first-class and not to be missed. Can you get us in there tonight? Say six thirty? A quiet, corner table preferably. That way we can hopefully make it to *Romeo and Juliet* at La Scala at eight o'clock."

The concierge laughed out loud. "Excuse me, *signora*, but do you have tickets for the opera? This is the *opening night* for *Roméo et Juliette* at Teatro alla Scala! Tickets have been sold out for many months." He glared at them.

Guy passed him a hundred-dollar bill. "Certainly you have connections, sir. We'd like to see *Romeo and Juliet* this evening."

"The tickets are *quite* expensive and *most* difficult to obtain. *Most difficult.*" The concierge spoke under his breath, obviously concerned someone might hear him, as greed spewed from his eyeballs like a garden hose on full strength. He rubbed the bill between the thumb and forefinger of his right hand.

Guy got the message. He passed another hundred to the employee. "Make that two *amazing* tickets for tonight's performance."

"Uh-huh. I will see what I can do," the concierge said. "Now about the restaurant. I will get you in at six thirty. You will have to dine quickly and then taxi to Teatro alla Scala. You must be seated in the theater prior to eight o'clock. You will not be permitted to enter if you arrive even a minute after eight. They request a dark jacket and tie for the gentleman and an evening dress for the lady. Perhaps not formal, but certainly dressy. Again, tonight is the *opening.* This is an occasion to be celebrated at Teatro alla Scala. All of high society will be there."

The concierge acted very busy while the investigators waited impatiently. "Funny, I just made the exact dinner reservations for the gentleman before you," he muttered. "Same place. Same time. But *he* already had his tickets for tonight's special performance of *Roméo et Juliette*. He has had them for some time." Before long, he produced two tickets from a drawer just in front of him and handed them to Guy. "Six hundred dollars, please . . . for the two. Or would you like the amount in euros?"

"Dollars are fine. Please add the tickets to our room charge," Guy said. He showed the number on his room key to the concierge.

"Certainly, sir." He looked up and down at the investigators. "We have a glorious boutique and a superb men's store right here in the hotel if you need something special to wear this evening."

As Claire and Guy walked away, Claire said, "I noticed you didn't flinch when he said the price of the tickets."

"Well, it is La Scala. On opening night of *Romeo and Juliet*. We need to go because DiNetto is attending. So we have no other choice. Massey will understand."

"And don't forget about the two-hundred-dollar tip to get these *special* tickets," Claire offered. "Not to mention, we need to find suitable clothes for tonight."

They found the shops, and each began to search for the perfect attire for the evening's festivities. Before long, both had disappeared into fitting rooms.

Guy emerged dressed in a midnight-blue bouclé jacket with understated black satin lapels, a stark-white Isaia cotton shirt, black slacks, dress shoes, belt, stockings, and a black-on-black-patterned tie.

Claire appeared a few minutes later wearing a sequined black dress cut low in the back and high-heeled black satin pumps. A matching velvet clutch finished the look.

They stood looking at each other for a long minute.

"It's amazing what a few nice pieces of clothing can do," Claire said, looking proud. "What a transformation, huh?"

"You look spectacular, Claire," Guy said. "Stay close to me tonight." He shot her his famous grin.

"You don't look so bad yourself." She smiled. "Very handsome."

"Let's go rest before we shower for the evening," Guy said. "I could use a nap."

"I'm hungry and I'm tired. I need to eat and sleep before we get ready to leave. Maybe I'll order room service," Claire said.

"Good plan," Guy said.

Within forty-five minutes, they had shared an order of angel-hair pasta topped with marinara sauce, tucked themselves into the inviting bed, and nodded off. They got up an hour later to shower and dress in their new evening clothes.

"I need to call Massey," Claire said, "and break all the news: the taxi crash resulting in one murder and another death; the menacing stranger in the car; the mysterious tray waiting for us in our room; nearly spotting DiNetto surrounded by his friends and admirers in the hotel lobby, then actually seeing him in the lounge; and the rather huge amount of money we've already spent—on our first day—for tickets to La Scala, appropriate clothes for the event, fancy dining, and on and on. This will not be an inexpensive investigation for the Miami-Dade Police Department, especially when you throw in the air travel, car rental, fuel, ongoing hotel charges, and food costs. Yikes! I wouldn't be at all surprised if he called a halt to the investigation and ordered us home."

"And don't forget about our investigation fees. We don't come cheap," Guy said. "Total it all together, and this is costing the department a pretty penny."

"Well, at least for tonight, we're on a mission. It should be interesting to watch DiNetto and take note of his every move," Claire said. "I hope it proves fruitful to our investigation."

They rode the elevator to the main floor and walked through the lobby to the hotel's front doors. The doorman on duty hailed a cab, and before they knew it, they were on their way. Claire had a small notepad in her velvet clutch and two pens. She was ready to start recording DiNetto's activities.

The driver dropped the two investigators at Conti Café, and they hustled inside. After Guy confirmed their reservation, the two were led to the perfect location—a table out of sight to the majority of the other diners, yet convenient for gazing out and seeing everything going on in the establishment. It would suit their snooping needs just fine. Straightaway, a server poured ice water into their glasses and delivered a basket of fresh, warm bread to the table. He handed both Claire and Guy a menu and said he'd give them a few minutes to peruse.

"I'm afraid we'll have to order immediately." Guy said. "We're going to La Scala this evening."

"Oh, opening night of *Roméo et Juliette*. How very fortunate for you. How very lucky you obtained tickets. What an honor. What a privilege. What a chance of a lifetime. I will take your orders at once and have you out of here in no time. Now, what will you have tonight?" the waiter asked.

While he prattled on, Claire quickly scanned the menu.

Guy looked at the server. "I'll let the lady order."

"Okay," Claire said. "We'll each have a misto salad to start, then we'll have the sea bass for two—the one baked with olive oil, potato slices, and Greek olives. Although I have to admit, both options for the sea bass preparation sound amazing."

"Good choices, *signora*. You will be pleased," the server said. "And to drink?"

"Two glasses of your best local red wine," Guy said.

"Of course. When in Italy, you must drink wine." The server ended his comment with a prolonged wink at Claire.

Nearly every table was filled in the busy restaurant, and servers moved around hurriedly as they delivered mouthwatering appetizers, entrées, desserts, and wines to the many patrons. Claire's eyes darted from table to table in the hope of locating DiNetto. She didn't see him at first. And then she did.

She caught a glimpse of his face when he turned to greet someone he obviously knew at a neighboring table. He sat three tables away from the investigators, with his back to them. Perfect placement to allow observation, she thought. At his table sat a striking younger woman. She had dark hair and eyes, and her strapless black evening dress showed off plenty of cleavage. From the looks of it, she was totally and utterly taken in by her male companion. They shared a bottle of wine and leaned across the table toward each other, obviously intoxicated by a cocktail of romantic conversation and alcohol. Claire looked on with interest. DiNetto pulled his chair closer to his female companion, gently cupped her chin in his hand, and slowly kissed her lips in a slow, seductive manner. Then he returned to his original position at the table.

"There he is," Claire said to Guy. "Three tables away, his back toward us. He's the one in the light-colored jacket. From what I see, he's quite the Don Juan. I've been watching him in action."

Guy located DiNetto easily. "And as Sergeant Massey predicted, he's with an attractive woman."

"Probably one of many in his stable," Claire said. "The woman is being charmed by a snake. I can see it in her eyes. Look. She's greatly impressed."

"Yeah," Guy said, glancing her way. "She certainly appears enthralled by whatever he's saying."

Claire reached for her notepad; recorded the date, time, and place; and penned their observations.

The meals arrived, and the investigators ate every savory morsel, all the while watching DiNetto at work—oozing his magnetism. Guy glanced at his watch. "Time to leave if we want to arrive at La Scala to be seated." They put the check on a credit card Massey had provided; finished the last of the aromatic, rich wine; and left the restaurant to join others already standing outside in the theater line, waiting for a taxi to deliver them to La Scala.

"Don't turn around," Claire said. "DiNetto and his date are standing several people behind us. She's wearing a mink wrap. I see them in my peripheral vision."

After a ten-minute wait, it was the investigators' turn. They jumped into the next taxi, and Guy directed the driver to take them to La Scala. The driver smiled as he pulled away from the curb.

To their surprise, the driver listened to radio tunes from the Beach Boys and the Doors as they made their way toward the famous opera house. And he sang along to all the words of every song in nearly perfect English. Halfway through one selection, he surprised Claire and Guy by turning the volume down and wanting to talk.

"Aah," he said. "Opening night of Gounod's *Roméo et Juliette* at Teatro alla Scala. Must be tough." He looked at the sleuths in his rearview mirror. "Mighty fancy stuff."

"Yes, we're looking forward to it," Claire said. She avoided his eyes.

"I heard tickets are hard to get," the driver persisted. "You must be VIPs. You Americans?"

"We are," Guy said. He volunteered nothing further.

The driver stopped asking questions and turned the radio volume back up. Aside from the familiar radio music, the occupants rode in silence the remainder of the drive.

Claire and Guy thanked the driver and paid the fare and a tip.

The two walked to the entrance doors of Milan's world-renowned opera house and stepped inside. Claire stopped and breathed in deeply. "*This is magnificent!*"

"La Scala is one of the leading opera and ballet theaters in the world. It's a spectacular structure," Guy said. "Nothing but the best for you, m'lady." He looked at Claire and kissed her forehead, near the cut beginning to heal from the accident just that morning. With her cut and his bruise, they were quite the pair. He grinned that wonderful grin of his. "Not a bad gig, huh?"

"*It's unbelievable!*"

Guy presented the tickets to an usher, and the woman handed them each a program and led them to their seats. It was exactly ten minutes to eight, and while the lights remained up, Claire and Guy took the opportunity to look around and search for DiNetto. But neither could spot him. Claire glanced at her program and noted there were 2,800 seats in the house. They were sitting in the orchestra section, only a few rows back from the stage on the house-right side. Perfect tickets to view the opera. Box seats ran several tiers high along the sidewalls of the theater, and Claire failed to see even one empty seat either on the floor or in the boxes. It looked like a sellout crowd. It wouldn't be easy to spot DiNetto. The theater was abuzz with eager patrons, all waiting in great suspense for the lights to dim and the heavy stage curtains to part. Gounod's opera was sung in French, but the seat back facing each patron had an electronic libretto that allowed them to read the lines of the opera in the language of their choice. Claire and Guy clicked on English.

The female investigator's eyes continued to scan the crowd until the lights had dimmed almost completely. Still no sign of DiNetto.

When the curtains parted at 8:00 p.m. sharp and *Romeo and Juliet* began, the patrons clapped madly. Attending an opening night at La Scala was a once-in-a-lifetime event—and the crowd's anticipation and appreciation of the moment was palpable.

The first part of the opera held the investigators' rapt attention. Not a sound could be heard from the audience, as complete contentment at seeing and hearing the brilliant Shakespearean tragedy sated each patron's highest expectation. When the curtains closed—indicating an intermission—uproarious and unrestrained whistles, clapping of hands, and shouts of "*Bravo!*" and "*Brava!*" reverberated through the opera house.

"*Spectacular!*" Claire said, eyes twinkling while clapping with great enthusiasm.

"*A—ma—zing!*" Guy said, also clapping wildly. He leaned over and kissed the woman he loved on her cheek.

As the commotion diminished, Claire and Guy left their seats and walked to the lobby. Lengthy lines had already started to form at the long counter offering beverages and sweets. The investigators took their place in the shortest queue.

"Coffee? Water?" Guy asked.

"I'd love a water, thanks," Claire said.

Guy ordered a water and a coffee when they reached the front of the line. The two then stepped to the edge of the room, standing apart from the milling operagoers crowding the lobby. People stood in small groups, eagerly discussing the splendid performances of the cast and the impressive set design.

Claire and Guy searched the lobby in earnest for DiNetto, but they still couldn't locate him.

"How strange," Claire said. "I know he's here. Why haven't we spotted him?"

Ringing bells signaled the next act was about to begin. The sleuths scurried to their seats and settled in. Claire continued to scan the orchestra seats and the tiers of boxes overhead. She realized it would be nearly impossible to locate DiNetto if he were seated in a box.

Nonetheless, just as the lights flashed for the last time before the curtains parted, Claire finally saw him! He was on the fourth tier up, in a box not far away from the stage. Strangely, though the next act was about to begin, he stood near the front of his box and looked down at the large number of people seated on the main floor. He seemed to be studying the audience with keen interest. Dressed in the light-colored suit they'd seen him in at the restaurant, he was now also wearing a white Panama hat, which made him stand out in the crowd. Most everyone attending the spectacular event that evening was dressed in black. Claire had to admit DiNetto looked both dashing and elegant, and she noticed others looking up at him as well. He certainly seemed to draw attention wherever he went, and he appeared to revel in it. As Claire continued to look his way, she caught a passing glimpse of the woman he'd dined with earlier in the evening. She stood close to him in the box. Claire nudged Guy and pointed to DiNetto. Guy's eyes located the man just as darkness fell upon the theater and the curtains opened.

About halfway through the act, and out of the blue, a piercing scream resonated on the opposite side of the main floor from where the investigators sat. The house lights came up suddenly, and the production stopped abruptly. Shrill shrieks of "*C'è un medico in sala?*" and "*Chiamate la polizia!*" followed.

Claire told Guy she'd be back in a minute, and she left her seat. She walked with rapid steps to the area where the screams emanated and pushed her way through the quickly gathering throng to get a closer look. There, sprawled on the floor in snow-angel formation, a mink wrap by her side, was the young woman DiNetto had dined with at Conti Café.

A man standing near her spoke loudly. "I am a doctor. She fell from a box and broke her neck. She's dead."

DiNetto was nowhere to be seen.

6

CLAIRE LOOKED UPWARD toward where the woman had been sitting. A scrap of her black dress clung to a protrusion on the exact box where Claire had earlier spotted DiNetto and his date. The same place she'd noticed DiNetto peering downward.

She raced back to fill Guy in on what happened.

"We'll have to let the police know," he said. "Obviously DiNetto needs to be questioned thoroughly."

The stage curtains closed, and an announcement came over the sound system indicating that under the circumstances, the opening night performance would not continue. Several police officers and an ambulance arrived at La Scala within minutes.

Day two
Milan

RAINDROPS PELTING the windows in their hotel room woke the sleuths. The overcast sky fit Claire's pensive mood. So much had happened the day before. She retrieved her notepad and pen, reviewed her notes from the evening before, and jotted precise additional notations about the incident at La Scala. She had created a written record of the evening: dinner at the Conti Café, where DiNetto and his younger, dark-haired female companion—wearing a black evening dress and a mink wrap—also dined; opening night of *Romeo and Juliet* at La Scala; DiNetto at the opera house wearing a white Panama hat, sitting in a box on the fourth tier with his female companion from dinner; the woman mysteriously falling to her death—with her mink wrap by her side—during the performance; and DiNetto's disappearance.

She picked up her global cell phone and dialed Sergeant Massey's number. Due to the difference in time zones, she knew she'd reach his voicemail. In her message, she updated him on their first eventful day in Italy. She began with the murder of the taxi driver and the death of the bicyclist, and ended with the tragic death of the young woman at La Scala. She also relayed the expenses that were quickly skyrocketing.

When she hung up, she looked at Guy. "Since we arrived in this enchanting country, death has been all around us."

"I wonder if DiNetto is the common denominator," Guy said. "He certainly has to be the prime suspect in the death of that young woman—that is, if the police determine foul play is the cause of her demise. And if they consider how he vanished from the scene immediately after it happened."

Claire walked to the door, opened it, and returned with the local newspaper the hotel staff had attached to the outside doorknob. The front page covered the La Scala incident with the headline: "*La Scala Tragedia.*" There was a photo of Anthony DiNetto and the young woman identified as Adelfa Pontillo, age twenty-seven. The article was in Italian, and the two sleuths struggled to decipher some of the words. Once they noticed the name Anthony DiNetto in the text they decided to ask the concierge to translate the article.

They dressed for the day, rode the elevator to the ground floor, and walked to the hotel's restaurant for a meal. The delightful brunch was just what they needed, and the two ordered strong American coffees. They ate quickly, then approached the concierge desk.

"*Buongiorno,*" said a different concierge than they'd seen the day before. "How might I be of assistance?"

"Good morning," Claire said. "Might we bother you to translate this article for us?" She pointed to the newspaper's front page. "We were at La Scala last evening when this happened, and we're curious to find out more about it."

"*Certo, signora.* This is no problem." He brought the paper closer and translated the entire article aloud in English. Guy passed the concierge the equivalent of five American dollars in euros, and both investigators thanked him for his help.

Then they returned to their room.

"Did you hear that?" Claire asked. "When Anthony DiNetto—'her companion for the evening'—was questioned regarding the incident, DiNetto stated that Adelfa stood up to visit the restroom during the performance, fell into a swoon, and tumbled over the balcony. He was unable to stop her."

"And?" Guy prompted.

"And? I don't buy it," Claire said. "I didn't see anyone else in his box, so I assume DiNetto rented the entire box for the two of them. That means there were no witnesses to the incident other than

DiNetto himself. *Very* convenient, wouldn't you agree?"

"You think DiNetto intentionally pushed the woman over the railing? Why?"

"I don't know yet," Claire said, "but his story doesn't sit well with me."

"We need to visit the police station and tell them we saw DiNetto with the woman at the restaurant earlier in the evening. Maybe they'll tell us what they know," Guy said.

They decided to take a taxi to the police station due to the insistent rain. Even though the hotel provided a large umbrella for them, this was clearly not a day for outdoor strolling. When the cab arrived, they moved hurriedly to get in. Rain fell heavily on the vehicle's windshield, giving the wipers a substantial workout. A glance at the sky suggested the wet weather would be sticking around for the entire day. Traffic slowed to a literal crawl, but the driver negotiated the busy streets like a pro. He knew the shortcuts and side streets and avoided the congested areas. Before long, he delivered the sleuths to the police station.

Guy paid the fare, and they sprinted to the front door, struggling to keep the umbrella directly above their heads as they ran. They entered through the glass double doors, walked up to the information desk, and identified themselves.

"We'd like to talk to a police officer or detective about what happened at La Scala last evening," Guy told the uniformed attendant. "We were there, and we might have important information."

"One moment, please," the man said. He made a call, informed them a detective would be out to see them shortly, and requested they have a seat on the chairs provided. He pointed to several stiff-looking chairs placed in a semicircle not far from the entrance.

The investigators waited about ten minutes.

To their surprise, the officer who walked out to greet them was the same officer who'd come to the hospital to speak with Guy after yesterday's horrific taxi ordeal.

"Well, well, well," he said, seeing Guy. He tapped his foot on the floor. "We meet again. I am Officer Bubbiano."

Guy extended his hand, and Claire introduced herself.

"You promised to call me," the officer said testily, staring into Guy's eyes. "What happened?"

"Actually, officer, I lost your card," Guy said. "Somewhere between the hospital and our hotel room. I apologize. I didn't pursue the matter because we had nothing to add to your investigation. Claire and I were talking at the time of the impact. We never even heard the shot. It happened so fast. The shot and the accident seemed simultaneous. Both Claire and I hit our heads quite severely when the car to our rear slammed into us. Claire actually lost consciousness. All of my attention was on her. I'm sure you understand." He paused. "By the way, have you determined who shot the taxi driver in the head?"

"No. Not yet," the officer said. "Seems nobody saw a thing. Typical with this kind of murder. It happens very quickly and without the slightest warning . . . like a strike of lightning. By the time people in the area figured out what had happened, the gunman was long gone. According to our lab, the single shot came from a rifle—specifically, a Beretta M501 Sniper with a Zeiss scope. That gun has a hidden harmonic balancer that reduces the barrel vibrations and assures accuracy. It's a deadly weapon."

He stopped to gather his thoughts. "While this resembles a mob hit, it might not have been. Certainly it came from someone who knew what he or she was doing. Hitting a moving target with that kind of precision requires expertise. The marksman may have been a sharpshooter in the army at some point."

He looked from Guy to Claire. "We have found nothing in the

driver's background to indicate he had any kind of a checkered past—no financial or gambling debts, no sworn enemies, no shady associates . . . " He cleared his throat. "So we remain unclear about the actual target of the shooting."

"What's your best guess at this stage in your investigation?" Claire asked.

"In truth, Ms. Caswell, the bullet might well have been intended to harm either you or Mr. Lombard." The officer watched Claire carefully to see if she would react to his statement. She didn't. "Perhaps now the two of you will share with me why you are here in Italy. What is your business?"

The officer's eyes drilled into Claire's.

"We're here to enjoy your remarkable country," she replied. "Does there need to be another reason?"

"Is there one?" the officer persisted.

"It's hard to believe that two Americans can't visit Italy without being questioned as to why we're here," Claire said. She shook her head. "I've always heard Italians are warm and welcoming people. But this doesn't feel like it."

Great, Guy thought. Keep it up, Claire. You're avoiding his questions admirably.

Suddenly, Officer Bubbiano backed off his line of questioning. "Tell me, why did you come here today? I am told it involves the death at Teatro alla Scala last evening."

"It does," Guy said. "Claire and I went to see *Romeo and Juliet*. We were there when it happened."

"On *opening night*? The two of you had tickets? How did you get them?" the officer asked, studying the two with his questioning eyes.

"Let's just say, we have connections," Guy said. He chuckled softly.

The officer was not amused.

"And what specific information do you have for me today?" the officer continued. He looked at his watch and rubbed his hands together. "I do not have much time. I have another appointment in minutes. So please, get on with it."

"We saw the young woman at dinner—at Conti Café—before the opera," Claire started. "We ate there too. In fact, not far from her table. We saw her again after dinner, waiting in the taxi line."

"Was she alone at the restaurant and waiting for the taxi?" Bubbiano asked.

"Oh, no," Claire said. "We saw her eating dinner and standing in the taxi line with the man identified in this morning's newspaper article—Anthony DiNetto. Then we saw the couple again at the opera house sitting in an upper-tier box—apparently the one the woman fell from. We noticed DiNetto in particular because he was dressed in a light-colored suit and wore a white Panama hat. Most everyone else dressed in black for the festive opening. He stood out in the crowd, as I'm sure you can imagine."

"Well, well, well," Officer Bubbiano said. He rubbed his chin. "Death certainly seems to follow the two of you around—first the taxi driver and the bicyclist, and now the young woman at the opera house. How do you explain this?"

"Things happen," Guy said. "We have no other explanation."

"We didn't know if this information might be helpful to your investigation of the woman's death. We wanted you to know about it," Claire said. "If I may ask, what is this DiNetto saying about last night's tragedy?"

"You can ask, Ms. Caswell, but I will not share that information with you," the officer replied. "DiNetto is a hero around these parts. The people love him. He made it big, and they respect him for that. He is philanthropic. Some of the money he makes in the US he brings back to us—to his home country. He builds parks and schools for the children. How can we not admire this selfless man?"

"How did he explain away what happened last night?" Claire persisted.

"Exactly *who* are you, Ms. Caswell? A policewoman from the US? You ask too many questions." He stared at the female investigator as if trying to pry the truth from her eyes. "What is your interest in all of this?"

Claire stiffened in her seat. "I'll tell you what our interest is, sir. The woman fell to her death only feet from where we sat at the opera house last evening. It's not the kind of thing one forgets. It was our first and only time visiting La Scala, and now this tragedy tainted our experience. If I were you, I'd want to examine her companion's story up, down, and sideways. He knows precisely what happened. He was with her in the box. How did he claim she managed to fall from a box with a solid railing all around it in front of the seats? How is that possible? Was she drugged? Something in her wine at the restaurant, perhaps? Did the medical examiner run a toxicology report on the woman at the time of the autopsy? Why did DiNetto not race down to help her when she fell? He was nowhere to be seen. It makes me wonder what really happened—"

"Okay, enough of this conjecture!" Bubbiano interjected. He flared his nostrils. "DiNetto claims she—his companion—suddenly became dizzy and fell forward when she attempted to stand up. He tried to help her, but it was too late. She plummeted over the railing before he could stop her. That's his story, and we have no reason to disbelieve it. And by the way, an autopsy wasn't ordered. There was no reason for it." The officer's tone was getting icier with each word. "Anything else, Ms. Caswell?"

Just then, another officer approached and handed him a folded piece of paper. Officer Bubbiano read it immediately, handed it back to the other man, and thanked him. Then he turned his full attention back to Claire and Guy.

"Well, well, well," the officer said again. "What a surprise. It's seems that the two of you are more than mere tourists to our lovely country. You are not being truthful with me. And I do not like this. I had you checked out after I was notified you were in the lobby today. The report just came in. Apparently you are private investigators from Miami Beach, Florida. Now I will ask you once again. Just what brings you to Italy?" His eyes bore into Claire's, then settled on Guy's.

Neither investigator said a word.

"Oh, so you are playing this the hard way? Is that what you are doing?" Officer Bubbiano asked. "Why will you not say why you are here? What exactly are you hiding?"

Claire thought quickly. Obviously, she didn't want DiNetto tipped off that she and Guy were tailing him. And based upon the Italians' loyalty and love for Anthony DiNetto, she knew that very thing would happen if Officer Bubbiano learned the truth. It would put their entire mission in jeopardy.

"Sir, we are investigators, that part is true," she said. "But does that mean we can't enjoy a vacation in your delightful country? We work hard at home, and once in a while we need some time off from our stressful profession. Isn't that allowed? You, of all people, can understand what comes with the territory."

Her words seemed to strike a chord with the officer. He exhaled deeply and sat back in his chair. "Whatever you do while you are here, please try to stay away from any more people losing their lives, will you?" He handed them each his business card.

"You have our word on it," Guy replied. "It hasn't been pleasant for us either, I can assure you."

"If you need anything while you are here in my country, let me know," Officer Bubbiano said. "Do not hesitate." He paused. "Oh, and one more thing. We pulled the body of a man out of a dumpster in a bad section of Milano early this morning. We found recent gunshot residue on his skin, on his clothing, and on the Beretta sniper rifle dumped with him. We believe it was the gun used to kill the taxi driver. The man had one bullet between his eyes—from another make of gun." He again glanced at his watch.

"The plot thickens," Guy said. It had become a favorite phrase of his. "Keep us posted."

The investigators thanked him, said their good-byes, and walked toward the front double doors to exit. Just before stepping out, Claire turned around to see Bubbiano standing only feet behind them. When her eyes met his, the officer gave Claire a wink. "*Ciao!*" he offered with a flirtatious smile.

As soon as the investigators were out of sight, the officer picked up his cell phone and made a call. "We have trouble," he whispered.

7

THE INVESTIGATORS SPOTTED a café across the street from the police station and decided to grab a cup of coffee. It was a sitting-down-with-a-hot-cup-of-coffee kind of day. The rain had paused temporarily, but the sky remained laden with heavy cloud cover, promising more precipitation at any moment. They walked across the street, sat down at an inside table for two near the establishment's front windows, and ordered espressos.

Claire grabbed her notepad and pen from her backpack and scratched more notes.

Two diminutive cups of strong black Lavazza coffee arrived with a plate of complimentary bite-sized iced cookies. Claire and Guy savored the hot beverages and sampled the tasty Italian sweets.

"This hits the spot!" Guy said. "I think I'll have another." He turned his head momentarily to flag down the server.

Claire's gaze fell on the police station across the street. To her shock, she saw Anthony DiNetto entering the building's front doors.

"Guy," she said urgently, "DiNetto just walked into the police station. Can you believe it?" She looked at her watch. Not twenty minutes had passed since the two investigators had walked out of the same building. "What are the odds?"

"I'm sure DiNetto will be tipped that the two of us are here in Milan. *Shit*! Just what we didn't want," Guy said. "Now trailing the man will become much more difficult."

"Look at this. I don't like what I'm seeing," Claire said, watching DiNetto and Officer Bubbiano exit the police headquarters and walk in the direction of DiNetto's dark gray Ferrari—parked illegally only feet from the entrance.

The two men got into the vehicle, and DiNetto sped off.

"I hope Officer Bubbiano has a damned good reason for this," Guy said.

"If only we could have followed them," Claire said. "It's really bothering me that an autopsy wasn't ordered on Adelfa Pontillo. At this point, Officer Bubbiano can't possibly be certain how or why she slipped or fell from the box at La Scala. Seems like extremely poor police work."

BACK AT the Hotel Principe di Savoia, Claire pulled out her notepad and reviewed her notes as they waited for DiNetto to return. Things were certainly getting interesting, and it really was just beginning. Only time would tell what the rest of this case would hold.

The investigators sat in the lobby—making a show of looking through the daily newspaper, even though they couldn't read it.

Claire had learned so much in her years as an investigator. But one truth stood out above the rest: things are rarely as they appear. Don't jump to conclusions, she told herself, not until all the facts are on the table. Right now, while it looked bad for Officer Bubbiano, there may well be a plausible explanation for driving off with DiNetto in his pricey car. But at that moment, she couldn't think what it might be.

Guy was hungry for lunch, so he and Claire walked into the fancy restaurant located on the hotel's main floor. They were delivered to a table that looked out onto the manicured grounds of the gated lawn. Each ordered iced tea and a sandwich. While eating, they discussed how following DiNetto around Europe was not going to be an easy task.

Activity at the restaurant's entrance garnered Claire's attention. When her eyes followed the noise, it was none other than DiNetto and several other Italian men coming in to dine. Thankfully, the group was seated across the aisle from the investigators, allowing a good amount of physical distance between them, but still affording the sleuths easy observation.

DiNetto was a character. There was no doubt about it. Unbridled charisma poured from his being. His voice was loud, deep, and commanding, and he thoroughly monopolized the conversation. He spoke using continual hand gestures, and his facial expressions engaged the others at the table. They laughed and howled at his stories, and DiNetto seemed to enjoy every moment, as if performing on stage for an audience.

"We need to follow him once he leaves the restaurant," Claire said. "I don't want to lose him again."

"We'll give it our best," Guy said. He called over the server and settled the bill.

When DiNetto and his friends left the restaurant, Claire and Guy got up and cautiously followed them out. DiNetto said his good-byes and walked toward the elevator. The investigators returned to the hotel lobby and sat down on comfortable chairs. They would wait until DiNetto left the hotel, no matter when that would be, and shadow him.

Outside, rain continued to water the earth.

While they waited, they talked.

"I wonder how Jin is doing," Guy said.

Claire looked at her watch. "Let's call him and find out. It's early there, so maybe try his cell."

Guy dialed the number, and Jin picked up after the first ring.

"Good to hear your voice, Mr. Lombard," Jin said. "Oh, and before you ask, everything is going well. No emergencies. A few calls. I took detailed messages and explained you were out of the office on business and would be back in several days. Nothing to worry about. How is Ms. Caswell?"

"Claire and I are both fine, Jin. Thanks for asking," Guy said. "Our case is getting more interesting by the hour."

"Oh, listen to this," Jin said. "I forward the firm's calls to my home when I'm not there—in case of any emergencies. I got a call around *2:00 a.m.* today. It rattled me out of my sleep. It was the strangest call. When I answered, a male voice said he was a long-lost relative of 'Lombard.' He didn't use your first name. He apologized for the horribly early call, but said it was important. Claimed he hadn't seen 'Lombard' in a long time. He asked all sorts of personal questions about the two of you. My antennae went up instantly. He gave me the willies. I thought you should know."

"Did he leave a name? Did you check caller ID?" Guy asked.

"No, and yes. He didn't give me a name. And the caller ID was blocked. It just showed up as 'No caller ID.' Believe me, I checked," Jin said.

"What specifically did he ask?" Guy queried.

"He chuckled between his questions, acting as if he should know these things, but just couldn't recall. Even asked me not to tell you he'd called. Said he'd be embarrassed if you found out." Jin paused. "I answered the phone, 'Caswell & Lombard, Private Investigation,' so I think he just grabbed the name Lombard to use in his questioning. Since he didn't use your first name, I figured he didn't actually know you. He asked questions like what types of cases you and the Caswell partner investigate, where you are right now, how old the two of you are, what you look like, et cetera, et cetera—both personal and business questions, I guess."

"What information did you give him, Jin?" Guy figured it was that other officer from the Milan police department who had checked on the sleuths for Bubbiano when they arrived at the station house. The time difference would explain the early-morning call.

"Nothing. Absolutely nothing. I kept answering that I didn't have the information he requested. He didn't learn a thing from me. I promise," Jin said.

"You handled the situation well," Guy said. "I'm pleased. Keep up the good work, and we'll check in with you later. Remember: never give out information about us to anyone. Under any circumstances. And in a case like this in the future, please call us right away and fill us in. It might be important."

"With the time change between us," Jin started, "I planned to call you in a couple hours."

"Good, Jin. You're doing well," Guy said.

He hung up and told Claire about the call.

"Interesting," she said. "Our trip to Italy is definitely niggling Bubbiano." She thought for a minute or two as she glanced all around the hotel lobby. "Someone may be watching us even now."

Just then, DiNetto appeared in the lobby. Claire turned her head to the side, and Guy looked down at an Italian magazine. They remained quiet and out of his line of vision. He stopped briefly and engaged the hotel employee at the front desk in meaningless chatter.

Then he walked outside. The attendant greeted him and ran off to collect DiNetto's Ferrari. Within three minutes, the unmistakable sound of the car's mighty engine could be heard approaching the hotel's front circular drive. DiNetto tipped the valet and talked with him like an old friend. He then jumped into his car, but continued to engage the valet with his gift of gab.

Claire had asked an inside valet for their Fiat just when DiNetto walked outside. The Fiat arrived and lined up directly behind the famous Italian sports car.

The rain had returned, hitting the pavement energetically. The air smelled clean and fresh.

The investigators ran silently behind DiNetto's car as he prattled on with the attendant, and they slipped into the Fiat without arousing attention.

As the Ferrari took off slowly, it left behind the roaring sound of the oh-so-powerful engine. The people huddled beneath the outside canopy looked up in unison, watching the Italian vehicle as it made its exit along the driveway.

The Fiat followed the Ferrari closely, but no one took notice of it.

As DiNetto drove the speed limit through the city, it was easy for the investigators to maintain a comfortable following distance and avoid attracting attention. DiNetto wheeled around and through the main streets of Milan, luring all eyes his way. He was a man who liked to be noticed, and he basked in the limelight his Ferrari provided. The distinctive vehicle telegraphed luxury, wealth, and speed.

As always, many taxis, motorcycles, mopeds, and other vehicles crowded the streets. DiNetto paraded his way to his destination as the Fiat skillfully tailed behind. Then, suddenly, like a bolt out of the blue, the Ferrari made an unexpected left turn and disappeared down an unmarked side street, leaving a trail of dust behind. Guy maneuvered the Fiat to the best of his ability in an attempt to shadow the Italian car made for speed. But other cars, bikes, and motor scooters made it impossible. The Fiat was hopelessly caught in the midst of the tangled traffic web and unable to make the turn.

"Lost him," Guy wailed. He pounded his fist into the dashboard.

The expression on Claire's face said it all. "Let's go back to the hotel. I wonder if he made us."

On the drive back, Claire pulled her notepad from her backpack and updated her ongoing summary of their surveillance.

Both DiNetto and the weather were making their task a challenge, to say the least. But it was still early in the game, and Claire remained encouraged that she and Guy would soon learn DiNetto's secret.

WHEN THEY returned to the hotel, the sleuths sat in the restaurant and sipped afternoon tea.

"We'll have another opportunity to follow him tomorrow," Guy said. "Let's hope so, anyway."

Jet lag grabbed the investigators.

"I must sleep," Claire said.

"You're reading my mind," Guy said. "Let's take an hour . . . or so."

They returned to their room, fatigued and disappointed from the day's events. In no time at all, they fell fast asleep.

In Claire's dreams, she walked alone down a dimly lit cobblestone street. It was dusk, and the area was vacant of other people. She felt someone behind her, but when she turned around to look, she saw no one. She heard someone behind her, breathing, yet when she turned around a second time, still no one was there. Her walking had quickened, and now she broke into a run. She sensed the presence of a person running up behind her. She turned again and saw nothing. All of a sudden, a large hand grabbed her around the neck and pulled her into an alley. The form was dark. She couldn't make out a face, but she knew it was a man. The smell of stale garlic and cheap wine permeated his clothing. She struggled as he pushed her against the sidewall of a brick building. She tried to knee him in the groin. He just laughed. He ripped at her clothing. She belted out a scream. She screamed louder and *louder* as she writhed to get away.

Suddenly, she felt a strong hand gripping her arm and heard a familiar voice. "Claire. Claire. You're dreaming."

She fought to open her eyes, then to focus.

It was Guy. She breathed in a deep breath.

"Another bad one, huh?" he asked gently. "You were wrestling with yourself and trying to scream."

"Yeah. Same as on the plane," she said. Her body was covered with sweat, and fear gripped her expression. She was shaken to her core. "I don't like this a bit. It's the second time I've had that same dream. Not a good harbinger."

"Don't worry, Claire. You'll be with me. Nothing is going to happen to you," Guy promised reassuringly. He pulled her close and held her for a long time.

Claire got up and stepped into the shower. She washed her hair, lathered her body, then let cold water beat down on her lower back. This recurring dream bothered her greatly.

THE SLEUTHS walked down to the hotel lobby and asked the concierge for a dinner recommendation. They were starving. As Guy entangled the hotel employee in frivolous conversation, Claire's eyes searched the reservation book sitting on the counter. The writing was upside down, and that made her task difficult. She scanned for the name DiNetto. Look for the double *t*, she told herself. She couldn't see it at first, but then she found it. Her eyes looked across the line for the restaurant name. She spotted it: "Da Ilia."

"What about Da Ilia?" Claire asked.

"Ah, Ristorante da Ilia," the concierge said. "Tuscan food. Very good place. There are three rooms of seating there. Time?"

Claire acted as if she were considering his question as she glanced back at the book for the time reserved for DiNetto. Then she looked at her watch. Guy took the lead and started to cough. The distraction allowed Claire the extra time she needed to glance back at the reservation book again.

"How about eight?" Claire said.

"Eight it is," the hotel employee said. "I'll make a reservation for a private, romantic table."

"Thank you," Guy said.

Claire and Guy walked into the lobby bar and took a seat. They had an hour to kill. Each ordered a glass of Chianti Classico, and they sat in cushy chairs at a small table. They agreed they should alternate between following DiNetto in the Fiat and in a taxi. That way, their chances of being detected would be lessened. The minutes passed quickly, and soon it was time to catch a taxi to the restaurant.

When they arrived, they were ushered to a back table in a long and narrow room. A bottle of Acqua Panna and a bowl of potato puffs—thin potato chips—were set in front of them without delay.

Claire looked around. Dark wooden planks lined the ceiling, and terra-cotta tiles finished the floor. Green plants hung from wall planters and also sat in pots. Large tables of Italians ate in merriment, while other guests at an adjacent table conversed in English. A white tablecloth, covered with a salmon overlay, topped each table.

The sleuths ordered salads with shaved Parmigiano-Reggiano

cheese and spinach ravioli with sage butter sauce to share. Claire decided on the Dover sole for her entrée, and Guy requested the veal Milanese.

Not long after the food was served, DiNetto walked into the restaurant, fashionably late. This time, a woman with short, wavy brunette hair accompanied DiNetto. Again, she was much younger, and she seemed over the moon in awe of him. They were seated in the next room, visible to the sleuths through a doorway. Claire and Guy watched with interest all the way through their crème caramel dessert and as they enjoyed after-dinner coffees.

This scenario was similar in every way to DiNetto's typical modus operandi. During dinner, he leaned over and passionately kissed the younger woman, the two laughed and flirted back and forth throughout the evening, and the bottle of wine on the table drained.

Claire looked at Guy. "I have a feeling we won't find out much about DiNetto while we're in Milan. Seems like he's just here to have a good time. But I think things might change rapidly once we leave this city."

Little did she know how true her words would prove to be.

8

BACK IN THE room, Claire and Guy relaxed.

Italy was, indeed, a magical place. The Italians were gracious and welcoming, the food and wine magnificent, the atmosphere charming, and their hotel room a study in luxurious comfort.

Guy eyed Claire with that look. She knew what was on his mind.

"Care to settle in early tonight?" he asked, a mischievous look appearing in his dark brown eyes. He raised and lowered his eyebrows a couple times.

"Yes, you silly thing," Claire said.

They tumbled into bed and sank into the deep mattress and thick feather pillows.

Guy kissed Claire on her neck. Slowly. Then he slid his lips onto hers and cradled her in his bulky arms.

"Ah, my favorite place to be," she said softly.

Day three
Milan

MORNING ARRIVED. The beginning of a new day in Milan. The morning newspaper carried a follow-up story on the death at La Scala. The official police report ruled the woman's untimely demise "accidental" and closed the file. The conclusion being that the young woman had consumed too much wine at dinner, got up during the performance to visit the ladies' room, tripped over her purse on the floor, and went flying over the box rail. It happened too quickly for DiNetto to do anything to help.

Over breakfast, the sleuths discussed the matter further.

"It didn't happen that way," Claire said. "I'll bet the woman found out something about DiNetto or saw something she shouldn't have seen. There's more to this story. I know it."

"You might be right," Guy said. "But proving it is another thing. I'll bet the folks around here will believe just about anything DiNetto tells them. He's a champion in their eyes—rich, famous, a hero, and a high roller. You'll never convince them otherwise."

"The truth usually makes its way to the surface, eventually," Claire said. "So we'll see . . . "

"We still don't know anything definite about the taxi driver or the bicyclist," Guy reminded her. "Maybe I'll call Officer Bubbiano and see if he knows anything more."

"Great thought, but he probably won't tell you a thing," Claire said. "Somehow I think the two were just innocent victims in the whole thing." She liked how Guy was getting into investigator mode more and more these days. He was a natural, and it was a pleasure to watch him show off his skills.

He used his cell phone to call the officer. After a rather short conversation, he hung up.

"The bicyclist was just in the wrong place at the wrong time, according to police findings. He was riding his bike to work, as he did every morning. Very sad. And the murder of our driver remains a mystery. The police have no leads on who might have wanted him dead. The investigation is open, but it's at a standstill. No witnesses have come forward, and the police have interviewed family, friends, and neighbors of the marksman, but no one can come up with a motive for his actions. He was a quiet retired man who lived alone. Bubbiano said the possibility is growing stronger by the day that you and I were the intended targets."

"Not terribly helpful," Claire said. "Sounds like no real proof of anything. Just lots of supposition. It's what I expected. They found the body of the shooter, and the weapon, but have no motive."

Claire peered out a restaurant window. It was a beautiful June day—sunny and clear—no rain in sight.

"Today is a perfect day," she said. "Let's go up to the room, grab what we need, and wait in the lobby for DiNetto to walk through. Maybe today we'll discover something helpful."

In the room, she dutifully updated her notes.

THE SLEUTHS sat in a far corner of the vast lobby, pretending to read magazines as their cover while waiting for DiNetto to appear. A full hour passed before they caught sight of the man making his way to the hotel's front doors. He glanced in the direction of the sleuths, but didn't appear to notice them. They trailed him outside and stood off to one side after asking the valet for their Fiat. It seemed there was always a huddle of people standing in front of the hotel, providing the sleuths with useful camouflage. Soon the familiar roar of the Ferrari's engine filled the air, and seconds later it rolled up to the hotel's entrance. The valet jumped out, and

DiNetto climbed in. There was no small talk today. He seemed in a hurry as he zoomed off.

Again, like a magnet, the well-built machine earned a glance from everyone present as it departed with a roar. The Ferrari exiting any scene was akin to watching the Lone Ranger mount Silver and ride off into the sunset. People watched until either disappeared from sight. There was something magical about both the masked man on the white horse and the famous Italian automobile with its distinctive purr.

The sleuths jumped into the Fiat and left the hotel's front driveway. They spotted the Ferrari in the distance and took off after it. Not too much time passed before they were a comfortable distance behind the vehicle and a lane over. As long as the Ferrari stayed in its place, they would stay virtually hidden from sight. Guy was impressed with the speed and pickup of the Fiat. While it couldn't keep up with the Ferrari at its top speeds, it did quite well otherwise.

The streets of the city overflowed with a myriad of vehicles. The investigators faithfully followed the Ferrari for more than forty minutes. Then, to their chagrin, DiNetto zipped through a yellow traffic light just before it turned red. The sleuths were left to wait for the green light. When it appeared, Guy pushed the Fiat to a good speed as he and Claire scouted in all directions for the Ferrari. After a time, he turned a corner and pulled the car over to the curb.

"We lost the son of a bitch again," he said loudly.

Claire didn't respond. He turned to look at her.

She held up the index finger on her left hand as she lowered the front passenger window with her right. "Listen," she said.

In the distance, Guy could hear the sound of the Ferrari's engine.

"Follow the sound," Claire said. "Hurry! It's coming from that direction." She pointed.

Guy peeled off. A few minutes later he pulled over again to listen. They could still hear the sound of the magnificent Italian automobile in the distance. He drove in the direction of the sound. He sped down side roads, nearly flying. Minutes later, he pulled over to the side of the road. The investigators discerned that the Ferrari was closer now. He let his ears direct his path as he drove. Soon, the powerful engine sounded very close. He slowed the Fiat.

Claire spotted the car, and Guy pulled the Fiat to the side of the road. Both investigators watched as DiNetto drove into a yard just outside a large abandoned warehouse and parked adjacent to the only other vehicle in sight, a bronze Alfa Romeo. DiNetto walked to the building, and with both hands, he slid its front door open far enough to allow his body room to squeeze through. Once inside, he pulled the door shut.

Guy drove to an area a short distance from the yard and parked the rental car behind a clump of bushes. Then the investigators hurried along the edge of the yard, moving stealthily. As they neared the old structure, Claire noticed some dirty windows. The two crept cautiously toward the windows, crouching low as they stepped. It was a very quiet setting, with no evidence of others anywhere nearby.

When they got close, Claire whispered, "Wait here."

She bent down even lower and sidled in slow, careful steps to take a look inside. The filthy windows provided enough concealment to let her peer in without being noticed.

What she saw shocked her.

She motioned for Guy to join her.

Just as he approached, he stepped on a twig. It produced a loud crack as it snapped in two, almost mimicking the sound of a muffled gunshot. The two investigators darted quick looks at each other, and Claire grabbed Guy's arm. "Let's go," she whispered urgently.

They sprinted to the end of the building and hid around the corner. Voices sounded outside almost immediately as the men ran out to see what had caused the sound.

"Stay very still," Claire warned in a hushed tone. "Don't move or say a word."

Soon the men satisfied themselves that no human was around and returned to their meeting.

"That was close," Claire said in a low voice once the coast appeared clear. "*Way too close.*"

"I don't like this," Guy said softly. "What if they have guns?"

"Well, one of them does for sure," Claire said. "He's a police officer. The man meeting with DiNetto is none other than our friend Officer Bubbiano."

"*What?*" Guy looked shocked. "Let's get out of here."

"Yes. I saw what I needed to see," Claire whispered. "DiNetto and Bubbiano were in there talking intently. Something is up, there's no doubt about it. But there's also no way to hear what they're saying, and it's probably too risky to stick around here any longer."

"We're leaving *now*," Guy said. He spoke low and firm. "Come on."

The two raced fifty feet away from the building and into the nearby brush that ran along the perimeter of the warehouse yard. They made it back to the Fiat and left in a hurry.

Back at the hotel, the two sleuths went up to their room.

It was too early back in Miami to call Sergeant Massey and report in. As much as Claire wanted to talk with him, she would have to wait until midafternoon. She summarized the day's events in her notes.

"Well, we've now confirmed Bubbiano is involved in whatever is going on with DiNetto," Guy said. "And coincidentally, the officer drives a pricey car as well."

"We don't know for sure Bubbiano is in on something illegal, but

I agree it could easily look that way," Claire offered. "There could be another explanation, though."

"*What*?" Guy demanded. "How much more do you need to see? I mean, think about it. We saw the officer walk out of the station house with DiNetto, get into his car, and leave with him. Now we see the two having an obviously clandestine meeting in what looks to be an abandoned warehouse far outside the city limits. But you're still not sure the officer is dirty?"

"I'm not. It does look bad, but we don't know what role Bubbiano is playing in all of this," she said. "Things aren't always as they seem. I'll reserve my judgment until I see more evidence. Maybe he's working undercover to bust DiNetto. Have you considered that possibility?"

"Okay, we'll wait until we collect more evidence," Guy said. "But I bet I'm right."

Claire stared straight ahead, going over the happenings of the morning in her mind. She wished she knew more about the confidential meeting at the warehouse.

"What's next?" Guy asked.

From her backpack, Claire pulled the itinerary Sergeant Massey had given them. "Well, according to the schedule, we leave in the morning to drive to Neuchâtel, Switzerland. DiNetto plans to be there for two days before returning to Milan. Massey's notes indicate it's 240 miles from Milan—or a little over a four-hour drive traveling sixty miles an hour. We'll have to be ready first thing in the morning, in case he leaves early."

Guy pulled the maps of Italy and Switzerland from his backpack and studied them. Mountains stood on either side of Neuchâtel, and the city was located on the northwestern shore of Lake Neuchâtel, surrounded by both hilly and heavily forested areas. A route had been highlighted for the investigators to take. Handwritten notes on the map also indicated Neuchâtel was a mainly French-speaking city. He informed Claire.

"I'm not fluent in French," she reminded him, "but I can get by."

Guy looked up. "Switzerland has some of the greatest driving roads in the world. Especially the back roads. No wonder DiNetto wants to drive his Ferrari there." He paused. "I've heard they might throw you in jail for speeding. Not something I'd like us to experience, obviously."

Then he stared at Claire as if assessing how the next thing he was about to tell her would affect their plans for the following day. "We have to pass through the mountains to get there. The roads look good, but believe me, there will be hairpin turns along the way."

Claire shrieked. "Oh, no. Sorry. I will not be riding in a tiny car through the mountains. No can do. End of story."

"We have to," Guy said calmly. "It's the only way to get there."

"I can't. I won't," Claire moaned. "You know how I feel about heights. And since driving up that mountain to Omalos in Crete, my fear isn't better. It's *worse*. Sorry. I can't do it! It's out of the question for me."

"Well, then you'd better figure out how we'll get to Neuchâtel. It's part of this case," Guy said. "We have to go there." He paused and looked at her. "I agreed to travel to Europe again after the incident in Greece. Do you think I wanted to? I did it because I knew you wanted to take this case." Suddenly, he appeared angry.

"You're *angry* because I have a fear that is absolutely real to me?" she asked. "I suffer from acrophobia. You know that. It's extreme and irrational, I know, but I have it."

"We both need to face our fears, Claire," Guy said. "I'm facing mine, and you'll just have to face yours." He seemed cold and unrelenting.

It was a side of Guy that cropped up every once in a while, and she hated it.

She swallowed hard. She felt trapped, and she struggled to breathe. Driving up the road to Omalos had almost done her in. She somehow made it the entire way in order to save Guy's life. But it still haunted her. Remembering, she suddenly felt dizzy and nauseated. Her mouth went dry, and she felt sick.

"I need to lie down," she said. "I'm not feeling well." She walked to the bed and got in. She pulled the covers up under her chin and closed her eyes. Jet lag still had her in its tight grip, and now this to deal with. She simply couldn't handle it.

Guy left the room, but not before he grabbed a cigar from his backpack. When she heard the door close behind him, she felt very alone.

AN HOUR passed before Guy returned to the room.

Claire opened her eyes when she heard him enter. She hadn't been able to sleep. She'd lain awake with her eyes wide open, paralyzed with fear, reliving her terrifying drive to Omalos again and again. She sat up.

"You won't believe what I just witnessed," he said.

9

"I WON'T TELL you unless you agree to ride with me in the Fiat to Switzerland," Guy said.

"That's not nice. Or fair," Claire accused. "And it's quite childish too." She was put off by his insensitivity to her very real situation.

"Well?" he said. "What's your answer?"

"My answer is—I'll take the train and meet you there."

"You're kidding, right?" Guy stared at her, nostrils flaring.

"No, I'm not kidding."

"Well, do what you must," he boomed. "I'm going in the Fiat." He stormed from the room, another cigar in hand.

Claire picked up the room phone, rang the concierge, and asked him to book her a ticket on the train. Round trip. First class. Milan to Neuchâtel. Two nights. Leaving the following morning. Returning to Milan the third day.

"Not a problem, *signora*. You will take the train from the Milano

Centrale station to Bern, Switzerland, and then hop on a connecting train from Bern to Neuchâtel. You will have only a very few minutes to catch the connecting train in Bern—fewer than fifteen. You are leaving first thing in the morning." He gave her the departure and arrival times for each leg of the trip.

"Please book the tickets," she said.

"Shall I book a second set for Mr. Lombard?" the concierge asked.

"No, thank you," Claire said. "I'll be traveling alone."

"As you wish, *signora*. And pack light. You'll be handling your own luggage along the way. There will be no one to help you on the trains."

The concierge hung up, booked her tickets, then picked up the phone. He dialed a number, lowered his head, and spoke in a whisper.

Claire threw some clothes, wigs, makeup, and toiletries into her backpack. She again looked at the itinerary Sergeant Massey had provided. He had made a reservation for a room at the Beau-Rivage Hotel in Neuchâtel. Handwritten notes on the schedule indicated: "Hotel is located on the lake, across the street from the main square. Bus and tram service next door, if needed."

She grabbed a sheet of notepaper from the desk and quickly jotted a note:

Guy,

I'll meet you in Neuchâtel at the Beau-Rivage Hotel tomorrow. Sorry we won't be traveling together. I'm taking the train first thing in the morning—Milan to Bern, and Bern to Neuchâtel. I'll probably be gone before you wake up. Travel safely.

Love, Claire
P.S. Don't forget to pack your disguises.

SHE LEFT the note on the desk, then crawled into bed. Sleep was just what she needed—to tackle the persistent jet lag and to forget about her fight with Guy. Before long, she fell into a deep slumber.

When Guy returned to the room, he failed to see the note. He sat in the chair beside the bed for a time watching Claire as she slept. He felt badly about the fight. He undressed and climbed in beside her. Gently, he kissed her on the back, but she didn't wake.

Day four
Milan to Neuchâtel, Switzerland

CLAIRE AWOKE early, quickly prepared to leave, and rode the elevator to the lobby. She approached the concierge desk.

"*Signora*, I have a taxi waiting for you. There is not much time to spare. Here are your tickets." He handed her an envelope. "I trust all is well."

Claire smiled at the man. "Thank you. I'll see you in a couple days when we return to the hotel. Make sure you hold our room."

"Of course, *signora*. We are fully booked, so it is wise to keep your room. Safe travels," he said.

As she walked from the hotel, the hotel employee picked up the phone and dialed a number. "She is on her way," he reported.

During the taxi ride to the train station, Claire felt downhearted. She would have preferred to be traveling with Guy, of course. But he could be so dismissive of her feelings. So utterly cold at times. Actions have consequences, she told herself. Now he'd have to drive in the Fiat without her. And she'd be alone on the trains as well. It would give them both some time to think. A single tear rolled down her cheek. She'd left without kissing him good-bye.

Claire arrived at the station and boarded the high-speed train to Bern. Then and there, on the spot, she decided she'd enjoy the three-hour journey—despite Guy's absence. She settled into her window seat and placed her backpack on the floor.

Just as the train was preparing to leave, a man rushed on board and sat down in the seat next to Claire.

"Morning, ma'am," he said, giving her a quick glance.

"Morning," she muttered. She turned her head and looked out the window.

She was not in the mood for small talk with a stranger.

The man, dressed in a business suit, set his briefcase on the floor just ahead of his feet. Although she couldn't identify the specific reason, something about him made her skin crawl. She decided not to speak any further to him.

Within a minute or two, the train started to move. Slowly at first, but then it picked up considerable speed and seemed to glide through the air. Claire took her train itinerary from her backpack, reviewed it, and noted it was an additional hour and a half from Bern to Neuchâtel. She laid her head back and closed her eyes.

"Have you taken this train before?" the man next to her asked in English.

Claire became slightly irked. Couldn't he see her eyes were closed and she was resting? She had no desire to talk to this ill-mannered man. Keeping her eyes shut, she ignored his question. Maybe he'd think she was asleep and leave her alone. No such luck.

"Is this your first time on this train?" he persisted.

She went from slightly irked to truly irritated. Again, she didn't answer the man and kept her eyes tightly closed.

"Perhaps you didn't hear me?" the man said in a louder voice.

Okay, that was it. Claire opened her eyes, grabbed her backpack, and stepped over the impertinent man's legs and briefcase to the aisle. She walked through the car to find a crewmember to assist her. She wanted to move to another seat. No one was there to help her, so she decided to walk to the next car. Suddenly, as she was moving between cars, she felt someone shadowing her. Turning in her tracks, she stared straight into the face of the man who had been sitting next to her.

"Did I disturb you, lady?" he asked.

"Please stay away from me," she said in a firm voice. She continued to move toward the next car.

He followed her.

She went from truly irritated to downright angry.

Once she stepped into the next car, she turned to face this bold, bad-mannered blockhead. "If you do not leave me alone at once, I will have the police arrest you when we reach Bern. *Comprenez?*"

Just then, the conductor appeared.

"Problem, *madame?*" he asked.

"Yes. This man is bothering me. He will not leave me alone."

"Return to your seat, *monsieur*. Now!" the conductor said. "And *madame*, you come with me. I will find you another seat."

The passenger glowered at Claire, turned, and retreated to the car he had come from.

"Not sure what his problem is," she told the conductor, "but he's giving me the creeps."

"The *creeps?*" he asked. "I don't understand."

"He's frightening me," she said. "Following me."

"This is not permitted," he responded. "It will not happen again. Not on my watch and not on my train. I can assure you. Or we will not allow him to ride this train again. We do not tolerate such behavior."

Claire breathed a sigh of relief. She thanked the conductor and followed him to another seat. There was a woman sitting in the aisle seat who smiled when the investigator sat down. The passenger greeted Claire in Italian and then said no more.

Once again, Claire found herself in a window seat. The train streaked along its route, affording almost no visibility of the outdoor scenery. She tucked her backpack securely between her feet and closed her eyes. Soon the speed and motion of the train rocked her to sleep.

At some point, she awoke with a start. She felt someone's touch. Opening her eyes, she looked directly into the face of the ill-bred man. It was a face she wouldn't forget—close, deep-set eyes; wide nose; and wiry hair. He was staring at her from inches away and tapping her on the shoulder. Unbelievable! Was there no end to this revolting character?

Claire looked around her. The female passenger who had been sitting next to her when she fell asleep was no longer there. She saw no one else in the car but this man. Fear gripped her.

"Everyone is gone. Except for you and me, pretty lady," the man said. "We arrived in Bern minutes ago. Everyone has exited the train." He gave her a noxious smile.

Suddenly, Claire remembered she had less than fifteen minutes to board her connecting train. She reached for her backpack, secured it tightly in her hand, got up, and pushed her way past the threatening man, almost knocking him off his feet. She ran for the exit and flew down the stairs. Desperately, her eyes searched the area until she spotted the other trains. Running like the wind, she refused to look back. She made it to the train marked Neuchâtel just as its doors were closing.

"I must get on board," she screamed to the conductor, waving the ticket in her hand. "*I must!*"

He reached for her hand and helped her up the steps as the train was pulling out.

"Thank you very much," she said. "Thank you!"

The conductor reviewed her ticket and led her to a seat.

As the train started out, Claire glanced out the window. To her horror, she saw the scary man beating on the train to let him on board.

Claire shook her head when the conductor looked her way, conveying her thoughts without words.

The conductor walked along the aisle, ignoring the man waving his arms outside. Soon momentum built, and the train was on its way to Neuchâtel. Claire emitted a long, deep sigh of relief. After her run-ins with the disturbing character, she couldn't wait to see Guy. Besides, she wanted to know what he'd seen that first time he left the room in anger. He still hadn't told her.

It wasn't long before Claire detected a slowing of the train's speed, and soon thereafter it pulled into the station at Neuchâtel. She grabbed her backpack and departed the train, relieved to be at her destination—and even more relieved to be rid of the repulsive passenger. She walked to the taxi stand and hailed a cab. Within a short time, the driver delivered her to the Beau-Rivage Hotel. She paid the fare and tipped him. A uniformed porter welcomed her to the grand hotel and walked her to the check-in counter.

"I'm part of the Caswell-Lombard party. Checking in," she said.

"First time visiting us?" the uniformed clerk asked.

"It is," she said.

"We have a very nice junior suite reserved for you for two nights," the hotel employee responded in English, "with a magnificent view of the Alps and the lake." He smiled. "One of our best. Room 316— on the third floor." He reviewed the reservation. "Is Mr. Lombard with you?"

"No, but I expect him shortly. I got an earlier start today," she said.

"Sign the registration form, and I'll give you a room key. I'll keep the other one here for Mr. Lombard when he checks in." He passed the check-in card and pen her way.

She signed, and he handed her a key.

"*Beau rivage* means 'beautiful shore.' I know your stay with us will be memorable," the employee said. "Our setting is relaxed and tranquil. And our staff is dedicated to meet your every need. Please let us know if there is any way we can assist." He smiled. "We are very close to the historic medieval town center of Neuchâtel. You can easily walk there. You must not miss the castle and the twelfth-century Collegiate Church. This is a special and charming city. Please enjoy all of it." He paused. "Will you need help with your luggage?"

"No, thank you. I only have a backpack," she said.

"Very well, *madame*," he said. "Again, enjoy your stay!" He pointed to the elevator.

Claire rode it to the third floor. She found the room easily and entered. The elegant suite was spacious and tastefully decorated in hues of creams, pale yellows, and soft blues, and it was accented with rich wood trim. The windows afforded a splendid panoramic view of Lake Neuchâtel and the Alps.

An immediate sense of calm overtook Claire. She breathed in deeply and exhaled slowly.

She spotted a Nespresso coffee machine on the bar, brewed herself a cup, and walked over to a high-backed armchair close to the windows. It had been a tough day, and she needed solitude. She sat down and sank into the chair's deep cushion. The view before her seemed surreal. White swans glided on the lake, and the mountains stood just behind like stately sentinels. As she enjoyed the steaming drink, she thought about Guy and their fight the day before. Oh, how she hated these disagreements. Fights between them happened infrequently, but they did happen. Both were strong-willed people, and neither one tended to give in easily.

This time, she couldn't have yielded. Although irrational, her terror of heights was visceral. Being the passenger in a tiny Fiat barreling through mountainous terrain was unthinkable. Guy, on the other hand, loved driving—anywhere, anytime. He couldn't comprehend her resistance to a situation that seemed to him so unremarkable, even pleasant. She thought about it longer. Why couldn't he put himself in her shoes? Why didn't he understand her fear—even if he didn't share it? She hated his lack of empathy for her terror.

The hot coffee tasted wonderful. She made herself a second cup and returned to the chair, and to her thoughts.

The man on the train had terrified her in a different, but no less palpable, way. She was alone and he was persistent. What would have been his next move had she not bolted from the car when she did? Traveling with Guy made her feel safe. The situation wouldn't have happened if he'd been with her.

Then, suddenly, her thoughts turned to the dream she'd experienced twice. Was the train incident a foreshadowing of things to come? Was it her recurring dream playing itself out? She shuddered and felt chilled. Even the coffee couldn't warm her.

She left the chair, put on her nightgown, walked to the bed, pulled back the covers, and crawled in. It was comfortable, and soon she'd feel warmer. Her head settled deep onto the down pillows, and she drew the comforter up around her. She fell asleep and began to dream.

Sometime later, she became aware of a presence. She felt someone next to her. How long had she slept? She didn't know. She was groggy, and her eyes stung. An arm came across her waist, and she thrust it away. Her body tossed and twisted. The arm returned. And then she felt a soft kiss on her cheek.

She awakened and saw Guy lying next to her.

"I'm sorry we fought," he said.

"I'm sorry too."

10

GUY TURNED TOWARD Claire, pulled her close, and caressed her. His body was warm against hers, and she could feel his breath on her skin and hear the beat of his heart. And she could smell the scent of his John Varvatos cologne—her favorite.

Claire felt safe in his arms, but thoughts of their fight still plagued her. Could she trust him completely? Would he blow up again the next time they disagreed on something? Walk out of the room and refuse to discuss the matter? Disregard her feelings? She had been forced to take the trains to Bern and Neuchâtel herself—and deal with the infuriating passenger who wouldn't leave her alone—without Guy's help. It all could have been avoided if they'd just traveled together.

He turned her toward him and kissed her full lips passionately.

"I love you," he said. "I was insensitive. I apologize." He buried his face in her neck and smelled her sweet skin. "I don't want this kind of thing to happen ever again. I worried about you on the train. And to be honest, I didn't enjoy driving all the way here without you, not one bit. Parts of the drive were tough, and it would have been very difficult for you. I realize that now."

His words melted her anger.

"A strange man on the first train kept bothering me. I wish you'd been there to help."

"If I had, I would have knocked him on his—"

"I know . . . I know," she said. "But you weren't."

After an hour, they got up and dressed for a late lunch. Both were hungry.

They walked to the elevator and rode it to the main floor. The hotel's restaurant, Restaurant O'terroirs, had seating inside and out. They opted to eat outside and were led to an umbrella-covered table. The investigators inhaled the fresh air and wallowed in the warm sunshine and the extraordinary setting. They ordered from the menu of the week, which promised a selection of innovative items crafted from locally grown produce to create a variety of mouth-watering appetizers, entrées, and desserts.

Over lunch, they each discussed the details of their trips to Neuchâtel. Guy commiserated with Claire as she told him more about the insufferable passenger she'd been forced to deal with on the first train.

"The *bastard!*" Guy said. "I only wish I had been there. This never would have happened."

Guy told her about driving the Fiat to Neuchâtel. The route was beautiful, but treacherous in spots and downright scary at times. And he didn't spot the Ferrari the entire way.

When they finished their stories, Claire looked at Guy. "What did you see at the Hotel Principe di Savoia in Milan? You never did tell me."

"I saw one of the concierges whispering with DiNetto. The same concierge who helped us book reservations for the spots DiNetto patronized."

"I would have loved to hear that conversation," she said. "Money for information, perhaps? We need to assume the employee told DiNetto we've been shadowing him." She paused. "That puts our lives in great jeopardy. I wonder if the concierge also informed DiNetto I'd be traveling alone on the trains today. DiNetto might have sent that repellent man to harass me . . . or worse."

"You're probably right on all counts," Guy said. "We need to presume DiNetto is on to us. That way, even if he isn't, we'll be even more cautious."

"Let's face it," Claire said. "To date, we have no solid proof of anything nefarious on DiNetto's part. We know only about the clandestine meeting he had in Milan with Bubbiano—in that abandoned warehouse—but we don't know why they met. Not yet, anyway. We know our taxi driver was murdered shortly after we arrived in Italy, and there's a chance we were the real targets of the hit. So we can't rule out the possibility DiNetto was the puppet master behind it. Especially if he somehow discovered we were arriving in Europe to investigate his activities. And there's the death at La Scala . . ."

"Well, we don't have many days on this case. Hopefully we won't let Massey down, and we'll get the goods on this DiNetto character to put him away for a long time," Guy said. "Maybe it will happen here in Neuchâtel."

"Yeah. I wonder why he's visiting this place. It seems so out of the way. It's a quaint tourist destination, not the sort of place you'd expect to find a worldly playboy." Claire pondered the thought. "We need to find out why he's here." She raised her eyebrows and pursed her lips.

"What's next on the agenda?" Guy asked.

"Let's walk over to the town center. I'd like to see the fairy-tale castle built in the Middle Ages," Claire said. "It might be our only chance. And the twelfth-century church too. I adore old structures. We can't follow DiNetto again until he shows up, and I'm going to assume he's not here yet. We haven't seen him—or heard his distinctive voice or roaring car engine. He's probably somewhere on the road to Neuchâtel in that showy Ferrari. Until then, I say let's see this medieval city."

The history-buff side of Guy was all for it. "I'd like that."

The two strolled to the town center and all around its streets, taking in everything about the charming city drenched in history and built in such a concentrated manner along the lakeside. Students from the French-speaking University of Neuchâtel and numerous other international schools filled the streets. Claire observed that most of the passersby spoke French, but occasionally she also caught snippets of German, Italian, and some English.

They passed three historic churches—including the Gothic-style Collegiate Church built in 1185—plus libraries, museums, countless street fountains, ancient fortifications, hotels, an observatory, and an ancient turreted prison tower. But it was the fairy-tale castle that garnered Claire's full attention.

It was a fascinating tour of the old city, and they enjoyed every minute of it. They could see Neuchâtel had so much to offer, even beyond the medieval architecture. It was a place for tourists to view the fine art collection of the Musée d'Art et d'Histoire, dine on rich foods and wines, and take in the city's charming eighteenth-century mechanical figurines. The temperature was in the low seventies, making the stroll delightful. They stopped along the way for coffee. When they sat, Claire pulled her notepad and pen from her backpack and jotted additional notations to keep her summary up-to-date.

She glanced at her watch. "We've used up a couple hours. I think we should go back to the hotel and see if we can spot DiNetto."

They ambled back to the Beau-Rivage and into the lobby.

As fate would have it, DiNetto was just checking in. Timing is everything, Claire thought.

The investigators scooted through the lobby and sat down in chairs positioned in a far corner. That way they could watch him, but he couldn't spot them easily. DiNetto had a loud voice, and people many feet away could hear him.

He seemed to celebrate the attention that followed wherever he went—not unlike the Pied Piper of Hamelin with the children of the town. Today, he even wore a bright red blazer. Patrons of the hotel gathered near him, some followed him, hoping for a chance to greet him. People whispered and pointed when he walked by. Others assembled outside the hotel's entrance, oohing and aahing over his exquisite dark gray Ferrari.

After completing his check-in, a bellman lifted DiNetto's small suitcase and led him to his room.

"Greetings, my fair people," DiNetto said boisterously in French, waving his right hand through the air. "*Bonjour!*"

"Who does he think he is?" Claire asked.

"Someone very special, obviously," Guy said. "Someone who has made it big and wants the world to know it. I wonder how he made his many fortunes."

"Not legally, according to Sergeant Massey," Claire said. "Or maybe it's all an act. If you want people to think you're rich and famous, you have to act that way. We don't know about his true financial situation. Not yet, anyway. Maybe he lives from scam to scam. And maybe he's currently out of money."

"Point well taken," Guy said. "But we know he lives in a multi-million-dollar home in a ritzy area of Miami Beach, and his cars alone are worth a fortune."

"Right," Claire said.

Within minutes, DiNetto reappeared in the lobby and made his way to the hotel's Lake-Side Lounge. The sleuths waited a few minutes to allow him time to get settled at a table. The restaurant was outside, facing the lake, and divided into two sections: a lounge with comfy seating and a more formal dining area. DiNetto sat at a table in the dining area, one a good distance away from other diners. A server delivered a drink to his table, and Claire and Guy watched as DiNetto placed his food order. He sipped his libation as he looked out over the water. He appeared pensive.

Claire pulled her hair back into a quick ponytail, lifted a scarf from her backpack, and tied it around her head. Then she put on a pair of black-rimmed glasses. She handed Guy a pair of tortoise glasses and a beret, and he put them on. From this point on, disguises seemed imperative, especially if the concierge in Milan had tipped DiNetto that the two sleuths were following him.

"Did you bring along your disguises, Guy?" Claire asked him.

"I did," he said.

Together, they made their way to the adjacent lounge area and sat down on one of the many orange sofas. They picked a seat behind a massive, leafy potted tree—one that would make them nearly invisible to their target. They ordered iced teas and sat back, eager to observe DiNetto.

Before long, a man in a dark suit joined DiNetto. They saw the visitor only from the back, so they didn't catch a glimpse of his face. The men exchanged handshakes. At first, quiet and private conversation transpired. Then the discussion grew more aggressive and dramatic.

Claire's inner voice predicted: *Things are about to get very interesting.*

The investigators watched as the two men ate and continued

their animated dialogue. At certain times, their words appeared friendly and uproarious, and at other times they dulled to a whisper as the men leaned closer to each other, as if worried about being overheard. There seemed to be a plan afoot, but what was it? The visitor pulled a sheet of paper from his case and placed it in front of DiNetto, extending him an ink pen with his left hand. Further conversation ensued, and then, unexpectedly, DiNetto shoved the paper back toward the visitor. The pen followed, sailing through the air and hitting the man squarely on his chest. DiNetto's voice grew louder, and his hands moved with great passion, but neither Claire nor Guy could make out his words.

Suddenly, the two men got up to leave the restaurant. As they turned to walk toward the exit, Claire's eyes widened.

"The second man," she said in an angry tone. "He's the despicable man I dealt with on the train! Now it's beginning to make sense. DiNetto must have arranged to have him bother me—to try to scare me off. The hotel concierge in Milan *must* have tipped off DiNetto that I was traveling alone on the train." She paused. "Now I'm wondering if this man is working with DiNetto on his scam."

"Damn DiNetto," Guy said. "And damn that other bastard. I'd like to punch his lights out."

"No!" Claire said. "We can't blow our disguises. We'll handle it the legal way—when the time is right. For now, we have another connection. This is becoming more and more curious. I have to call Massey today and fill him in on everything we're finding."

The investigators paid their tab and followed the men out, staying a safe distance behind.

DiNetto and his visitor shook hands reluctantly before parting company. DiNetto walked directly to the elevator and disappeared behind its doors.

Claire and Guy waited a few minutes and returned to their room.

Claire called Sergeant Massey. He answered after the first ring.

"It's Claire Caswell."

"I've been waiting for your call," he said. "Tell me everything."

Claire pulled her notepad from her backpack and filled him in on everything that had happened, beginning with their arrival in Italy.

"The taxi accident makes me worry," the sergeant said. "Also, the man on the train, Ms. Caswell. Stay safe. There's more to this DiNetto than meets the eye, and it sounds likely that he's on to you. Find out what you can, but never jeopardize your safety. Abort the mission if it becomes necessary. And that's an order. Do you understand what I'm saying?"

"Loud and clear," she said. "Based on what we've seen so far, something is about to break. We can feel it building."

"Keep me posted. Be safe," Sergeant Massey said. "And make sure you and Gaston try the Neuchâtel chocolates while you're there," he added in a lighter voice. "They've been called the 'food of the gods' in the past. I did some research. The city has many well-known chocolate makers. Throw a couple of those chocolate bars into your backpack to bring back for me, will you?"

Claire and Guy freshened up and returned to the hotel lobby to watch for DiNetto. About an hour and a half passed before he showed up. When he did, he went straight to the concierge desk. The conversation between the two men was lively and friendly. When DiNetto finished, he shook the employee's hand robustly. The employee nodded a thank-you for the handsome tip DiNetto had passed his way.

DiNetto walked outside.

Claire approached the concierge.

"Is there anything fun to do in the city tonight?" she asked.

"Well, aside from walking around the town center and seeing it lit up, which is always delightful, the annual masquerade ball is tonight, from eight until eleven. It's a party hosted by the city. Some tickets remain. In fact, I just reserved one for another guest."

"Oh," Claire said. "Mr. DiNetto?" She smiled. "We just saw him standing here."

"Yes, he will be attending. Do you know him?" he asked.

"Who doesn't know him? Or should I say, who doesn't know *of* him," Claire said. "He's famous in these parts." She chuckled.

"I'd say so," the employee said.

"Yes," Claire said. "I'll need two tickets to the ball. Is there a place we can rent costumes?"

"Certainly, *madame*," the concierge said. "There is a store in the city center." He scribbled the address on a small piece of paper and handed it to Claire.

"It's a popular event. I recommend you go to the costume rental shop soon, before everything is gone. I'll have your tickets waiting here at the counter. Pick them up on your way to the ball." He paused for a moment. "And have a *fabuleux* time this evening."

Claire rushed back to Guy and filled him in.

"Let's go costume shopping," she said. "Tonight's an ideal opportunity to watch DiNetto without him knowing we're there."

The costume store was fascinating—filled with feathered boas, hair accents, hats of all kinds, old-fashioned gowns, period apparel for men, masks, and a multiplicity of other items. The sleuths felt like kids in a candy store.

A salesclerk approached.

"English?" she asked.

"Yes," Claire said. "Will you please assist us in putting together two outfits for tonight's masquerade ball?"

"It would be my pleasure, *madame*," the woman said.

Within minutes, the clerk had pulled together two magnificent costumes.

They thanked her, paid the rental bill, and walked back to the hotel.

The sleuths showered and donned their costumes for the occasion.

"Remember," Claire reminded Guy, "we'll be incognito, but so will DiNetto."

11

CLAIRE AND GUY stood in front of the bathroom mirror in full costume.

"We look good," Guy said. "Actually, we look amazing."

"Good enough to be close to DiNetto without him recognizing us," Claire said.

"We'll find out."

Guy dressed in an ivory suit jacket with tails. The jacket was decorated with heavy gold buttons and piping along the lapels and around the cuffs. A mass of lace ruffles popped out from under a gold-buttoned vest made of print-on-print ivory brocade. Matching tightly fitted white pants, cuffed just below the knees, were secured by bows. White tights clung to his legs. Heeled ivory shoes—the buttoned type—and an ivory three-cornered hat with matching gold piping completed his ensemble. He carried a walking stick topped with gold filigree. A black-and-white checkered mask with openings for his penetrating dark eyes covered the top half of his face. It was a period costume that required the wearer's full commitment, and he wore it well.

Claire's cap-sleeved gown was a brilliant mix of rich reds. Cinched tightly at the waist, the skirt consisted of layer upon layer of matching scarlet lace. A golden-blonde wig of long ringlets, elbow-length sheer crimson gloves, and sequined pumps in an intense red embellished the look. But the crowning glory of her costume was the asymmetrical, delicately ornate red mask. It was bejeweled and patterned with elaborately raised swirls, and it featured a scarlet feather dangling from one side. The mask covered her face from high on her forehead to the tip of her nose. It molded perfectly over the structure of Claire's face and showcased her striking green eyes in a mysterious way. Her full lips, covered with a vivid, glossy, ruby lipstick, looked luscious. And she carried a matching silk evening bag to complete the look.

"Look at you, Claire!" Guy said. "You look gorgeous—arousing! Every man at the ball will be after you. There's no doubt about it." He shot her his famous grin.

"But I only have eyes for you," she said. She batted her lashes. "And what about *you*, Mr. Handsome? You'll be in high demand tonight too."

After locking their room, the investigators made their way to the lobby and past the hotel's front doors. The bellman stopped to look at the pair, winked, and hailed a taxi.

"To the ball," the bellman instructed the driver. "Enjoy your evening," he said to the passengers.

Claire looked over at Guy with a sweet smile.

"Who would have guessed we'd be attending opening night of *Romeo and Juliet* at La Scala, and now this—an old-fashioned masquerade ball?" she asked softly.

"Not me," said Guy. "I came into this case without expectations. But this? And La Scala? No. Never. Not in my wildest imagination."

"We'll have to try to locate DiNetto and see what we can find out about him tonight," Claire said. "Hope we can get close."

The old building hosting the formal masquerade ball was immense and ideal for the occasion. Its ground floor was open and spacious, and a wide staircase curved up to a second floor of nearly the same size that overlooked the main floor. Scores of partygoers, all dressed in elaborate costumes, had already arrived and crowded both floors. It was a sight to behold. The painstakingly chosen costumes were magnificent, so much so that each attendee's attire and mask seemed to outdo every other. The sleuths had never seen anything like it.

And everyone present was totally unidentifiable.

Suddenly, Claire remembered that the salesclerk at the costume store had given her a faux diamond to apply to her lower lip. She pulled it from her clutch, stripped off the protective coating on the adhesive, and stuck it to the left side of her lower lip. It was particularly sparkly for a fake stone, and when Claire glanced into a mirror as she and Guy made their way out onto the dance floor, it twinkled like magic under the room's perfect lighting.

Guy looked at Claire. "May I have this dance, m'lady?"

"Why, yes, handsome sir. I thought you'd never ask." She gave him a coy smile.

He whisked her into his arms, placing his left hand around her diminutive waistline, and with his right hand he held her left at shoulder level. She gripped his upper right arm with her right hand. For a moment in time, the couple felt like Cinderella and Prince Charming. They displayed their ballroom dancing skills to the music of the live string quartet. It was a fairy-tale moment. As they floated flawlessly around the main floor, Claire's and Guy's eyes searched the crowd for DiNetto. They knew his height, weight, build, and more importantly his voice, and they hoped these factors would help identify him. But, alas, many men seemed to fall into his physical description. They needed to hear his booming voice. It set him apart, and they were sure they would recognize it.

The merriment was in full swing—the atmosphere filled with intrigue and mystique. Dancers swirled, dropped, and dipped as they traversed the dance floor. Everyone laughed, chatted with a partner, and soaked in the grand time. Some even tried to guess who was under certain masks.

Guy and Claire moved up and down and around in a lively manner, then danced their way to the beverage counter. Each ordered champagne. The bartender excused himself, stepped away momentarily, then returned holding two full glasses of the white sparkling wine.

As they sipped the refreshingly cool, bubbly beverages from crystal flutes, the investigators watched the gala from the sidelines. It was as if they had stepped back into a previous century. The medieval costumes and obligatory masks intrigued them. People seemed to be flirting and dancing with anyone available, never knowing exactly who was hiding under which disguise. Some revelers wore half masks, while others wore masks covering the whole face. Some even covered the entire head. Still others carried stick masks they held over their eyes with one hand. A number of the handcrafted masks were seductive—and a few were downright grotesque. Claire and Guy noticed that several mimicked animals, others resembled Pinocchio's when he told a lie, and a large number featured beads and feathers. Many masks appeared to be created from top-quality papier-mâché. Ribbons—attached to elastic bands and tied to the back of the head—secured most face coverings in place.

Each woman's exquisite gown required a great deal of fabric.

Extravagant boas, hats, and other adornments accented each costume to suit the desire of its wearer. The men's costumes—mainly old-fashioned tuxedoes with long coats, tails, and top hats—were equally as grand, representing the heyday of the masquerade tradition. Some couples even dressed as kings and queens of the period.

The entire main floor bubbled with color. It swirled with the sweeping movements of the gowns and capes and the fluttering of handheld fans. The extreme gaiety dazzled the eye.

"How will we ever find him?" Claire asked.

"I don't think it's possible in this collection of costumes," Guy said.

Just as he finished speaking, a masked female pulled Guy's champagne glass from his hand, set it down hard on the counter, and tugged him to the dance floor. He looked back at Claire with *sorry* written across his eyes.

And in the next moment, Claire's glass was grabbed from her hand. A man dressed in a royal-purple velvet tuxedo rushed her onto the dance floor. His full mask was stark white, and he carried a scepter. He held her tightly, and no words were exchanged. While dancing to music from *The Phantom of the Opera*, Claire searched the room for Guy on every turn, but her eyes could not find him.

"At last," the man murmured, placing his lips next to hers. She could smell alcohol on his breath.

She tried to pull away, but his grip strengthened.

Just then, a man put his hand on her arm.

"May I cut in?" the male voice asked.

Claire whirled toward the voice.

She hoped it was Guy, but it wasn't. Another costumed man— this one dressed in blue satin from head to toe with a matching half mask—yanked her to him. She looked around frantically. The man in purple had completely disappeared into the crowd. The new dancer pulled her closer and began to twirl her around and around in circles. She felt dizzy. She wasn't sure if it was the champagne, the heat of the room, the dancing, or a combination of all three, but soon her knees buckled from under her, and she fainted.

She fell headfirst into the dancer's arms.

When she woke up, she found herself lying on a bed. Still in costume. Still wearing her mask. Her evening bag by her side. She looked around.

"Where am I?" she demanded.

A costumed and masked female appeared at her side.

"You are resting in an upstairs room," she said. "You passed out on the dance floor. How are you feeling?"

"How long have I been here?" Claire persisted.

"Maybe an hour or so," the woman said.

"I have to find Guy," Claire said. "He doesn't know where I am."

"Who is Guy?" the woman asked.

Claire didn't take the time to answer. She bolted from the bed and rushed out of the room. She stopped at the railing of the second-floor balcony, gazing downward as she searched the main floor for Guy. She didn't see him. She flew down the staircase and ran between and around the dancers on the main floor, needing to find her partner. But she couldn't locate him.

A masked man dressed in green grabbed her around the waist, then embraced her, trapping her arms flat against her sides, and forced her to dance. She tried with all her might to free herself from the costumed patron, but to no avail. When the song ended, the dancer relented slightly, enough that she could push him away and run toward the front door.

Just then, another man caught her by the arm. He was dressed in solid black and wore a black mask that covered his whole head. His black hat, trimmed in silver, was that of a court jester.

"You will dance with me, pretty lady," he whispered. "I have waited all night for this dance. You are the loveliest at the ball."

"I can't dance now," she said firmly. "Please let go of me."

"No," he said. "You will dance with me now."

He pulled her too close. She felt uncomfortable and struggled to put distance between them. He was strong, and she couldn't break away.

As he moved her around the dance floor, he brought his mouth close to hers.

"I will bite that diamond off your lip in time."

"No, you will not!" Claire said loudly. "Let me go!"

He danced on as if he didn't hear a word she said.

With all the might she could muster, she jammed the heel of her red sequined pump down onto the top of his foot. He winced in pain and loosened his hold enough for her to pull free. Just as she did, he ripped the faux diamond from her lower lip with his hand.

She screamed, grabbed the skirt of her gown to make sure she didn't trip on it, and dashed from the dance floor.

The man yelled after her, "You'll regret this!"

She approached the event organizers standing close to the front door and asked for their help.

"I've lost my partner," she said, allowing her anxiety to show. "I fainted earlier, and I haven't seen him since I woke up. I'm afraid something has happened to him. Please help me!"

She nervously looked over her shoulder for the jester, but didn't see him.

"What does your partner look like?" one of the planners asked.

Claire described his height, weight, and costume.

"It sounds like the man resting upstairs," one of the organizers said. "He also fainted. He hit his head on the floor and had to be carried upstairs to a room. I believe he is still there. We hire a nurse for this event in case of situations just like this, and she is looking after him. I will take you to him."

Claire agreed to go with the man. As she ascended the stairs by his side, she looked down onto the dance floor. The man in the jester costume wasn't visible. She was led to a room at the far end of the upper floor.

There was Guy. Still in full costume and mask. She rushed to his side.

The nurse spoke. "He has been out for some time." It was the same nurse who had tended to Claire in a different room.

Claire bent down and gently kissed his lips. "Honey?" she said. "Please wake up. I want us to get out of here."

He opened his eyes groggily.

"I must have hit my head. It hurts," he moaned. He reached up and touched the back of his head.

"Take these pain-killers," the nurse instructed. She handed him a short glass of water and two pills.

"Is he able to leave?" Claire asked.

"Yes, but make sure he gets a good night's rest," the nurse said. "And you too, *madame*. It's funny that the both of you fainted."

With the help of the organizer who'd led her to the room, Claire walked Guy down the staircase, through the front doors, and outside into the fresh evening air. Back inside, the gala remained in full swing.

The doorman hailed a taxi. When it arrived, Claire helped Guy into the backseat and jumped in next to him.

"To the Beau-Rivage Hotel, please," Claire instructed the driver.

As they pulled away from the building, she noticed a figure standing to the side of the drive, hiding in the shadows. She strained her eyes as they passed and could make out the faint outline of a medieval jester's cap.

12

BACK AT THE hotel, the investigators walked arm in arm to the concierge desk and stopped.

"We had an interesting time at the masquerade ball," Claire told the hotel employee.

"You left early?" he asked.

Claire smiled. "A bit. Gaston had a headache."

"I'm so sorry. Let us know if you want anything sent up to your room," the concierge said.

"Thank you," Claire said. "There were so many incredible costumes at the event this evening. You should have seen them!"

"I only wish I could have, *madame*," he replied.

"Oh, by the way, we wanted so badly to see what costume Anthony DiNetto wore to the ball. We knew, whatever it was, it would be spectacular. But of course, we couldn't identify him or anyone else because of the masks. Maybe you know how he dressed for the ball this evening?"

"I wish I could help you, *madame*, but unfortunately I cannot. He did not leave the hotel dressed for the evening's affair. He must have changed elsewhere."

Claire smiled. "Thank you. Good night."

They returned to their room, changed into pajamas, fell into the awaiting bed, and discussed every detail of the strange happenings at the festive celebration—including the excessively unpleasant men Claire was coerced to dance with and the most eerie fact that the two investigators had both fainted.

"Tomorrow we'll return the rental costumes, and the masquerade ball will be only a memory," Claire said.

She reminded herself to update her case notes in the morning and closed her eyes. The night had been eventful, to say the least.

Day five
Neuchâtel

THE NEXT morning, Claire awoke first. She pulled her notepad and pen from her backpack and jotted notes furiously. So much had happened, and she wanted to record the latest events while they were fresh in her mind.

She made a coffee, sat in a chair by the window, and watched Guy sleeping. Suddenly, her thoughts went to marriage. She had said no each time he had asked, and now she secretly feared that one day he would find someone willing to marry him—and he'd leave her. The formal union seemed so terribly important to him. But that wasn't the case for her. She loved him. And he loved her. They were together in a committed relationship. So what did it really matter? They had struggled with this issue for some time now, and she worried what would happen if it went unresolved.

Why did the thought of marriage frighten her so? Was it just that she had seen several of her friends get married only to split a couple years later? Or was there more to it? Was there something deeper?

She tasted the hot beverage and pondered the issue.

Claire missed her parents and made a mental note to call them in the late afternoon. She and Guy had left so hurriedly for Europe that she hadn't called to let them know—something she always made a point of doing.

Soon Guy stirred and sat up in bed.

"Morning, my beauty," he said sleepily.

"How's your head?" she asked. "I'm sure it's still sore." She looked at him sympathetically. "First you hurt your head in the taxi accident, and now last night you fell on your head. You poor, poor thing."

He touched the back of his head. "Actually—and thankfully—there's hardly any pain this morning. I think I might have a hard head." He let out a half-suppressed laugh. "That masquerade ball was quite something, wasn't it?"

"I'd say so," she said. "We were literally pulled apart, and I didn't see you again until they brought me to the room with the nurse. I was afraid when I couldn't find you."

He listened with interest. "We were pulled apart, and then we both fainted. Strange coincidence. Mighty strange."

"I don't believe in coincidences," Claire said.

"Meaning . . . "

"Meaning, I think someone instructed the bartender to put something in our champagne. I think *someone* wanted us to pass out, so that *something* could happen. So we'd be separated. So one of us would have to dance with someone. I think it was deliberate."

"Slow down, Claire. Tell me exactly what you think happened."

"I think we were drugged. You more than me," she said. "Remember how after we ordered our drinks, the bartender disappeared for a few seconds and returned holding the flutes. It could have happened then." She thought for a long minute as Guy looked at her. "It would have been a short-acting substance—one that wouldn't show up in our bloodstreams after a few hours. And we obviously can't go back and test our glasses for residue. So we'll never know for certain." She wrinkled her forehead.

"Shit, Claire. Why didn't you tell me this last night?" Guy asked.

"Because you had enough to deal with." She sighed. "I think it was all arranged so DiNetto could dance with me. Perhaps to question me—or threaten me."

"How was he dressed—the man you think was DiNetto?"

"I'm sure as a jester. A medieval jester. All in black. Wearing a black jester's cap with silver trim. He forced me to dance with him, and as hard as I tried to pull away, I couldn't. Finally, I jammed the heel of my shoe onto his foot to break free. As I ran away, he said, 'You'll regret this.'"

"Dammit. And once again, I wasn't there to help you." Guy grimaced.

The two showered, dressed for the day, and took the elevator to the main floor. They walked into the hotel restaurant that served breakfast, sat down, and ordered. Over strong black coffees and full plates of food, they discussed the previous evening in even greater detail. Afterward, the two returned to their room and packed the masquerade costumes and accessorics into two shopping bags. They walked briskly to the town center and entered the costume shop.

"We had a riveting time at the ball last evening, because of you," Claire said to the salesclerk. "The costumes you picked for us were hits." She smiled broadly.

They handed the bags to her.

"Oh, we were wondering," Claire said. "We saw a really fun costume at last evening's gala, and we're curious who was under the mask. The man was a great dancer, and it would be fun to know who he is. He was wearing a jester's costume. Dressed all in black from head to toe with a full-head black mask. And his jester's cap was also black with silver metallic trim."

"Well, I am not supposed to give out that type of information," the clerk said.

Guy placed the equivalent of fifty US dollars in euros on the countertop.

"It's important," Claire said. "Please. We must know."

"I guess I could make one exception," the woman said, chuckling nervously. She grabbed the money and put it in her pocket. "But you didn't hear it from me. I will deny it if anything comes of this." Her eyes darted around the shop to make sure no other customers were present.

She pulled a box of index cards closer to her. "I keep everything recorded here." She searched for a time. "Oh, yes, here it is." She lifted a card from the box. "His last name is Bubbiano. He told me he is visiting from Milan."

That name came as something of a shock.

"Are you certain?" Claire asked.

"Quite sure. He used a credit card to rent the costume. I have his information right here."

"Did you rent a costume to a man named DiNetto as well?" Claire asked.

The clerk scanned her cards. "No, I do not see that name."

The investigators thanked the woman and exited the store.

"I was so sure the jester was DiNetto . . . " Claire said.

"What the *hell* is Bubbiano doing here?" Guy asked. "And why was he at the masquerade ball?"

"Obviously he's connected to DiNetto. We just don't know why yet. DiNetto went to the Milan police station, met Bubbiano, and they drove off together in DiNetto's Ferrari. They also had a secret meeting at that abandoned warehouse. Now Bubbiano just happens to be in Neuchâtel while DiNetto is here."

Claire thought for a moment. "There was another offensive man at the ball, dressed in purple. He made me dance with him and whispered, 'At last.' I wonder what that meant. And I wonder who he was. Maybe he was DiNetto, if the jester was Bubbiano. They're about the same size. Or maybe the man costumed in purple was the obnoxious man from the train? We know he's associated with DiNetto too." She paused again, still trying to read the clues. "There was another man, dressed all in blue. And one dressed in green. All of them were overly aggressive, to say the least. DiNetto could have been any of them. "Funny, I was sure the jester was him."

Guy hesitated. "You know, I was rather aggressively passed around while we were separated too. Several masked women took me by the arm, one after the other, and held on tightly. I had to dance each time until the music stopped. I couldn't pull away either." He sighed. "I looked for you the entire time I was dancing."

"Well, after agreeing to stick close together while we're in Europe, we did one heck of a job last evening going our separate ways." Claire shrugged her shoulders and tipped her head.

"Going forward, I promise to stay by your side at all times. Enough is enough!" Guy declared.

Claire stared straight ahead, and Guy left her to her thoughts. He knew the look and never disturbed her when it appeared on her face. Minutes passed.

"There's a leak," she said. "Someone seems to be reporting our every move—that I'd be traveling alone on the train from Milan to Bern and then on to Neuchâtel, and that we'd be attending the masquerade ball. Maybe DiNetto is paying a concierge at each hotel to spy for him."

"Makes sense," Guy said.

"In retrospect, I wish I'd ripped the mask off the man in purple. He wouldn't have been happy, but at least I could have discovered his identity. Now the jester, he was a different story. He had a full-head mask that would have been impossible to remove."

They walked back to the hotel. DiNetto's gray Ferrari was parked next to the entrance, so they knew he wasn't far away. They asked the valet to retrieve their Fiat, then took seats in a different section of the lobby.

Before too long, DiNetto sauntered up to the concierge station.

"Late night?" the concierge asked him.

"Yes. Late night," he said. He was not his usual talkative self, and his tone seemed to indicate he was in a bad mood.

DiNetto walked through the double front doors and paused outside. He chatted briefly with the bellman, walked over to his car, dropped into the driver's seat, and sped off.

The investigators followed in their black rental car, once again making sure a vehicle or two stayed between the Ferrari and the Fiat at all times.

This was the last day in Neuchâtel, and if DiNetto had business to do, it would have to be done today.

Twenty minutes passed. The Ferrari suddenly veered off the road, turning onto a side street and entering a residential area. The Fiat followed behind at a slow speed. Claire spotted the dark-gray sports car parked on a side street in front of an unremarkable house. She signaled to Guy, and he turned the car around, drove a short distance, and pulled over to park.

The sleuths crept carefully as they made their way toward the house. But just as they approached, the Ferrari sped off.

"Dammit!" Guy shouted. "He made us. I thought he was out of the car."

The investigators returned to the rental car, and Guy drove away.

A concerned look appeared on Claire's face. They'd been cautious, but now there could be no doubt that their cover was blown. And this was not a good thing.

"When we return to Milan, we'll have to get a different rental car. There's no choice. He'll be looking for a black Fiat now. And we'll have to start wearing disguises whenever we're out. That's it. Disguises at all times from this point forward. No exceptions."

"Just what we didn't need," Guy said. "We'll have to lay low until we leave Neuchâtel. To be safe."

Claire grabbed his arm. "I have a hunch. Park here, and let's walk back. I have a feeling DiNetto returned to that house."

Guy pulled over and parked. They were two blocks away. The two ran the distance back and hid around the corner at the end of the street. From their vantage point, they had a full view of the house. And Claire had been right. The gray Ferrari was parked out front. They waited for several minutes, and then DiNetto and an older man exited the property's front door. Each carried five small corrugated cardboard boxes—one stacked on top of the other, for a total of ten—to the Ferrari and placed them in the trunk.

Claire's eyes scrutinized the boxes with keen interest. Each appeared to be the exact same size—she guessed they were approximately eight inches by eight inches and four inches high.

The men shook hands, and DiNetto drove off.

Claire took a good look at the older man as he returned to his house. Once he was back inside, she walked down the street and made a mental note of his address.

The sleuths returned to the Fiat.

Claire pulled out her notepad and recorded the physical

description of the homeowner, his street address, the number and size of the boxes, and the interaction between the man and DiNetto. When the investigators reached the hotel, the Ferrari hadn't returned. They took the elevator to their room.

"Those boxes," Claire said. "Wonder what's in them."

"Good question," Guy said.

"Hmm," Claire said, deep in thought.

"I'm traveling with you on the train back to Milan tomorrow morning," Guy said. "I'm returning the rental car here this afternoon. We're not traveling separately again. The stakes on this case are too high." He picked up his cell phone and made arrangements with the car rental agency in Milan to leave the Fiat in Neuchâtel and pick up a different rental car in Milan.

"Thank you," Claire said. "I appreciate it more than you know."

It was the crack of dawn in Miami Beach, but she dialed her parents, Don and Abbey, to let them know she and Guy were in Europe on a case and would be home in a few days. Hearing their voices comforted her instantly. She loved that they lived close to her and Guy, and she promised to meet for dinner soon after they arrived back in the States. After she hung up, she called Sergeant Massey and filled him in on everything that had happened since her last contact, including a detailed report of the masquerade ball and the boxes DiNetto had picked up.

"Things are heating up here," she concluded. "I think we're close to having an answer for you—but we don't have it yet. We're obviously making some people very nervous. That's always the case when we start closing in."

"Well, again, be careful, Ms. Caswell. I don't like what I'm hearing," Sergeant Massy said. "DiNetto knows you two are on his trail, and believe me, he could become very dangerous if pinned into a corner. I don't want either of you to take any unnecessary chances. Do you read me?" he boomed. "If things get too hot, get out and return home at once!"

"Of course. We're professionals," Claire said. "We'll protect ourselves at any cost. Never doubt that. And if our lives are in jeopardy, we'll parachute out."

"According to the itinerary, you and Gaston will return to Milan tomorrow. Then the following day, you'll travel south to the Italian Riviera—spending one night each in Porto Venere and in Portofino. Then on to Montpellier, France, for two nights. From there, you'll drive to Paris and hop on the flight home. You have a lot of driving ahead of you. And not easy driving, by any means." He stopped for a moment. "Keep me posted. Once you arrive in Montpellier, you'll have exactly two days to wind things up before flying home. Two days! No extensions. No excuses."

That evening, the investigators ordered room service. Afterward, they dropped into a heavy sleep.

13

ANTHONY DINETTO SAT in a comfortable chair in his room, drinking AVIV 613—a special vodka new to the market. After his first taste, it quickly became his drink of choice. Now it was the only vodka he'd consume. He toted a bottle with him wherever he went, in case he came upon a restaurant or bar that didn't stock it.

He stared at the tall triangular-shaped bottle of AVIV—with its clear glass on two sides and its frosted front with black lettering. Depending on the lighting and how he held it in his hands, he could see the hidden symbols and messages cleverly incorporated into the bottle's clear sides. He picked it up and carefully read the statement on the front:

TEL AVIV, Israel—AVIV 613 Vodka is crafted by a family of master vodka artisans whose Russian ancestors moved to the Kabbalistic town of Tzvat, Israel, in 1824. It is created using a 6.1.3 formulation process from a masterful blend of wheat, barley, olives, figs, dates, grapes, and pomegranates. Its fresh, crisp water is sourced from Israel's natural aquifers and the Sea of Galilee, which contributes to its smoothness. AVIV is Hebrew for spring, symbolizing renewal.

HE POURED a shot and took a sip. The taste started out smooth and ended slightly sweet. He now craved its flavor. He emptied the glass and poured another. Drinking it slowly, he savored the quality of the irresistible liquid.

A look of wry amusement came over his face before his expression turned grim as he disappeared into his thoughts. Lots of things . . . and people . . . seemed to be getting in his way lately. And these annoyances irritated him to no end.

His biggest con ever was almost within reach, and now a pair of nosy investigators from the US wanted to foil his plans. They were closing in on him. He could feel it. An employee on his payroll had warned him early on about this Claire Caswell and Gaston Lombard. And even more recently, a concierge in Milano had warned him that the two seemed to be going everywhere he went. And now, sure enough, they showed up in Neuchâtel. His concierge connection at the Beau-Rivage warned him the two were also going to the masquerade ball. His thoughts consumed him.

What were they after? Who hired them? What had they discovered about him and his plan? He had been so careful—always looking over his shoulder. But had he ever missed the investigators? Slipped up and failed to cover his tracks? Had they seen anything that could pose problems down the road? Or eventually take him down? The duo seemed tenacious, even relentless. And that presented a problem he'd have to manage. The thought was not pleasant.

His mind drifted further. He had already dealt with a problem that arose on the opening night of *Roméo et Juliette* at Teatro alla Scala. His female companion had met with an unfortunate "accident" because she had poked her nose into his private business. He had caught her listening in on a phone call—a *business* call—earlier that evening, before they had dined at the Conti Café. He'd been forced to slip something into her wine at dinner when she visited the ladies' room. When she became confused during the performance and complained of a whirling sensation in her head, he had merely *helped* her up and over the box railing—tumbling to her death in the fur wrap he'd given her as a gift. The fall had ended tragically. Poor girl. But she left him no other choice. It looked like an accident to everyone present, and his testimony had hammered down that conclusion. The investigation was quickly closed.

The day the investigators had arrived in Italy, he'd arranged for a warning shot at their taxi. The sniper had been instructed not to shoot to kill—only to take out a window and scare the sleuths into turning around and going home. But no such luck. The sniper's aim had been off, and the driver had become an unfortunate victim of circumstances, as had the very unlucky bicycle rider. Mistakes happen when you hire someone incompetent, he reminded himself. He'd been forced to put a bullet between the eyes of the sloppy shooter when he came to collect payment for the errant job. The nerve. The audacity. The man should never have shown his face after his foul-up, but there he was holding out an open palm and demanding money. That was his second mistake. And he paid dearly for it. His body was found in a dumpster the next day, and police ruled it a mob hit. DiNetto was never even a suspect.

Why were people always putting him in positions that required unpleasant, but inevitable, actions? He couldn't understand it. Why did he always have to clean up loose ends?

And now one of his lesser partners in the big scam—a thug, really—had threatened to pull out of the deal if DiNetto refused to sign his name on a contract. DiNetto slammed his fist down on a chair arm. His word was as good as gold. He had never signed a written contract. Never in ink. How dare the partner demand a signature? *How dare he*!

DiNetto set his drink down and walked to the mirror in his room. He stood there admiring his image for some time. Then he recited a motto he said each night before retiring:

Say it with diamonds,
Say it with mink,
But never ever say it with ink.

IT WAS the adage he'd lived by for years. His Italian father, his tata, had taught him early in life never to sign his name to *anything*—to do business only on a handshake, or not at all. Like his father, he was a man who would never sign in ink. People dealt with him on his word, or they didn't deal with him at all. It was that simple. A handshake should suffice in any situation. If pressed to sign on the dotted line, he would nix the deal and walk away. He gave it no further thought; he never looked back.

DiNetto dropped onto the bed and settled his head into the pillows. He shut his eyes and shifted restlessly for several long minutes. No position felt comfortable. When at last he nodded off, he talked in his sleep as he wrestled with his thoughts. He dreamed about his family. His tata. His mamma. His younger sister. And his thoughts returned him to his ten-year-old self on that day just six months after they arrived in the US. The day his life changed forever.

The school administrator called him into the office that fateful afternoon to inform him his entire family had died in an automobile collision. A drunk driver had plowed head-on into their vehicle. He recalled the man's exact words to him: "You're an orphan now, son. You need to adjust and adapt to your new life. Be a man." What cold words to offer a grieving ten-year-old, DiNetto reflected. They were so cavalier, without a hint of empathy or concern. He'd fought tears, afraid if he set them free they would flood the room. He had replayed the administrator's words often since that day.

He was shuffled through several foster homes and ultimately went to live with a great-aunt—his father's relative who had moved to America from southern Italy. A woman who was never even remotely close to his family. A woman who was mean, unmarried, and childless. The last thing she wanted was to raise the orphan boy, but when the courts had contacted her and offered her money to bring him into her home, she agreed. Raising Anthony didn't appeal to her, but the money did. In exchange for a monthly check, she agreed to provide him a place to live until he reached the legal age. It was a business deal, and one without heart.

Life with his great-aunt was harsh. She used a belt on him whenever he looked sideways, and he grew to hate her. He became withdrawn, and he dreamed of his older brother, Carlo. If only he hadn't chosen to end his life, he would have been there to help Anthony. But eventually Anthony had to let go of the fantasy. Carlo was gone. His parents were gone. Even his sister, Esmeralda, was gone. He was alone.

Years later, when Anthony was in his teens, a neighbor discovered his great-aunt's body, beaten to death in her home, her valuables stolen. The police blamed her demise on an intruder, Anthony recalled, because the glass in the back door was broken and the door kicked in. But a suspect was never apprehended. No one even considered it was poor, orphan Anthony who had killed her.

Since then, he'd lived on his own. He liked it that way. He inherited his aunt's house, and the court held the property in trust until he was old enough to assume proper ownership. He dropped out of school and went to work. Relationships in his life became convenient, short-lived, and purposeful. He used others as he saw fit, then moved on. People were simply a means to an end—there to provide something he needed or wanted. He wasn't necessarily proud of the person he'd become—a man devoid of any true feelings—but it was too late to change now.

His mind continued to spin as he slept.

He relived pushing the young woman over the box ledge at Teatro alla Scala. Then he envisioned the taxi driver's life ending, without warning, with a single bullet to the head. He even pictured the man on the bicycle, who died so suddenly. He flashed to a memory of ending the sniper's life. He, Anthony DiNetto, was responsible for all these deaths. He groaned in his sleep.

Sweat encompassed his entire body, and he twisted uncontrollably. His devoutly Catholic mamma had told him about God as a child, prayed with him and for him, and read him the Ten Commandments each night before tucking him into bed. To this day, he could recite all ten in order. The fifth one, "Thou shalt not kill," echoed through his head. His mamma had explained that "kill" meant "murder." She had tried her best to impress upon him the importance of keeping God's laws. He hadn't forgotten her words, but he hadn't kept the commandments either. At some point, he would need to ask for forgiveness, he realized, but not now. His mamma's words continued to haunt him: "Keep God's laws, my child. Always keep God's laws."

He squirmed toward the bottom of the bed, arms and legs flailing.

His thoughts turned to Claire Caswell and Gaston Lombard and how he'd have to handle these investigators who had the audacity to intrude into his personal and private life—*to follow him*. How dare they! He dreamed of ways to take care of the meddling pair of sleuths.

And then his wild thinking turned to his current scheme—to the plan he had worked on for some time, a plot to increase his wealth tenfold. To the partner who kept demanding he actually sign the contract for payment. "Never!" he shouted in his sleep, but it emerged as an inarticulate gurgle. He would deal with him at a later date.

He finally fought himself into an exhausted all-out slumber, but not before muttering, "Never! Never in ink!"

In the morning, DiNetto was exhausted. He picked up his cell phone and made a call. He needed to check in with his mole in the US. He paid the person well and expected results. Then he had other calls to make.

Day six
Neuchâtel to Milan

CLAIRE AND Guy readied for a day of travel. Guy had confirmed their travel arrangements the day before. They would take the train—traveling first to Bern, then switching trains to reach Milan. He also made certain another rental car, of a different make and color, would be waiting upon their return to Milan's Hotel Principe di Savoia.

The sleuths shared the shower and dressed for the day. They packed the duffel and backpacks and went to the restaurant off the lobby to eat breakfast. After consuming toast, scrambled eggs, juice, and coffee, they checked out of the hotel and walked outside. A doorman hailed a taxi, and before they knew it, they were on their way to the train station.

"I'll be relieved when we leave this place," Claire said softly. "Way too many strange things happened here."

"You can say that again," Guy responded in a low tone. "And now that DiNetto has figured out we're following him, I'm not sure how safe either of us will be until we leave Europe altogether."

"The thought has crossed my mind more than once."

Guy pulled out the itinerary and a map, studying both as he talked. "We'll be in Milan only this one last night. Then lots of driving lies ahead for us. From the looks of it, the schedule becomes terribly aggressive from this point on. One thing's for sure: DiNetto doesn't waste much time anywhere he goes. It's as if he's on an important assignment."

"I think he is. And time is running out for us to solve this case." Claire grimaced. "We have to figure out what DiNetto is up to. We need to find out what's in those boxes he picked up in Neuchâtel. They hold the secret. The Miami-Dade Police Department is depending on us. We need to find out what he's hiding."

"It's getting more dangerous by the second," Guy said. "DiNetto will be looking for us. Count on it. And my guess is he'll try to stop us however he can. More than ever, we'll need to watch our backs. We need to stay together at all times. I want to get through these next few days using extreme caution, and when it's time for us to leave, *we leave*—case solved or not."

"We'll solve it." An unmistakable look of determination appeared in Claire's eyes.

Once at the train station, the two investigators boarded the train to Bern and settled into their seats for the short ride.

When the train ride was underway, Guy took out some reading materials. Not too many minutes passed before his head fell back on the headrest and he was fast asleep. The momentum of the train seemed to act like a sleeping pill to lull its passengers into the Land of Nod.

Claire got up to visit the ladies' room. She made her way to the connecting passageway, walked through it, and began to step toward the restroom in the attached car. Strangely, it was devoid of passengers. As she approached the ladies' restroom door, which was on the right-hand side, the door of the adjacent men's room opened. A man stepped in front of her, grabbed her, and pulled her into the men's room, locking the door behind them. The quarters were tight, leaving barely enough room for the two of them to struggle. Before she could scream, the man cupped his hand over her face and pressed his body into hers. He uttered the words, "At last."

Horror owned her. This was the same appalling man she had fought off on the train ride from Milan to Bern, the same man lunching and arguing with DiNetto at the outdoor restaurant in Neuchâtel, and the same obnoxious man dressed in the purple velvet tuxedo and white facemask at the masquerade ball.

"I couldn't get to you on the other train," he whispered, "or at the masquerade ball, but I've got you now." His breath was close and pungent.

Claire couldn't speak, but her eyes said it all. She was terrified. With all her might, she tried to wiggle free, but couldn't. She tried to scream, but her pleas emerged as agonized and muffled gasps.

"It's no use," the stranger said. His voice was low, harsh, and grating. "No one follows DiNetto and gets away with it." He pulled a knife from his pocket. "I need to teach you a lesson."

Claire pounded her fist against the wall until the man forcefully grabbed it.

At that very instant, Guy kicked the door in.

"*Bastard!*" he screamed. He grabbed the man by his neck, yanked him out of the tiny room, knocked him to the floor, jumped on top of him, and started to strangle him.

Claire bolted past the two and pulled the train car's emergency cord.

Train officials, including a licensed security guard, swept onto the scene within seconds and pulled the men apart.

Claire screamed out, "This man attacked me!" She pointed to the stranger. "He has a knife!"

The guard secured the man's hands behind his back with plastic zip tie cuffs and led him to the front car to keep an eye on him for the remainder of the trip. The conductor found the knife on the bathroom floor and bagged it with his gloved hand. He called ahead to have police waiting when the train stopped and assured Claire and Guy the man would be arrested.

The investigators returned to their seats, trying to act as natural as possible in front of the other passengers.

"That was close," Claire said. "If you hadn't come when you did . . ."

"I woke up, you were gone, and I assumed you went to the restroom," Guy said. "I followed you to make sure, and when I approached, the ladies' room door was swinging wide open, and I heard a loud pounding in the men's."

"That was the same man who wouldn't leave me alone on the train to Bern, Guy—the one we later saw having lunch with DiNetto at the Beau-Rivage. And he was in the purple costume at the masquerade ball. He admitted it all." She paused. "DiNetto set him up to hurt me. Or worse."

"We'll talk to the police when we stop. Then we're aborting this mission!" Guy said in a loud, deep voice. "No further discussion."

"No. I'm okay. We'll make it through. We can't give up now. We're too close," Claire said.

"We're flying home from Milan on the first flight out. We're not staying in Europe another night. This case is not worth our lives."

"I'm not leaving," Claire said firmly. "You go, if you must. I have a case to conclude. I've never walked away from one yet, and this won't be the first."

"Shit, Claire. Use your head. We need to leave," Guy pled with her.

"As I said, go ahead. But I'm staying in Europe to finish the job."

"You're being bullheaded. To your own detriment!" he yelled.

She stared at him, not at all happy with his tone or his words.

The other passengers on the car stared open-mouthed at the novelty of such a dramatic display on what was usually a quiet journey.

The sleuths didn't speak to each other the remainder of the trip to Bern.

14

JIN IKEDA SAT at Claire's desk and then at Guy's, trying to decide which location suited him. His own desk was fine when the investigators were present. But when they were away, it only seemed appropriate he should sit at one of their desks at the front of the office, instead of at his in the back corner.

Claire's desk was closest to the front door, and Jin opted for that spot. He made a hot cup of tea in her flamingo mug and leaned back in her chair, settling his feet comfortably on the desktop. For a minute, he closed his eyes and imagined a rosy future. He liked the idea of having his own prestigious business one day soon—a computer forensics investigation service that would rival the best of the best. He smiled, pleased with his new circumstances. Claire Caswell and Gaston Lombard were just the two to help him make his dreams come true. He felt proud to be working for the esteemed investigators.

While he was still in thought, a deep voice abruptly startled him back to reality. "Is the office open?"

Jin jolted upright and wrenched his feet to the floor. "Yes, sir. How can I help you?"

"I'm looking for Claire Caswell or Gaston Lombard—the private investigators," the man said. "Are they in?"

"No, not at this time," Jin said. "But I can assist you. I'm an associate with the firm. What brings you to us?"

Officer Monty Figg sat in the chair across from the desk. His demeanor was formal and his Miami-Dade police uniform was neatly pressed.

Jin listened to the information he relayed with keen interest, jotting notes.

"I see," Jin said. "Very interesting." He scratched his chin. "You've come to the right place."

The officer continued to tell Jin the intricate details of the matter that brought him to the investigation firm, and Jin continued taking copious notes. He interjected occasionally with a salient question. As he listened, he structured a game plan in his mind—a way to tackle the issue and reach a proper resolution. This was his chance to prove himself to his new employers.

"I can help you," Jin said with confidence. He outlined the fee schedule and asked Figg to sign the firm's standard contract.

"Get it done fast," the officer said. "We don't have a lot of time to play around. A slow leak can flatten a tire in no time if it's not tended to."

Jin nodded. "Exactly." He paused, then asked, "Where does he spend time when he's not at work? I need to know every place you're aware of."

"I overheard him talking on his cell in the office a few days ago. He repeated an address in South Beach where he planned to meet someone. I wrote it down." Figg handed Jin a slip of paper with the address and several photos of the subject.

After Figg left, Jin finished out his time at the office for the day— reviewing his notes and anxiously glancing at the clock every few minutes. There was work to be done on this new case, and time was of the essence. When it was finally time to go, he grabbed the photographs, locked the office door, and set out on his first assignment.

He drove to South Beach, parked in a ramp, and strolled to the address the firm's newest client had provided—a bar. Happy hour was in full swing when he arrived. The place was crowded and tawdry. Jin pushed his way to the bar and ordered a drink. Just then, a man vacated a barstool, and Jin claimed it. He glanced at the nearby patrons and in short order realized he was sitting in a gay establishment. The young man on the stool next to Jin looked over and smiled coyly.

"Come here often?" the young man asked. "Don't think I've ever seen you before. My name's Robert."

"No. First time," Jin replied. He didn't offer his name, and he glanced at his watch repeatedly.

"Looking for a good time?" the young man asked.

"No. I'm waiting for someone," Jin lied. He surveyed the room.

"You're a good-looking guy," Robert persisted. He conspicuously eyed Jin up and down.

"Thanks," Jin said, again glancing at his watch, acting at once unimpressed and uninterested.

"If you get stood up . . . I'm here," Robert said. He raised his eyebrows up and down three times in rapid succession.

"Sorry, bub. You're not my type. Nothing personal," Jin said.

Robert promptly stood and poured his drink over Jin's head before sauntering away.

The bartender rushed over and handed Jin a fistful of tissues. "The guy's got a problem. Happens on a regular basis. Sorry about that."

"No worries," Jin said. He blotted the remains of the martini from his face and clothing.

Jin continued to scan the bar as he finished his first drink and ordered another. As he sipped slowly, he stared straight ahead into the massive wall mirror behind the bar, trying desperately to spot the subject of his search. People came and people left—sometimes alone, sometimes in pairs or threesomes. But mostly the patrons mingled and made the rounds, chatting with strangers and trying to have a good time. He didn't spot his target.

Just when Jin had decided to go home—convinced tonight would not be the night to find whom he was looking for—the subject of his search walked in. Jin recognized him immediately from the photos. The man was dressed in midnight-navy slacks and a matching shirt. His hair was the color of soot, with a lighter gray at the temples, and his build resembled a brick house. Jin quickly realized that meeting up with that man in a dark alley should be avoided at all costs.

The law student swallowed with difficulty.

The sturdy man made his way to one of the crowded stand-up tables, flagged a waiter, and ordered two beers.

Jin abandoned his stool and meandered around the room, eventually ending up closer to the table where the man stood. Jin looked around as if he were trying to spot someone, moving in a manner that drew attention.

It wasn't long before the man noticed Jin.

"Can I buy you a drink?" he asked.

"I guess," Jin replied. "I'm actually waiting for a friend."

"Isn't everyone?" the man asked. He gave Jin a once-over. "Well, until your friend gets here, perhaps you can keep me company."

"Why not?" Jin said unenthusiastically.

"Looks like someone held a hose to you."

"No, it was just a martini with olives," Jin said. He attempted a feeble smile.

"Now, that wasn't nice. You must have made someone real unhappy."

Jin gave the man a dismissive shrug.

"When someone makes me unhappy, I don't pour a drink on his head," the man said. "I go for the jugular."

"Ouch. Sounds painful. And serious."

The two beers arrived, and the husky man shoved one over to Jin.

"I'm only and always serious," the man said. "What brings you here? Never seen you before."

"I'm supposed to be meeting a friend, but so far he hasn't showed. He's late."

"Seems like my lucky night, then," the man said. "I'm Randy. Who are you?"

"Andrew," Jin said. It was the first name that popped into his head. Now they both were using false names.

"You seem nervous. First time?" the man asked.

"First time? Oh, ah, no," Jin said. "Why do you ask?"

"You're acting sort of naïve—innocent. I find it refreshing . . . captivating." He stared at Jin.

"This really isn't my scene," Jin said. "My friend . . . *he* wanted to come here. Not me. And now he stands me up. Go figure."

"Uh-huh," the man said.

Jin sipped the beer. It was his third drink of the night. He'd be careful to simply nurse it or act as if he were drinking it, but he wouldn't finish it. He wanted to be cognizant of his surroundings and stay alert.

"So, Randy, what do you do?" Jin asked.

"What do I *do*? Isn't that a bit personal? After all, we've just met." He rubbed his chin suggestively.

"I mean, what do you do *for a living*?" Jin asked. "Just conversation."

"Oh, that. I . . . I think it's far too early in the game to ask me questions, Andrew. That's what I think. I like it a whole lot better when everything remains anonymous." Randy paused. "Now, how do you like it? What's your preference?"

Jin had to think quickly, or things could go downhill rapidly.

"I told you, I'm waiting for someone," Jin said, feigning annoyance at the direct sexual question. "What don't you understand about that?"

"You're a testy little dickhead, aren't you?" Randy asked. "Irritating as all hell. No wonder you ended up with a drink in your face." He cleared his throat. "But I have to admit, I like feistiness in a pretty man."

This was not going well at all. Jin needed to befriend Randy so he'd answer some questions, but he didn't want to be *that* friendly. He decided to try a different tactic.

"I agreed to have a drink with you, buddy, while I waited for my friend," Jin said. "Nothing more. Nothing less. *Comprenez-vous*?"

"Ooh, speak French to me, baby," Randy cooed. "Turns me on." He stared in a way that made Jin feel wholly uncomfortable. "You're not getting away from me tonight."

Jin was in a bind. He needed answers, but this situation was quickly getting out of hand. He wanted to prove his worth to Claire Caswell and Gaston Lombard—prove he could be trusted to handle a matter in their absence—but he had stepped in over his head. It was time to get out.

"I have an appointment," Jin said. "I'm afraid I need to go."

"Not so fast, you twerp!" Randy boomed. "You baited me, got me interested, and now you're walking?"

"Hey, man, that's your problem. I never encouraged you. Thought we could have some conversation while I waited. That's all. Sorry to disappoint you."

"I bought you a drink, you little fucking asshole," Randy barked.

"Yeah? Big deal," Jin said. He reached into his pocket, pulled out a twenty, and threw it at Randy. "That ought to cover the beer, and then some."

"Nobody treats me like that," Randy thundered. "Nobody! Watch out, Andrew. This isn't over."

Jin quickly made his way through the crowd. Once outside, he sprinted to his car in the nearby lot. He jumped in, locked the doors, and sped off. This was his first foray into the world of private investigation, and he realized he'd done just about everything wrong. He would have to reconsider his strategy and come up with a new approach. He wanted to impress his bosses, so he wouldn't give up. Now that Randy could identify him, though, he'd have to be exceedingly careful about his next moves. He'd have to work completely behind the scenes to get the information he needed. But he mulled over watching Randy at the bar one more time—if he could only get his courage up.

He knew one thing for sure: Randy had something to hide. Officer Figg had said Randy was married with children. But Randy had a big secret: he was gay. And Jin suspected he'd do just about anything to keep his secret life hidden from his wife and his employer.

Jin drove home, frequently glancing into the rearview mirror to make certain he wasn't being followed. He didn't take Randy's threat lightly. The law student had stepped into a potential hornet's nest and now had to proceed with extreme caution. He pondered the situation. Should he tell the investigators about this new case the next time they called to check in? Would they fire him if they found out how he was investigating the matter? He wasn't sure how to handle it.

As he was weighing his options, something hit him. If he had discovered Randy's secret life, then someone else might have too. Randy was a ripe target for blackmail.

15

IN BERN, THE sleuths boarded the second train. Still no words had been exchanged between them since their argument.

Claire closed her eyes to think. From now on, disguises would be required at every juncture. She would take no chances. She hoped Guy would stay to complete the case, but if he chose to fly home, she couldn't stop him. But her intent to uncover DiNetto's secret remained unwavering.

She looked over at Guy. His eyes were shut, but she knew he wasn't sleeping.

"You awake?" she asked softly.

He didn't answer.

She grabbed a brochure on Neuchâtel from her backpack, got up from her seat, and walked up and down the aisle of the train car to stretch her legs.

Why Neuchâtel, she thought carefully as she browsed the

brochure. Why had DiNetto and his goon traveled there? Not to mention Officer Bubbiano. According to the store clerk, he'd rented the court jester costume for the masquerade ball. But had he actually worn the costume, or had DiNetto? There was no way to know. And what was the connection among the three men? What were they up to? And those boxes DiNetto collected from the elderly gentleman in the residential neighborhood—what was in them? She had to find out. She continued to turn the glossy pages of the brochure as she strolled the aisle.

Much of the city's seventeenth-and eighteenth-century architecture showed a French influence and was constructed from local yellow sandstone. Claire chuckled out loud when she read that Alexandre Dumas—the French writer of historical fiction—had described Neuchâtel as appearing "like a toy town carved out of butter." It was an apt description.

The locals spoke a dialect of Swiss French, she recalled—the closest dialect to standard French spoken outside of France. And the next destination on the itinerary—after one additional night in Milan—was France. DiNetto was headed to France. Was there a French connection here? Why had DiNetto traveled to the picturesque capital of the Swiss canton of Neuchâtel—a city tucked under the ridges of the Jura Mountains and surrounded by fields and forests of the Swiss flatlands leading to the Bernese Alps? Why had he traveled to this place offering modern and Gallic street cafés, designer boutiques, outdoor markets, nightclubs filled with students, and three shimmering lakes dotted with boats? Her mind filled with questions, but no answers.

Why Neuchâtel? They had lost track of DiNetto for long stretches of time there. What had he been doing when they could not trail him? Had he engaged in secret meetings?

Without reaching any conclusions, Claire returned to her seat.

She pulled her notepad and pen from her backpack and updated her writings. She made a note to call Sergeant Massey and check in when they reached Milan, and also to contact Jin to see if everything at the office was in good shape. She looked at Guy. He was sleeping hard now. She felt restless. She got up again to continue pacing the aisle. Her inner voice warned her to be alert. But she didn't know why.

Suddenly, she became aware of a female passenger staring at her with overly keen interest. Claire walked toward the woman and stopped alongside her seat. "Have we met?" Claire asked.

The woman looked down as she spoke. "Not formally," she said in English. She extended her hand, looked into Claire's eyes only briefly, and then returned her gaze to the floor. "I believe I saw you at the masquerade ball in Neuchâtel. You were the one in the dazzling red dress."

"Yes, I did wear red," Claire said. "I'm surprised you recognize me. I was also wearing a mask." She studied the reserved, almost introverted, woman with curiosity. "How did you know it was me?"

"The way you carry yourself. Your posture, height, weight, élan."

Claire was impressed. "I'm Claire," the investigator said. "And you are?"

"Françoise," she said. "I live in Paris."

"Pleasure to meet you," Claire said. "Have you been to the masquerade ball in Neuchâtel before? Or was this your first time?"

"Oh, my dear. I've gone each year for the past nineteen years." Her eyes looked forlorn. "You see, I danced with a man the first time I attended, and I have never been able to get him out of my mind. He was . . . " She paused to find the right word. "Unforgettable." Her eyes drifted off as if she were remembering their first meeting in great detail. "There was something about him. I felt I had known him for many lifetimes. Each year I have returned, hoping to see him again. Alas, it has never happened."

"How would you recognize him in costume?" Claire asked.

The lady smiled. "I would know him anywhere." She looked to the floor again.

"I'm sorry," Claire said.

"When I saw you dancing with that tall gentleman of yours—the one sitting next to you over there—it reminded me of dancing with the special man I met so long ago." Her eyes misted. "We were like that too. A magnificent pair."

Claire waited a few moments before her next question.

"Do you know Anthony DiNetto?" she asked.

"We all do," the woman replied. "He is a legend around this area. Whether you are in Italy, Switzerland, or France, most everyone has heard of Anthony DiNetto." The woman stopped to gather her thoughts. "There was a time when he was good. Rumor had it he always helped the poor. As the years passed, however, he changed. He became greedy, stealing from the rich to make his own life better and better, plowing down anyone who stood in his way. He stopped helping those less fortunate long ago." The woman searched Claire's eyes. "Why do you ask me about Anthony DiNetto?"

Claire thought fast. "He was staying at our same hotel in Neuchâtel," she said. "He strutted around like a celebrity, so naturally I'm curious about him and what he's all about."

"Stay away from that man," the French woman warned. Her eyes narrowed. "Don't cross him. He has powers."

"Powers?" Claire asked.

"Friends in high places. You could end up dead."

The woman reached into her purse for a pen and a piece of scratch paper. She jotted something down and handed it to Claire. "Here is my contact information, in case you ever come to Paris. Look me up. We will meet for tea and chocolate croissants."

Claire thanked the lady and put the folded piece of paper in her sweater pocket.

She returned to her seat. Guy woke up as she stepped over his legs.

"Where were you?" he asked, rubbing his eyes.

The rest had done him good. They seemed to be on speaking terms again.

"Chatting with a woman." She turned around to point out the lady to Guy, but her seat was empty. "That's odd," Claire said. "She was there a moment ago." Claire reached into her pocket and pulled out the contact information the woman had given her. But when she unfolded it, the only thing written on it was: "STAY AWAY FROM HIM!"

THE TRAIN sped along on its way to Milan. When it arrived, both of the investigators were happy to be back in Italy. They cabbed to the Hotel Principe di Savoia.

Claire couldn't wait to be back in the opulent room. She yearned to sink her head onto the comfortable feather pillows on the luxurious bed and pull the freshly laundered cotton sheets and thick comforter up under her chin. She was tired, and she needed a nap. She'd talk to Guy later in the day about staying to complete the mission.

Upon arrival, the valet informed them a rental car had been dropped off earlier in the day. He handed Guy the keys. "It's over here, sir, just down the drive," the staffer said. He pointed to a blue two-seater BMW Z4 Roadster hardtop convertible. "It's the sDrive28i model—with a TwinPower Turbo four-cylinder engine and a six-speed manual transmission," the valet said, smiling. "A car built for speed. The car I want to own one day."

Certainly not inconspicuous, but then it probably wasn't likely to attract undue attention in a land of fast, expensive cars mixed with small, eco-conscious models. Regardless of the car's make and model, they couldn't chance any of the valets tipping off DiNetto about their new vehicle.

"Keep quiet about our new rental car, will you please?" Guy asked. "And ask the other valets to do the same." He passed the valet the equivalent of fifty US dollars in euros. "We like to keep a low profile, if you know what I mean." He winked.

"No problem, sir. I understand. Thank you." The valet winked back.

As the two walked to the hotel's front doors, they noticed DiNetto's dark gray Ferrari parked to one side of the entrance.

Claire and Guy stepped into the lobby as quietly as possible. They talked to no one, made their way to the elevator, and rode it up to their room. As soon as they settled in, Claire ordered room service. It was past lunchtime, and they were starving. She ordered a pizza and salad to share.

"Certainly, Ms. Caswell. Welcome back to the hotel. I trust you and Mr. Lombard enjoyed your time in Switzerland. The food will be up shortly," promised the room service employee on the other end of the line.

"Okay. Now that had a bit of a creep factor to it," Claire said, filling Guy in on the conversation. "They certainly do keep a close watch on the patrons of this hotel. So much for staying out of the limelight."

"I'd say so," Guy replied. "A little too close a watch for my liking."

"From this point on, from the minute we leave this hotel, we must be in disguises," Claire said. "That is, if you plan to stay here and finish the case with me. Or are you still set on flying home early?" She looked at Guy squarely in the eyes, awaiting his answer.

"And pass up the chance to drive that amazing vehicle we

rented?" He flashed his famous grin. "No, Claire, I'm not leaving you here alone. I'm in it until the end. The bitter end."

"Bad choice of words, Guy, but I do appreciate you staying."

WHEN THE tray arrived from the hotel kitchen, Guy opened the door, and a waiter came in to set up the service on a coffee table.

"How was Neuchâtel?" he asked. "And the masquerade ball?"

"The masquerade ball?" Claire repeated quizzically, as if not understanding the question. She immediately wondered how yet another employee could possibly have known they attended.

"Oh, *signora*. You are too modest. I heard all about it. You and Gaston Lombard were the hit of the event," the man said. "A friend of mine at the Beau-Rivage e-mailed me photos of the two of you in your costumes. You looked *molto elegante!*"

Claire and Guy were blown away, but did not let their surprise show. The audacity of the situation seemed overwhelming, to say the least.

"Well, so much for costumes providing anonymity," Claire said, forcing a smile. She refused to talk further to the nosy hotel employee.

"How long will you be staying with us?" the hotel employee persisted. "We do so enjoy having—"

"Not sure," Guy broke in. "Now, if there are no *further* questions . . . " He'd reached his limit. "Thank you and good day." He handed the man a tip.

The employee made his way to the door. "Excuse me for being . . . friendly. I thought you Americans liked being sociable. I guess I am wrong. *Mi scusi*." When the door closed behind him, he reached for his cell phone and dialed a number.

THE INVESTIGATORS ate in silence.

"I'm taking a nap," Claire announced as she finished. "I'm exhausted."

Guy said, "Good plan. Tomorrow we drive to the next stop. Getting some rest now is just what the doctor ordered."

The two slept like babies, cradled in each other's arms.

Just outside their room, the waiter held his ear to their door, trying desperately to hear anything the two investigators might be discussing. Money for information was something he could always use. He held a cleaning rag and a bottle of spray polish in case other hotel patrons might pass by and wonder what he was doing. He'd been on DiNetto's payroll for a long time and knew the routine well.

16

THE INVESTIGATORS WOKE from their shared nap refreshed and reenergized. It was their last night in Milan, and they needed to shadow DiNetto.

Claire wove her hair into a loose braid. She pulled on a pair of dark-framed tortoise eyeglasses, applied pink frosted gloss to her lips, and placed a black beret on her head. To top it all off, she tied a synthetic clump of raven hair to her braid.

"What do you think?" she asked Guy. "Am I recognizable?"

"It's good," he replied. "Changes your look completely."

"Now for you," she said.

For the next few minutes, Claire adjusted the long, curly salt-and-pepper wig on Guy's head. She brushed the curls until it looked natural. Then she tied a black scarf around his neck and handed him a pair of perfectly round silver-framed glasses. She had him insert a set of fake front teeth that dramatically altered his jawline.

"Take a look in the mirror," she said. "Even I wouldn't recognize you."

Guy gazed into the mirror and had to agree. "Nor would I."

The two dressed in black jeans and dark tops. Avoiding detection at all costs was the name of the game.

Claire also put on a pair of very high heels to change her height. Guy couldn't easily change his height, but she could. And hopefully the two of them as a couple would look very different with her appearing taller.

She placed a call to Sergeant Massey and brought him up-to-date. While she spoke to Massey, Guy phoned Jin to check in. Jin informed him all was well and nothing was new, pressing, or urgent.

The sleuths locked their room and rode the elevator to the lobby. It was time to wait for DiNetto to surface for the evening. They went to the lounge and sat down at a table away from the bar. They each ordered a glass of red wine. Acting like new lovers, the two laughed quietly, told stories, and kissed from time to time. To the average onlooker, the couple appeared quite taken with each other. Anyone would assume they were on their honeymoon or involved in some other romantic encounter. That image was exactly what they desired to portray.

More than an hour passed with no sign of DiNetto.

Claire glanced at her watch. It was seven.

Another hour passed.

Suddenly, Guy nudged Claire. DiNetto had entered the room. He walked to the bar without haste, took a seat, and ordered AVIV vodka straight up. The hotel had honored his special request to carry the cutting-edge spirit and now kept a private stash of it just for DiNetto.

The drink was served, and DiNetto enjoyed it at a slow pace, savoring every bit of its remarkable qualities until he emptied the glass. Soon he looked at the bartender—who was dressed elegantly in a dark suit, starched white shirt, and silver bow tie—and shook his empty glass. Within seconds, it was refilled. People—women and men alike—began crowding around DiNetto, as seemed to be the established pattern, and they tried to engage him in conversation. He was thunderous, jovial, and seemingly eager to entertain his fans.

Many couples packed into the Principe di Savoia lounge. Some were patrons of the hotel, and others appeared to be locals. Claire and Guy found it easy to hide among the energetic crowd and observe their target. Another hour passed. By now, DiNetto had polished off several rounds of his favorite drink. He got up and walked through the room to the exit door, staggering only slightly. The sleuths followed him out, lagging a comfortable distance behind. DiNetto made his way to the hotel's Acanto Restaurant—known for its elegant presentations of Milanese cuisine—and was led to a table. Claire and Guy watched from a distance and observed that a man quickly joined DiNetto at his table. They couldn't get a good look at the man because he sat with his back to them.

After a time, the sleuths walked into the dining room and requested a table near the windows. The hostess led them to a nice spot overlooking the hotel's courtyard garden. Their vantage point showcased an enchanting eighteenth-century fountain. DiNetto and his dinner companion occupied a table on the opposite side of the room. The sleuths made certain he couldn't see them.

Claire and Guy ordered pumpkin ravioli with butter, sage, and pecorino cheese as a first course, and hazelnut-crusted beef filets for the second. The food tasted remarkable, and its presentation was fit for a magazine cover.

"Our compliments to the chef," Guy said to the waiter.

They watched DiNetto's table the entire time they dined. The conversation between the two men appeared cordial but stiff as they appeared to enjoy their repast. After the men finished desserts and coffees, the dialogue between them turned gravely serious. Their hands flew through the air expressively, and their voices increased in volume and intensity. DiNetto pulled a box from his briefcase—alike in size and shape to the boxes they'd seen him stash in the trunk of his Ferrari in Neuchâtel. Instead of standard cardboard, though, this box appeared to be crafted of a lightweight wood laminate, plastic, or lacquer material of some kind. DiNetto handed the box to his dinner companion, who pulled it onto his lap, opened it, and peered inside.

DiNetto watched for his reaction.

"*Superb!*" the man exclaimed with enough volume that the investigators could hear him clearly. "This is an amazing piece," he added without lowering his voice. The man closed the lid of the hinged box, set it on the table in front of DiNetto, and drew a folded sheet of paper from his shirt pocket. He thrust it toward DiNetto, along with an ink pen. "I need a written guarantee."

At first, DiNetto didn't respond. He merely stared at the other man. But after a moment, DiNetto flew into a rage. He grabbed the paper, ripped it to shreds, and stuffed the torn pieces into his wine glass. He tossed the pen into the air, and it fell with a thud to the floor. He got up from the table, grabbed the box, and left in a huff.

His embarrassed companion paid the tab, looked around nervously, and stepped hurriedly from the room. Now that they could get a more thorough look, Guy and Claire saw that the man reeked of old money.

"What is in those boxes?" Claire asked. "We have to find out."

"And what about the paper?" Guy asked. "Perhaps it's a contract of some kind. The man told DiNetto he wanted a *guarantee*. Looks like he doesn't like to sign contracts. Or doesn't want to sign this one. Or maybe he can't provide a guarantee."

"Whatever the reason, that paper and pen sure seem to inflame DiNetto's ire. Wonder why." She looked at Guy with penetrating eyes.

The investigators settled their bill and left the restaurant. They walked to the grandiose lobby and sat alongside a small square table. They ordered black coffees. None of the hotel staff greeted them as they passed, which seemed a good indication their disguises were effective.

"I wonder if DiNetto retired to his room for the evening," Guy said.

Claire glanced at her wristwatch. "It's eleven now, so I'm going to assume he did unless we see him reappear in the next few minutes. He seemed violently angry when he left the restaurant. He's likely in no mood for company."

Ten minutes later, DiNetto appeared. He walked through the lobby to the hotel's front doors, as if on a specific errand, and stepped outside. Claire volunteered to check it out and casually made her way in his direction. She followed him outside and stood off to the side as if waiting for a taxi.

"Can I give you a lift?" DiNetto asked, noticing Claire.

She was caught off guard. "*Oh, non merci*," she said, faking a French accent. She didn't smile, and she turned her head to the side.

"Certainly a pretty lady like you would appreciate a ride in my exquisite Ferrari," he said. He walked toward her.

"*Non, monsieur, merci*," she responded. She avoided his eyes and hoped he would leave her alone.

"I noticed you in the bar," he persisted. "That man you're with needs a haircut."

She almost chuckled under her breath. Instead, she glanced over her shoulder toward DiNetto. "*S'il vous plaît, aller loin*," she said firmly. Her French vocabulary was limited, and she wondered just how long she could go on speaking the language if he didn't give up.

"Did you actually just tell me to go away?" DiNetto snarled. "I'm not used to being shunned by a woman. Not now. Not ever. I'm no longer asking. I'm demanding you take a ride with me. Understand?"

With one arm, he grabbed her around the waist and hustled her to his car as she struggled. He opened the passenger door, shoved her in, and locked it. Claire tried to open the door, but couldn't. DiNetto flew around to the driver's side door, unlocked it, jumped in, then relocked his door. He started the car's famous engine, put the accelerator to the floor, and roared off. The valet on duty watched it all happen, but didn't dare disturb DiNetto in action.

DiNetto looked over at Claire. "Your door can be unlocked only from the outside," he said. "All my cars are made that way. It's a custom feature."

Claire tried to open the door again, but it was securely locked. I'm in trouble now, she told herself. Stay calm. Her inner voice told her to get out and run whenever an opportunity presented itself. She stared straight ahead, thinking of ways to escape.

"*Je suis effray*ée," she said boldly. "*Arrêtez, s'il vous plaît!*"

"You want me to stop?" DiNetto asked, exploding into a sinister laugh. "Relax, my dear. Enjoy the ride. It's not often you get to ride in a car of this quality."

BACK AT the hotel, Guy was worried. Claire hadn't returned to the lobby, and he couldn't understand what was taking her so long. He walked to the front doors and stepped outside. The Ferrari was gone. And so was Claire. Attempting to alter his voice, which by now was recognizable to the valets, he asked the two employees on duty if he'd seen his date leave the hotel. He described Claire in her disguise.

"Oh, yes, sir, we did see her," one of the young men said. "Mr. DiNetto offered the young woman a ride in his Ferrari, and she accepted. They left only minutes ago." The valet winked at Guy. "The man's got a thing for the ladies. They all like him."

CLAIRE WAS getting more frantic by the second. She needed to find a way out of the situation. She couldn't keep up the French-speaking facade much longer, and she feared DiNetto would figure out she was a fraud, realize who she really was, and hurt her.

Minutes passed, and the Ferrari and its occupants had traveled far from the hotel.

Without warning, Claire felt DiNetto's hand on her thigh.

She slapped it, and he drew it back.

"*Non! Laissez-moi sortir!*" she shouted.

"You want out?" He seemed to enjoy her fright. "Okay. I'll let you out."

He pulled over curbside. The street was dark and wide, and Claire saw only a few lights emanating from the nearby buildings. It was after midnight, and the last thing she wanted to do was walk alone through an area she didn't know. DiNetto exited the vehicle, stepped around, and unlocked the passenger door. She swung it open and lifted herself from the low seat.

"Have a pleasant stroll back to the hotel, *mademoiselle*," DiNetto said, smirking. "I'm sure you'll enjoy it."

She walked off in her high-heeled shoes with her head held high. She refused to let DiNetto see she wasn't at all comfortable being dumped in a dark and unfamiliar area far from the hotel. She pulled her cell phone from her backpack and dialed Guy's number.

"Honey, it's me," she said. "I need help."

He detected fear in her voice, despite her effort to sound calm.

"Where are you?" he asked frantically. "Are you okay?"

"I'm okay for now," Claire said. "I'll fill you in when I see you. DiNetto dropped me in some pitch-dark area, and I'm scared." She looked all around for a landmark. "Please come get me!"

"I'm on my way," he said, walking down the street from the hotel to the rental car. "Where are you? What are you near? Which way did DiNetto turn when he left the hotel? Give me something, anything . . . "

"I don't know where I am," she said. "But I remember he turned left."

"Stay on the phone with me, and keep walking until you see some street signs or any landmark that will help me find you. Anything."

Claire kept up a fast pace. She walked along the cobblestone streets, desperately searching for a clue to her whereabouts. She pulled her heels off and carried them. The moon provided a sliver of light, but mainly she felt enveloped by darkness. She became chilled and wanted in the worst way to be back at the hotel with Guy, cuddled between the sheets. Warm. She saw no signs or other people as she walked. Her gait and her fear increased tenfold. She hated the situation she was in. Anthony DiNetto—one day he'll pay for everything he's done, she promised herself. Now she wanted him behind bars more than ever. She wanted the man held accountable for what he'd done to her and his other victims—and for all his as-yet-undiscovered crimes. If need be, she'd single-handedly make certain it happened.

"Claire? Stay with me," Guy said. "Are you there? Are you seeing anything to help me find you?"

"No, I'm not," she moaned softly. "There are some old buildings around, but I don't see numbers on any of them."

Just then, Claire thought she heard footsteps behind her. She turned and looked, but saw no one and heard nothing.

"Guy, find me!" she wailed. "I need you to find me!"

Footsteps.

She heard them again.

They came from behind.

She broke into a run.

"*Help!*" she screamed into the phone. "*Help me!*"

17

GUY WAS BESIDE himself.

"Claire!" he screamed into his phone. "Claire! Answer me!"

She didn't.

She was running for her life with a pursuer hot on her heels. The cobblestone streets were slippery from an earlier mist, and the air smelled like early-morning dew. Claire could hear her heart thumping as if each beat were amplified in another plane. Her throat was dry, and she yearned for a swallow of water—cool, clear water. She breathed heavily as she bolted forward, knowing every step was vital. Outrunning her would-be attacker seemed her only chance of escape. She couldn't afford to trip, stumble, or fall. A surge of anxiety engulfed her. *Keep running! Don't stop! It's your only chance!* Her senses were on high alert, and she could feel her pursuer closing in.

She bellowed out the words she had memorized on the plane,

"*Chiamate la polizia! Chiamate la polizia!*"

Ahead, she saw only empty streets with a few scattered buildings locked up tightly for the night. No houses. No people. No lights. No hope. "*Chiamate la polizia!*" she yelled again in a desperate roar. She told herself to stay on the main street and avoid any side roads, praying it would help Guy find her.

The footsteps behind her sounded heavy, and she guessed they belonged to a large man. He moved quickly for his size, and she could tell he was gaining ground. She heard him panting. He was almost upon her.

Then it hit her! This was the premonition she'd had on the plane. This was the unpleasant dream that caused her to wake up shaking. The nightmare was playing itself out. She remembered how it ended. "*Help!*" she screamed. "*Help me!*"

At that instant, she felt two giant hands grab her shoulders from behind. She fought valiantly as her attacker pulled her to a stop with a sudden jerk, forced her to the ground, and dragged her kicking and screaming several feet to an alleyway. She wished she had a gun, a knife, or an assault flashlight. Anything to help defend herself.

The attacker didn't speak. He yanked her up and shoved her against a cold, concrete wall. As she struggled, her shoes, cell phone, and backpack fell from her grasp and landed on the ground. She kicked at him and tried to knee him in the groin, but he was too large and held on too tightly. "*No!*" she screamed. "*No!*" She reached up and scratched the man's face deeply with her fingernails, drawing blood. If nothing else, she'd provide DNA evidence of her attacker.

He knocked her to the ground and wrestled with her, trying to restrain and dominate her. She fought back with a strength she didn't know she possessed. She would fight to the finish. He slapped her face, and her glasses and beret sailed into the air. Her hairpiece fell off.

"*Stop!*" she cried out. "*Stop!*"

The attacker ripped at her clothing.

"*Polizia!*" Claire screamed. "*Polizia! Help!*"

GUY LISTENED on the other end of the phone in horror. Totally unable to help the woman he loved. He had been driving like a madman through the streets surrounding the hotel, but there was no sign of her. She could be miles away, and he knew he couldn't find her. Terror, disgust, and utter helplessness cloaked him. He felt powerless and weak.

JUST WHEN Claire thought the fight was over, help came. She heard the blaring of a siren and could see flashes of a blinking red light very near. Seconds later, two uniformed officers pounced on the assailant and heaved him face-first onto the damp pavement of the alley. One policeman helped Claire to her feet, and she quickly gathered up her hairpiece, glasses, beret, and shoes, stuffing them all into her backpack. She found her cell phone and held it tightly.

The officers wrenched the attacker to his feet. One of them pulled his hands behind his back and slapped handcuffs tightly around his wrists. The other shackled his ankles.

The assailant glared at Claire as the officers led him to the squad car and shoved him into its cramped backseat. He had a face she didn't recognize, but would never forget.

"You okay, *signora*?" one officer asked, kindness evident in his voice.

"If you hadn't arrived when you did, things would have been much, much worse," she said, fighting back tears. Her breathing was difficult. "That monster needs to be locked up."

"Another car should be arriving soon," the officer informed. "We will take you to the station and get a formal statement. By the looks of his face, you probably have some of his DNA under your fingernails. Good for you! We will process that evidence to help with the prosecution."

"Hold on, please," Claire said. She held up her cell phone. "Guy?"

"Claire!" he said. "Are you okay? Did he hurt you?" The anguish in his voice deeply touched her heart.

"No. The police came just in time," she said, choking back overpowering emotion. "I need you."

Through tears, Claire asked the officer for the address and directions to the police station and then relayed both to Guy. "Please get there fast," she pleaded.

"I'll be there before you are," he said.

Claire turned to the officer. "How did you know I needed help? Did someone hear me scream?"

"An elderly man said his dog would not stop barking. The dog must have heard you. The owner put him on a leash and took him outside. He lives only two blocks from here. As they walked this direction, the owner heard your cries for help and called the police from his cell phone."

"Please thank him for me. And his dog too," Claire said. "They saved my life."

"I have already done that," the officer said.

Just then she thought she heard the distant roar of a Ferrari, but she couldn't be sure. All instincts told her DiNetto set this up.

TWENTY MINUTES later, Claire sat in a hard metal chair at police headquarters with Guy by her side. He listened as she provided a detailed written statement of the car ride and the attack. Her fingernails were scraped for DNA. The police informed her the collected materials would go to the lab for analysis. When they learned Claire and Guy would be leaving Italy the following morning and returning to the US within days, they videotaped her statement—to be utilized should the assailant refuse to confess and the matter go to trial. Her taped interview, together with the lab results, would be the prosecutor's key evidence. Further strengthening the case, Claire easily picked the man out of a book of known offenders.

The police informed her the culprit had a long rap sheet and had served time previously for assaults on women. He'd been out of prison for less than a month. "This should put him back behind bars for a long time," one officer assured Claire.

Guy didn't leave her side. She'd never seen him so quiet. He seemed dazed and filled with remorse that he had been unable to help her, once again, when she needed him most. His eyes were moist with tears. Finally, he spoke. "Your dream. On the plane . . . "

Claire nodded. "I know. It happened just as my premonition warned." She shuddered. "DiNetto sent this man after me. Like the one on the train. I just know it. Probably found this thug on the street after he dropped me at the curb and paid him to attack me. The police will question the assailant to see if he'll come clean and implicate DiNetto," she said. If her theory were true, she realized, that meant DiNetto had recognized her despite her disguise. The thought occurred to Guy simultaneously.

"DiNetto sees us as a threat, and he's not going to relent until he destroys us," Claire concluded.

"If he destroys you, he destroys me, and he knows that," Guy said. "We're going to get that bastard if it's the last thing we do."

"I'm committed to it."

THE INVESTIGATORS fell hard asleep when they arrived back at the hotel. Rest was what they needed, and staying wrapped in each other's arms provided much-needed serenity after the night's ordeal.

Day seven
Milan to Porto Venere, Italy

MORNING BROUGHT with it a hazy day.

Claire awoke extra early and cracked open a window in the room. The outside air felt cool, and sounds of the city flooded in.

When she turned around, Guy was sitting up in bed watching her.

"How are you feeling after last night?" he asked, his expression grave.

"Fair enough, I think. Thankfully, the ending turned out okay. I'm blessed it didn't go further. I hope to *never* be faced with *anything* close to that situation again. And I plan to learn how to use a gun when we get back to Florida. I refuse to be so utterly vulnerable and unable to defend myself ever again," she said boldly. "Not that a gun would have helped me here. Guns aren't allowed in Italy. But at least in Florida . . . "

"I agree," Guy said. "When you think about the business we're in, and what we've gone through on recent cases, it's time we carry— probably past time. I plan to learn right along with you." He paused. "What do think about continuing with the case? After what you've been through, I hate to even ask. I wouldn't blame you one bit if you said you wanted to go home."

"Are you kidding? A team of wild horses couldn't pull me away," she declared, displaying profound courage. "There's *no* possibility I'll let DiNetto skate. I'll find out what he's up to—if it's the last thing I do!"

"I was hoping you'd say that," Guy said. "My thoughts exactly! I'm energized like never before. That bastard will pay for everything he's done—and for what he's planning to do. You have my word. So let's make that, 'if it's the last thing *we* do!'"

Claire brewed two cups of coffee, and the investigators enjoyed each sip. Afterward, they showered. Claire stayed under the water for an extra-long time. She scrubbed her body with lots of soap and hot water; she wanted any trace of the scumbag who attacked her removed forever.

They dressed, packed up, and took the elevator to the lobby, where they stopped for a quick breakfast before checking out. Beginning the last portion of the mission was good news for the sleuths. It spurred them onward, in part because it meant their return home to Florida wasn't too far off. That thought made them both deliriously happy. First, though, they needed to find evidence that would put DiNetto behind bars—completing the job the Miami-Dade Police Department had started.

The two walked to their rental car and jumped in, ready to begin the next part of the journey.

BACK IN Miami Beach, Jin was perplexed. He was about to embark on his second evening of investigation on behalf of the firm's new client, Officer Monty Figg. The law student had become fixated on making a good impression on Claire and Guy, and he could accomplish that goal only by single-handedly making their new client exceedingly satisfied with the firm's work. After careful consideration, he decided another night of hitting the South Beach bar scene was a necessary evil. He certainly didn't relish the task, but he had to try it one more time.

He walked to a mirror in his apartment and took a long look.

He needed to change his appearance. Using plenty of hair gel, he slicked his hair back. Then he dressed in a dark gray shirt and black slacks. But it wasn't enough. He glanced around his apartment. He found a pair of old blue-tinted sunglasses—not dark sunglasses that would look out of place in a bar, but decorative glasses with gradient lenses that would hide his eyes. He took another look. He definitely looked different from the first night of his investigation. He locked up his place and drove to the same area of South Beach where he'd seen the person of interest before. He entered the same bar and located a remote standing table in a dark corner. He ordered a beer and watched the festivities unfolding before his eyes. Last time, he over-engaged with the subject and almost backed into an impossible corner. Tonight he would stay in the background.

He sipped his beer straight from the bottle. It was cold and comforting. A man came up to him and asked if he could join him at his table. Jin declined, saying, "I'm waiting for my partner." The same exchange happened several times.

Suddenly, he noticed the target of his investigation drift into the bar. A young man, looking not a day over twenty-one, accompanied him. The two sat down at the bar and ordered drinks. A number of patrons had clustered around the area where Jin sat, making it possible for him to hide and watch.

The man he was surveilling was Cane Dougan, aka "Randy," a thirty-five-year veteran of the Miami-Dade Police Department and of Irish descent. Dougan was partnered with a rookie officer, Monty Figg. Figg was certain something was amiss with Dougan, which was why he'd brought the matter to Caswell & Lombard. In fact, he suspected Dougan was a dirty cop. On the take. Exchanging information and favors for money. He also suspected—but had no proof—Dougan was hiding a deep secret. If that were true, it could set the officer up to be blackmailed. Retirement was within range for

Dougan. That gave him extra incentive, and possibly a very strong motive, to line his pockets with easy cash. And lots of it.

According to Figg, a number of things had happened at the precinct over the last few months that caused the officers to raise their eyebrows and scrutinize each other. Someone in their ranks was betraying highly confidential police information. Numerous leaks to the press and private individuals—and several instances of vital evidence vanishing from lockup—had all the officers on edge. According to Figg, Sergeant Massey had interviewed each officer, but to date had failed to identify the mole.

The sergeant had ordered the officers not to discuss the leak situation with anyone outside the office, citing that the problem was an internal matter that should be resolved within the confines of the department. But Figg had noticed a troubled look on the sergeant's face lately. If it became public knowledge that one of his own was dirty and leaking confidential information, the sergeant would have a hard time living it down. The ensuing scandal would surely result in demands for his resignation. It would also destroy his reputation for being a tough—but fair, honest, and ethical—police sergeant.

Young and eager to make a name on the Miami-Dade Police Department, Officer Figg had stepped forward and decided to hire the private investigation firm to poke around and see what they could find out about Dougan. Figg had overheard Massey sing the private investigators' praises many times and was convinced they could successfully handle the case.

Figg wholeheartedly believed Cane Dougan was the problem. Though Dougan had an uncanny ability to come up with plausible explanations for his questionable actions whenever the finger seemed to point in his direction, Figg didn't believe him. Figg smelled a rat, and the rat's name was Cane Dougan, as far as the newbie was concerned. But he needed proof.

Jin's gaze fell to Dougan. The man acted like a high roller, throwing around money as if it were water, buying drinks for his boy toy and everyone else at the bar. The veteran officer seemed to relish in his ability to draw devotees; he was apparently unconcerned or unaware that free alcohol was the real lure. He acted important and demanded respect.

Unexpectedly, Dougan got up and walked directly toward the restrooms in the back of the bar. He walked right by Jin, but thankfully didn't appear to recognize or acknowledge him. Jin got up and followed a few yards behind Dougan. But Dougan wasn't interested in the bathroom after all. He was headed for an old-style pay phone hanging on the wall just outside the men's room.

Dougan dropped the appropriate coinage into its slot and punched in a number. A pay phone couldn't be traced to a person, and Jin assumed that was the reason Dougan used it.

Jin edged closer until he stood just outside the coved area housing the restrooms and the pay phone. Dougan faced the wall, and Jin was able to pick up on some of the officer's short conversation.

"Unharmed," Dougan said. "On to the next act. I'll keep you posted."

Jin walked back to his table and ordered another beer. If only he knew who was on the other end of that call. That would reveal a lot, he thought. He finished his drink, paid his tab, and exited the bar.

When he approached the parking lot to retrieve his car, like a strike of lightning a blow hit the back of his head. He raised his hand to the injured area and squinted as two men raced around in front of him. He swooned dizzily as he tried to grasp what was happening.

"Teach him a lesson he won't forget," Jin heard a voice say from the shadows. It was Dougan's voice. Jin was sure of it.

His two attackers proceeded to pummel Jin in the stomach with their fists. First one man, then the other. Reeling from the initial hit to his head, Jin was in no condition to fight back.

He dropped to the ground in a heap.

18

JIN WOKE IN a hospital bed.

He tried to move.

"Ooh, that hurts," he moaned. "Everything hurts."

A nurse rushed to his side. "Please don't try to move, sir. Lie still."

"How did I get here?" he asked.

"An ambulance delivered you to the emergency room last night. You were unconscious when you arrived," the nurse said. "The doctor had to put some stitches in the back of your head. That's why the bandage is taped there. And you have a couple of broken ribs too. That's why your upper torso is bound."

Jin reached up to touch the back of his head. "Oh, that smarts," he said, grimacing. "Will I make it?"

"You will," she said. "How are you feeling otherwise?"

Jin thought for a moment. "I've got a bad headache, and I'm nauseous."

"I'm not surprised. You sustained quite a blow to your head." She got up and walked from the room, returning moments later with a capsule and a glass of water. "Here," she said, passing both his way. "Take this. It'll help you feel better."

Jin dutifully complied. Then he focused on the nurse's name tag. "Have you been the one taking care of me, Julia?"

She nodded.

"Thank you," he said as he closed his eyes.

GUY AGREED to drive the BMW Z4 Roadster while Claire watched the map. The two had learned never to rely solely on a car's GPS because it had proven inaccurate on occasion. Nowadays, the investigators used GPS in conjunction with an old-fashioned road map to ensure they reached their destinations as efficiently as possible. After they heard the Ferrari pull away from the hotel, they waited fifteen minutes before following. The Ferrari was a faster car, and they assumed the short wait would provide the necessary lag time they needed to avoid being spotted.

The next stop on DiNetto's itinerary meant the sleuths needed to drive mostly southeast and then south, in the direction of Bologna. She traced the route with her finger. "We'll be traveling from Milan to Parma, then through Reggio, Modena, and Maranello. We'll stop in Porto Venere for a night, and then drive west to Portofino. Both cities are on the Italian Riviera. Massey reserved a hotel room for us for one night in Porto Venere and one night in Portofino."

Claire looked at the distances and estimated it would take around six hours of driving to take this indirect route from Milan to Portofino, traveling first to the village of Porto Venere for a night. Even the route from Milan to Porto Venere seemed indirect. Claire wondered why DiNetto chose this route. There had to be a reason.

Perhaps he had specific plans, and he was literally going out of his way for them.

She glanced up at the sky. A covering of clouds filled all of it, strongly indicating more rain was coming. The sleuths had decided not to follow too closely behind the Ferrari—the risk was too high. Arriving at their destinations sometime after DiNetto offered the best odds he wouldn't discover he was still being tailed.

But on the outside chance the two vehicles might meet up or pass on the road—or that DiNetto might spot the sleuths in one of the stops along the way—Claire threw on her short red wig, making sure to securely tuck under all her strawberry blonde hair. She tied a colorful scarf around her head, threw a turquoise cardigan over her shoulders, and put on very large dark sunglasses to hide much of her face. Guy donned his fair-haired crew cut wig and a pair of aviator sunglasses. He raised the collar of his rain jacket up around his neck. To onlookers, the two would appear to be common tourists.

Soon they were on their way.

The Italian countryside offered amazing vistas. They passed farms, factories, and numerous buildings constructed in shades of mellow yellows. That morning, they shared the road with tall, narrow transport and commercial trucks, as well as Audis, Fiats, Peugeots, and a variety of other automobiles. DiNetto's Ferrari was not in their line of vision.

Rain burst forth and quickly turned into a downpour. The wiper blades could barely keep up. A succession of what can only be described as sheets of water dropped heavily on the BMW, and Guy fought to maintain the vehicle in his lane.

Claire peered out through her side window and squinted. Through the heavy and unrelenting precipitation, she spotted numerous old light-colored brick buildings dotting the roadside. Some were overgrown with ivy. The buildings were surrounded by fields of grasses in vivid limes and golds. They appeared connected by a long line of tall, beautifully formed cylindrical trees, each covered with foliage from the ground on up to their pointed tops. She also noticed a Shell Oil station and a delightfully structured pink building.

Mercifully, all at once, the rain lessened, making it easier to navigate the road. Claire heard Guy exhale a sigh of relief.

"Tough driving," he said, keeping his eyes peeled to the roadway.

The rental car passed over arched white bridges as the investigators neared Parma, Reggio, and Modena. Soon they entered the city of Parma, and Guy slowed the car.

"Parma and Reggio are very near each other," Claire said, looking at the map. "And Modena and then Bologna aren't far. There's a notation here that Parmigiano-Reggiano is among the finest Parmesan cheeses in the world. It's made here—in the regions of Parma, Reggio, Modena, and Bologna. Fascinating."

"You're making me hungry," Guy said. "I could go for a huge bowl of pasta right now, drowning in tomato sauce and heaped with Parmesan cheese." He grinned.

"You're in luck," Claire said. "Guess what I see." She paused. "DiNetto's Ferrari parked right in front of that restaurant." She pointed. "Let's pull up to the next block, walk back, and eat at a place across the street. The city looks small, but it's crawling with restaurants. And I bet they're all good." She stopped and glanced around. "That way, we can fill our stomachs and keep our eyes on DiNetto at the same time."

"Help me find a spot to park," Guy said. "I'll eat anywhere."

Moments later, the investigators walked into a corner restaurant filled with windows. They requested a table that allowed them to look outside. The menu was filled with pastas and thin-crust pizzas, and Claire and Guy quickly made their decisions.

Next to the sleuths sat a table of three Italian men. With sparkling eyes and wide smiles, the trio stared at the Americans and soon attempted to engage the sleuths in conversation. One of them spoke English as his second language, the others only Italian. The men introduced themselves as Marco, Roberto, and Ermes. With helpful translations thanks to the Italian who spoke English—Roberto— the five engaged in remarkably easy conversation. Roberto informed Claire and Guy that none of the three had ever been to the US.

Claire's eyes darted to a group of skinheads sitting at a table several feet away. They seemed overly interested in gawking at the Americans and made her feel uncomfortable. She chose to ignore their overt, unfriendly stares.

All of a sudden, Marco pointed outside to DiNetto's Ferrari. His eyes lit up like a child's at an amusement park.

"Ferrari!" he said. "DiNetto!"

"You know Anthony DiNetto?" Claire asked.

Roberto smiled. "Of course. We all know Anthony DiNetto. He passes through our city whenever he visits Italy. He drives one of Italy's masterpiece cars, and he makes a grand appearance each time he arrives—and eats at all the restaurants. Parma is a city of great food, music, and art, and he shows us he loves it all."

Soon the sumptuous food arrived, and the investigators ate while the dialogue continued.

"Other than cheese, what products is this area known for?" Guy asked.

"Oh," Roberto said, smiling. "We produce the *real* foods—the *necessary* foods." He laughed. "Not just any Parmesan cheese, but *authentic* Parmigiano-Reggiano cheese! There is none better." He looked amused. "And then, of course, Parma hams, Culatello salami, sausages, delicious mushrooms—pore fungi. White and black truffles, the sweetest-smelling wild strawberries, raspberries, and bilberries. And confections of all sorts—from biscuits and panettone to Italian-style ice cream." He paused to catch his breath. "Also, liqueurs—alcohol with infused fruits. Like *nocino,* made from the hull of the green walnut; *erba luigia,* made with lemon verbena leaves and rosemary; and *citronella,* made from lemongrass leaves. And Lambrusco—a sparkling red wine we say has a purple-violet-ruby color. It's the predominant wine of this area. It has only a mild alcohol content."

Roberto stopped to assess whether the investigators were impressed with the list he rattled off, and he continued on when he was satisfied that they were. "And I must not forget to mention the balsamic vinegar of Modena. It's made from our finest grapes and aged in wooden barrels from twelve to twenty-five years. It's aromatic and dense, and its flavor is simply outstanding." He stopped again, happy to have a chance to brush up on his English. "DiNetto arranges to have many of these products sent to his address in the US every time he visits."

Just then, Marco pointed to the Ferrari parked outside and uttered something in Italian.

"He says the Ferrari is leaving," Roberto translated.

Ermes had ordered chilled shot glasses of *bargnolino*—a special drink of Modena made from the sloe fruit of the blackthorn plant—for his table and for his new American friends. The server delivered the sweet reddish liquor to the tables, and Claire and Guy each took a quick taste.

"Good!" Guy said, nodding.

Claire and Guy looked out in time to see DiNetto getting into his famous Italian car. They heard the recognizable thunder of the engine as he started the car and drove off.

"I'm afraid it's time we must leave," Claire said. "It's been an absolute pleasure meeting and talking to you all." She left money on the table to cover their check.

"And thank you for the drinks," Guy said. "We enjoyed tasting *bargnolino*. It's *magnifico!*"

Good-byes were exchanged all around, and with pleasant, friendly smiles the Italians waved to the Americans as they walked from the restaurant.

"Nice people," Guy said as the sleuths stepped from the Italian eatery and hustled down the street to their car.

"Amazing," Claire said. "On another note, did you notice the table of skinheads?"

"I did. Their shaved heads and 'Anarchy' T-shirts gave them away. I was surprised to see them here."

The sleuths reached the rental car, jumped in, and were on their way.

They passed through nearby Reggio, then entered Modena—an area filled with vineyards and houses with tile rooftops and bright golden-yellow and sherbet-orange stucco. Unexpectedly, they heard the distinctive reverberation of a Ferrari engine directly in front of them. DiNetto's car was too close.

"Slow down, Guy. Drop back," Claire said. "We can't let him see us."

He trailed behind at a safe distance to avoid detection, but they could still see the Ferrari ahead.

Signs indicating the Maranello exit was approaching drew the sleuths' attention. They watched DiNetto take the exit and motor along, presumably heading in the direction of the Ferrari plant, given his obsession with the brand and Maranello's lack of other attractions. The investigators, leaving a wide margin between the two vehicles, shadowed him. As DiNetto turned into the city of Maranello, the distinctive sound of many Ferrari engines filled the air.

DiNetto drove several blocks to the Museo Ferrari and

automaker's plant. He parked his car in the lot and walked inside.

Guy pulled their rental car into a spot on the opposite end of the lot, and the sleuths began to stroll toward the main building on the premises. When they were only feet away from their car, a dark green van pulled in and drove slowly past. Claire glanced up and noticed it was filled with the group of skinheads they had just seen in Parma.

"It's the skinheads from the restaurant, Guy," she said. "Think they're following us?"

"Let's watch and see."

As Claire and Guy walked across the parking lot, they observed a full-sized racetrack in the distance on the property. They would soon discover that several new Ferrari models were being tested on the track for quality-control purposes.

The investigators arrived at the doors of the main building and walked inside. It was crowded with Ferrari fans and curious car lovers. Part of the building housed an impressive shop that sold everything Ferrari—clothing for children and adults, shoes, mugs, key chains, gloves, mouse pads, replica toy cars, and more. The sleuths spent a few minutes strolling through that area, staying on high alert for DiNetto. Then they spotted a food counter offering sandwiches, sodas, coffees, and ice creams.

Claire finally spotted DiNetto. He was at the head of a long line of people standing two by two. The sign hanging directly above the crowd indicated "Tours." Her gaze fell to a blackboard positioned on an easel near the front of the line. Its message said, "Next tour: 3 minutes." The message was printed in chalk, and just as Claire read it, an employee of the plant erased the "3" and replaced it with a "2."

"He's taking a tour of the plant," Claire said, nodding her head in DiNetto's direction. "We need to buy tickets as fast as we can and make it into his group."

Guy noticed a cashier stand and stepped over to purchase two tickets.

"We're all sold-out for this tour, sir," the attendant said. "You'll have to wait for the next."

"Sorry. Can't wait," Guy said. "We have a long drive ahead of us today, and this is the only chance we'll have to go on the tour. We came all the way from the US to experience it. Please make an exception and let us in."

Guy saw Claire motioning to him from the sidelines, frantically pointing to her watch. "It's starting," she mouthed. Guy looked over and saw that the people in line were already moving into another area. The tour was underway.

"Please," Guy said again. "Have a heart." He smiled.

The attendant had mercy on him and passed two tickets his way. "These are on the house. I cannot take money for them now because it's already started. Just go. You had better hurry!"

Guy shook the woman's hand and passed her the equivalent of twenty-five dollars in euros.

"Thank you, sir!" she said under her breath. "Enjoy!"

Claire and Guy quickly moved over to join the tour crowd, stepping in at the very back just as a cord was being strung across the entrance, closing it off.

"A minute later—" Claire said.

"No, actually one *moment* later," Guy said, "and we wouldn't have made it."

The excitement of the tour group was palpable.

Claire could see DiNetto at the very front of the horde. Several women on the tour had surrounded him. And just behind DiNetto and his harem, unbelievably, she spotted the group of skinheads.

19

THE HOSPITAL RELEASED Jin and sent him home with a prescription for pain-killers. He taxied to his car in the lot near the South Beach bar. The attendant refused to charge Jin once he learned the reason the car had remained there so long.

"We wondered," the car parker said. "Hope things work out for you."

Jin drove to a pharmacy, filled the prescription, and headed home. He walked in, locked the door, and got comfortable on the sofa. He decided he would return to law school classes and work the following day if he felt better. He turned on the television and pulled a throw over himself. He was miserable, and he just wanted to hide. Maybe forever. When Gaston Lombard and Claire Caswell next called him, he'd have to fill them in on the debacle he'd created—and apologize. Or maybe it was best to keep things quiet for now. He remained unsure.

He thought about the botched investigation he'd undertaken and reviewed the incidents that had led to his current situation. Things couldn't have gone worse. Lying in a prone position, he thought long and hard whether he was cut out for the business of private investigation. He'd stepped outside the parameters of his contract with Caswell & Lombard, something he'd learned in law school could be termed a "frolic and detour." He could only imagine what might happen once his new bosses found out what he'd done. He sighed. He'd have to call the client too and confess what had taken place. "Ugh," he grimaced. No more stakeouts in South Beach bars for him.

He soon fell asleep and dreamed of sitting at a beautiful, polished desk while performing computer forensics on a criminal case. That's what he was best suited for, and he knew it. The life of an investigator was demanding and onerous, and he wasn't sure he could ever meet the challenge. Even in his sleep, he groaned at the realization.

THE TOUR of the Museo Ferrari and plant was in full swing. The guide was a pleasant Italian woman who conducted the tour in English. She explained she'd be leading the group through a variety of buildings on the grounds and reviewing the entire history of the famous Italian automobile, from the first one built in 1947—after World War II—to the current models. The tour's final activity would be a walk-through of the parts assembly plant, where each person would be afforded an up-close look at all aspects of how the handcrafted luxury vehicles were built. The guide encouraged them to ask questions along the way and informed the group that buses would transport them between the buildings. "Please feel free to use one of our umbrellas," the guide said, "when we walk or wait outside."

Claire and Guy had popped on heavy-framed glasses. With disguises in place, they felt confident they could blend in with the crowd of thirty to forty others. They stayed close to the rear.

As they walked through the first exhibit, the guide asked the group for the original color of the Ferrari. Many guessed red. But she shook her head and informed them yellow was the first color used.

As the tour progressed through different buildings, the group learned all about the Italian car and what made it so special. Eventually, they toured a building housing Ferrari race cars and were given the opportunity to walk among them and peer inside each model. Soon they were moving to their final destination, the parts assembly plant.

The structure was enormous and spotlessly clean, with trees growing inside the work area. State-of-the-art robots performed certain functions, and live workers hand-stitched the interior leather elements of each Ferrari being built.

The investigators were enthralled by it all. Claire stopped to watch a certain robot named Romeo and Juliet. Romeo—half of the automated machine—dipped valve rings one by one into a bath of liquid nitrogen. Then with the help of his other half, Juliet, who held the cylinder head, Romeo set each valve ring in place. The process fascinated her. The machine performed flawlessly.

Assuming Claire was at his heels, Guy strolled off to look at a completed engine.

Moments later, when Claire turned to look for Guy, she noticed DiNetto standing on the floor some thirty feet away, staring directly at her. She turned her head and walked off in the direction she'd seen Guy travel. As she turned down an aisle, she abruptly realized she was totally separated from the rest of the group. Without warning, two skinheads stepped in front of her and blocked her path.

"Is there a problem?" she asked cockily.

"There is," one of them said. "Come with us."

"I don't think so," she said.

Without delay, each grabbed one of her arms, lifting her slightly off the ground. She let out a loud yelp, but no one heard her. They force-walked the sleuth through a nearby exit door. No one else was outside, and Claire felt highly vulnerable. Rain fell lightly. The two men glared at her. After the recent attacks she'd experienced, she wasn't about to succumb to another.

"What do you want?" she demanded.

"We want you to return to the US, where you belong. You and that man of yours. Without delay," one of the skinheads said.

"Is that clear?" the other asked.

"I'm not sure I understand," she said. "*You're* telling *me* what to do? Is that correct? Where do you get off?" She refused to dilute her boldness.

"You're wasting our time," the thinner of the two said.

"More importantly, you're wasting mine," she said defiantly.

The stockier of the two men rolled up his right shirtsleeve to just under his elbow, revealing a limb decorated with heavy tattooing. Claire's eyes darted to the exposed indelible ink designs just as the man raised his arm high in the air. Before she realized what was happening, he brought his arm down speedily and with steady control, slapping his hand squarely across her face in a manner designed to cause the maximum pain. The sting was unbearable, but Claire refused to show it. Her face reddened.

"Okay, now that was uncalled for," she said. "Didn't your mother teach you to never strike a woman?" She bellowed out at the top of her lungs, "*Help!*"

The skinheads became agitated when she wouldn't be cowed, and they ran off.

Claire raced back into the plant, searching desperately for Guy.

The tour guide saw her searching for him and pointed toward the building's far corner. The female sleuth ran through the plant until she reached him.

"Claire, where have you been?" he asked. "I searched the plant for you. You look terrible. Your face is bright red."

"We shouldn't have let ourselves get separated again," she said. She filled him in on what happened.

Guy looked around. All the skinheads had left the building. DiNetto remained with the group, watching the final assembly of a Ferrari with keen interest.

"DiNetto's responsible. *Again!*" Claire said. "That animal is behind this. He's been behind everything bad that's happened to us, and in particular to me, since the day we arrived in Milan. He's trying to get to me in any way possible. To scare me—us—away. He'll stop at nothing." She touched her face gently. It still smarted. Her anger toward DiNetto soared to new heights with this last episode, which earlier today she would have thought impossible.

Claire looked over at DiNetto. He turned his head and stared straight into her eyes. He held his eyes open, refusing to blink. He smiled a despicable smile, as if to say, "I dare you to prove it was me." Claire glared back at the man.

"This is not over," she said more to herself than to Guy. As the blood boiled in her veins, her face grew redder, changing her appearance. She was intent on putting DiNetto away. And in her mind, the mission was now hers alone. No one and nothing could dissuade her from putting the pig where he belonged—in a barred pen. She clenched her fist.

Guy continued to stare at DiNetto too. "Your time is running out," he mouthed with an icy look.

The tour ended, and the crowd dispersed from the factory. Both DiNetto and the investigators got into their cars and departed on the drive to Porto Venere, where they'd spend the night. Claire and Guy drove in silence. The trauma Claire had experienced on this case would take her some time to deal with. For now, however, she shoved it out of her mind. There was a case to complete.

She pulled her pad and pen from her backpack and furiously scribbled additional notes.

JIN AWAKENED from his rest. His head throbbed, and he gulped down a pain pill. He had missed his classes at the law school that morning, but decided he'd better go in to the Caswell & Lombard office to make sure everything was in order. He felt a great responsibility for the firm, particularly because the investigators were away and depending on him.

He got in his car and drove to the office. Once inside, he immediately noticed the light on the answering machine blinking to signal new messages. He grabbed a legal pad and pen and sat down. There were four new messages—three in short succession from Officer Figg. In each he requested a callback and an update on the case. Jin twisted his face into an ugly expression. What could he report? That he'd found out absolutely nothing of any substance? That he was beaten at Dougan's request and hospitalized with a head wound? He'd sound like a rank amateur. He'd be deemed totally incompetent. He swallowed hard. Maybe he could put the client off until he had something concrete to report. But how?

The fourth message was from Gaston Lombard, calling to check in. He said he'd try back later.

Soon Claire Caswell and Guy Lombard would return to the US and the office. Jin couldn't wait. He may have taken on a job he didn't have the skills to perform. But the firm's reputation was on the line. Something had to be done to help the client.

He picked up the phone and called Officer Figg's cell number.

"Officer Figg? Jin Ikeda reporting in, sir."

"Been trying to reach you. What have you discovered?" the police officer asked, not disguising his impatience.

"This case is new. It is in progress, officer. It's an open investigation, so I'm afraid I'm not at liberty to reveal anything to you today. But hopefully soon," Jin said. He crossed his fingers that this answer would buy him more time.

"Very well, Ikeda. Keep me posted. The sooner the better."

"You've got it, sir," Jin replied.

Jin's headache worsened. He didn't know what his next step should be. He popped another pain pill and held his head in his hands with his eyes shut. Suddenly, an idea came to him. He called Figg again.

"I'll need a list from you indicating each time a breach of confidential department information occurred and the name of each reporter who announced the private information to the public. I might have something," Jin said. He wasn't exactly sure where he was going with this, but at least he would have something in writing to analyze.

"Not a problem," Figg answered. "You'll have it soon."

Jin glanced at the wall clock. It was a good time to try calling Claire and Gaston. He dialed Guy's cell number and reached him in the car.

"Mr. Lombard? It's Jin, reporting in. I got your message."

"Jin, good to hear from you," Guy said. "How's everything at the office? You putting out any fires?"

Jin chuckled. "Not really, sir. How's your case going?"

"We'll fill you in on all the details when we arrive home. For now, I'll just report that it's been hugely challenging, to say the least. Dangerous. The kind of case an investigator dreads. The kind of case you think might be easy, initially, but then it turns out to be anything but," Guy said.

"Well, stay safe, you two, and get back here," Jin said.

"Any new clients?" Guy asked.

It was the question Jin had tried to avoid. Now he had to answer.

"Actually, the firm does have one new client, sir," Jin started. "It's a matter I can handle. I don't want to trouble you with it now. As soon as you come home, I'll fill you in." He paused briefly to swallow. "It involves a confidential matter, and I don't think discussing it over the phone would be wise."

"Okay," Guy said slowly, suddenly leery. "You aren't a licensed private investigator, Jin. Remember that. You were hired to man the office and do computer research. I thought we made that clear. Don't detour from your job description, Jin. You'll get us all in trouble."

The tort of "frolic and detour" again entered Jin's mind. As a lawyer, Guy would know Jin had studied the concept in law school. An employee acting outside the scope of his employment could cause big problems.

"Yes, sir," Jin said.

"Very well, then," Guy said. "We will be in touch."

Worry oozed over Jin like icing on a cake. So far, he hadn't technically crossed the line. He'd merely been out at a bar twice— nothing more than that. He had puffed his abilities to Officer Figg, though. Jin twisted in Claire's chair. Everything he'd worked so hard for could blow up in his face if he crossed the line and engaged in unlicensed activities. He was hired to do office work, not to be a third investigator for the firm. His specialty was forensic computer analysis, not undercover work.

He got up, made himself a cup of hot tea in Claire's pink flamingo mug, and resituated himself in her chair. Then he picked up the phone and ordered in sushi.

As he ate, he pondered his situation. I'll sit behind a computer and figure this out, he told himself. I'll do it my way.

For the first time since the attack, his headache felt better.

He lifted his head, turned on the computer, and got started.

GUY DROVE the rental car like a pro through the rain bearing down on the motorway. They were nearing the turnoff toward Porto Venere. The Ferrari raced forward, and Guy lagged a protective distance behind, making sure never to come within view of the high-speed Italian automobile DiNetto manned.

Before long, Claire spotted the exit ramp. As Guy made the turn, he saw the tail end of the Ferrari ahead at the far end of the exit.

He slowed to a crawl.

20

CLAIRE FOCUSED HER thoughts on the investigation. In two days, she and Guy would drive to France, the third and final European country on DiNetto's itinerary—specifically to the city of Montpellier, located in the southern part of the country. If they were unable to determine the nature of DiNetto's activities in the few remaining days of the trip, all would have been for naught. They would have to board a plane and fly home as scheduled. No matter what. And their time for solving the case would have run out.

A single-minded drive to discover DiNetto's secret possessed her. She could think of nothing else. She remained infuriated about the attacks DiNetto had foisted on her. He had crossed the line several times over, and there was no way back. He wasn't going to just walk away. She fumed. She needed to find evidence of his scheme—concrete evidence—that would put him away for a long time.

Her blood continued to boil, and questions about the case

whirled through her head. What was DiNetto plotting? How was Officer Bubbiano involved? Had DiNetto planned the attack on the taxi when they first arrived? Had he pushed the young woman from the box at La Scala? Did he direct the hideous man on the trains to first harass then later attack her? Who'd been behind the black jester's costume at the masquerade ball? Had Bubbiano merely rented the costume for DiNetto? Did DiNetto arrange the attack on her after dropping her on the dark street? What was the connection among Milan, Neuchâtel, Porto Venere, Portofino, and Montpellier—destinations that had them traversing Italy, Switzerland, and France? How were the skinheads involved with DiNetto?

And the key question: What did the boxes contain? As a seasoned investigator, she knew they held the secret to solving the case. She needed answers.

Guy drove on in silence, also deluged by thoughts pouring through his mind. He mulled over everything he and Claire had been through since they arrived in Milan. He replayed in his mind's eye the taxi ride that had resulted in the deaths of two people—and nearly in the deaths of Claire and himself. He reviewed each and every heinous deed DiNetto had arranged to inflict harm upon Claire since their arrival. She had been the sole target of the subsequent attacks, and she'd remained so strong through it all.

He sighed deeply. They had no proof whatsoever DiNetto was behind the attacks, but they knew it was him. He had the motive and the opportunity. It was time to stitch it all together and locate confirmation of DiNetto's current illegal scheme. To stop him, they needed evidence that would stand up in a court of law.

Since exiting the expressway, the drive to Porto Venere was curvy and descending as it spiraled toward the water's edge. Guy traveled at a slow speed to avoid showing up in DiNetto's rearview mirror. When at last they reached the Italian Riviera coastline, Guy navigated a narrow two-lane road in the direction of the hotel. Cars whooshed past, speeding along in the opposite direction. He discovered that driving along the stretch of road bordering the blue waters of the Ligurian Sea was exhausting. It called for maximum concentration and left no room for error. To make the situation even more uncertain, the road was crowded with bicycles, motor scooters, motorcycles, and pedestrians—all moving at the speed of light. There were objects in motion all around them. The nerve-racking driving required quick, constant maneuverability and vigilance, without a second's reprieve.

The rain had disappeared since they left the motorway, and now the sun was shining, providing a comfortable temperature. With some difficulty, the investigators found their way to the Grand Hotel Porto Venere, located just off the waterfront. Their room had a panoramic view of the Italian Riviera with the castle and old fort remains on the nearby hillside and the many old fishing boats and luxury yachts floating in the pier. The buildings lining the harbor resembled a painting of faded memories.

Spent from the day's events, Claire and Guy took an hour-long nap. Then they left the room to explore the waterfront and pier, sporting altered disguises. After walking for a time, they stopped at a restaurant—marked by a life-sized, yellow, wooden fisherman—for dinner. Most everyone dining around them spoke Italian. But one family, at the next table over, spoke English.

Claire and Guy greeted them, and conversation ensued. The sleuths learned that the family—a husband and wife from Australia, together with their three children—was in the midst of an extended three-month vacation. They were spending time in England, Israel, Spain, France, Italy, and South Africa before returning home. The children were excited about taking a boat ride to the famous Cinque Terra—five connected villages built into the terraced, steep hillside of the area—the following day, and they could talk of nothing else. One child explained that if the sea was too rough to take a boat on the excursion, they would take a train. Claire and Guy welcomed the chance to converse easily in English and wished the family a wonderful time together.

The investigators walked for another half an hour after dinner and then returned to their room to retire early. Tomorrow promised to be a long and difficult day of driving, and a good night's sleep was in order.

They saw no sign of DiNetto in Porto Venere, but they knew he was there. When they returned to their room, a slip of paper had been inserted under the door. It read: "Enjoy the Italian Riviera." It was unsigned and printed in pencil. The paper was blank except for those four words.

"DiNetto wrote this," Claire said. "He knows we're here."

"He's playing with us," Guy said.

"He wants to make sure we know that he knows we're trailing him. Disguises or no disguises. He always seems to recognize us. It's a mind game. And I think he rather enjoys it." She hesitated. "Seems he has a concierge on his payroll at every stop. We have DiNetto under surveillance, but he also has us under surveillance."

The look on her face told Guy she felt great frustration.

She walked to the only window in the room—a large wood-framed window without a screen—and pushed it wide open. Cool evening air rushed in. Night had fallen, and she peered outside at the scattered lights dotting the shadowy landscape. They added little illumination to the darkness, but twinkled under the cool moonlight. There was enough light for her to make out the moored boats heaving and swaying gently on the Italian Riviera. She took in the colorful, tightly nestled buildings of blue, yellow, beige, pink, peach, and coral that stretched alongside the water's edge as if the side walls were glued together to form one long row. The scene was framed by the surrounding sharp hillside. On the streets below, horse-drawn carriages provided transportation for tourists to experience Porto Venere's magical nighttime scene.

She inhaled deeply the smells of the nearby salty sea. She felt like a child who had stepped into a picture book that was hers to absorb. She heard the sounds of people below enjoying a nighttime stroll, and it seemed as if she could almost taste the flavors of the Mediterranean. Her eyes were drawn upward to the ancient castle sitting so majestically high on the hillside, subtly illuminated with colored lights in the darkness.

Claire looked down again, this time focusing on the walkway bordering the entire length of the pier. Her eyes were drawn to the far end of the pier, where three large yachts were tied. Curiosity gripped her as intermittent dock lighting allowed her to witness a man exiting the middle craft. As he walked along the dock in the direction of the hotel, she recognized the form was DiNetto. He'd visited a specific boat. And he toted a bag large enough to hold two of the boxes.

"Guy, come here," she said. "Look who I see."

As they peered out, the large boat DiNetto had been on left its position at the pier and slowly disappeared into the dark waters of the Italian Riviera.

Day eight
Porto Venere to Portofino, Italy

THE FOLLOWING morning, the sleuths awoke early, refreshed. They dressed, packed, and checked out of the hotel. They walked to a nearby restaurant for a quick breakfast, and soon they were en route to the famous nearby city of Portofino. It was an hour-and-a-half drive west along the motorway. This would be the penultimate stop on the itinerary before the last destination—Montpellier, France—the next day.

Portofino—famous as an Italian fishing village and upscale resort—was also located directly on the coastline. Just like yesterday, reaching their destination today required focused driving once they left the main road. Similar to the drive to Porto Venere, this route took them down a steep hillside to the water's edge and then along a narrow road paralleling the sea. As they headed toward Portofino's picturesque harbor—the location of the hotel—the road left little to no margin for driver error, and was horribly congested. It seemed a dangerous mix of bicycles, mopeds, motorcycles, automobiles, and pedestrians. Everyone competed for space in the limited confines of the cramped passageway without slowing from a breakneck speed. Someone suffering from claustrophobia would be hard-pressed to avoid extreme anxiety in the chaotic and compressed environment, Guy thought.

Glancing down at the map, Claire mentioned, "I read that Portofino is a place celebrities visit."

"That doesn't excite or interest me," Guy said.

"Me neither." She looked up. "Watch out!" she screamed.

BACK IN the office, Jin worked hard. He decided to find out everything he could about Officer Dougan while sitting behind a computer. For this work, he needed to use his own computer, so he pulled it from his bag. His personal computer contained a number of software packages that would accelerate his search.

He plotted a strategy as he hunted the Internet. He began by looking at public records, the national criminal database searches,

Florida criminal history records, genealogy records, and vital records. He looked for information on Dougan using e-mail and reverse–e-mail searches, and he foraged for newspaper, magazine, and e-publication articles that might have mentioned his name. Jin wanted to learn everything there was to be found about Officer Cane Dougan.

Instead of mindlessly punching keywords into a search engine, he considered each step before he clicked. He used common sense and logic. He didn't rush or rifle through an endless sea of information. Blind searches never produced the results he needed. He targeted his efforts by asking himself where he would likely find information on a police officer.

Who would potentially know more about this individual? Close friends? Other officers on the force? Sergeant Massey? After some thought, he ruled out other officers and the sergeant at this time. It was too early, and the client wanted Jin to steer clear of any police involvement in the investigation.

Focusing on the lead of close friends, Jin looked at social-media interfaces Dougan might have used—Facebook, Twitter, LinkedIn, MySpace, and so on. He even looked at a site that checked many social-media networks at once. If the privacy setting had been implemented on any of these pages, Jin had a backdoor way to scrutinize the particular search sites for cached versions of personal pages. He knew information on a subject's friends often showed up this way. If he obtained the names of Dougan's friends, he could also check their social-media sites to learn more about Dougan.

Jin decided to hone in on gay chat rooms and blogs. Suddenly, an idea struck him. He picked up the phone and dialed Officer Figg.

"Does Officer Dougan use any nicknames?"

"Not publicly," Figg told him. "But one time when he was on his cell phone, I did overhear him whisper, 'Yeah, this is Sugarcane.'"

"*Sugarcane?* Well, his given name is Cane, so that makes some sense," Jin said. "That's what I needed. Thank you."

Jin returned to gay chat rooms based in the Miami area, searching for Sugarcane. He hit pay dirt. The name appeared in many chats on a website that had been shut down. Jin smiled. He gained access to the site using a Trojan horse method and scoured everything he could find about Sugarcane. He took scrupulous notes on his discoveries and saved some telling screen grabs.

Now he had some useful information to pursue.

"THAT WAS close!" Guy said in a shrill voice. "I almost hit that motorcycle."

"Or he almost hit us," Claire said. "Not sure which. He came up so fast on the side. I didn't see him coming."

"Neither did I," Guy said. He inhaled deeply and exhaled slowly. "I can't wait until we're there. This driving is not for me."

"Seems like there's a constant stream of impossibly close calls. I've been watching. People honk horns, swear, laugh, show a hand gesture, and simply keep moving. It's like everyone agrees to drive crazy, and it works. No one stays mad for long," the female investigator said. "It's nerve-racking for us, but I guess we're just not used to it."

"It looks like driving a motorcycle in this mayhem would be even more difficult, so I guess I'm happy we're in a rental car." His face betrayed his stress level. "Seems to me that traveling to either Porto Venere or Portofino would best be done by boat. This driving is for the birds."

"I'm glad it's you and not me," Claire said. "Thank you."

The two passed through a small village bordering the water. The streets were jammed with pedestrians—shoppers, walkers, talkers, people enjoying gelato cones, and those simply out to take in the lovely day. Guy pushed onward toward Portofino.

Finally they arrived at the famous city clustered around a pier and sitting in an inlet of the Ligurian Sea—a part of the strikingly blue Mediterranean. The water was filled with boats of every size. Most of them white. A number of luxury yachts were moored next to one another at the end of the cove. It was a scene not unlike what they'd experienced in Porto Venere. Portofino was smaller than Claire had expected. Cobblestone streets led to, from, and around the immediate area surrounding the water's edge, and each was lined with shops—mostly designer in nature—and also restaurants. It was a walking area only. Guy found a garage three short blocks from the water's edge and about two blocks from the Splendido Mare hotel. They parked in a ramp and walked to their lodging, taking turns pulling the duffel bag along the uneven stone streets. Upon checking in, the investigators were led to a spacious room on the main floor. The windows opened directly onto the walking plaza surrounding the pier and afforded the two a spectacular view of the marina and neighboring area.

"This room," Claire said, "is the perfect place to observe everything that's happening here. We couldn't have asked for a better spot. Massey certainly outdid himself this time." She grabbed her notepad and updated her case notes. "Speaking of the sergeant, I should give him a call." She reached for her cell.

"Sergeant Massey? It's Claire Caswell. I know it's early there. I usually don't have the chance to reach you at a reasonable hour. I apologize." She filled him in on all happenings since their last conversation.

"Glad you called. I planned to call you when I got in to the station. How close are you to finding out what DiNetto is hiding?"

"I'd say close. We know it has to do with those boxes I told you about. We're on our way to France tomorrow, and I have to believe something big is going to happen there. It's all been building to this."

"Well, there has been a slight change of plans, Ms. Caswell," the sergeant said. "DiNetto amended his itinerary. I just received a text from the travel agent on our payroll, and DiNetto is now stopping in Cannes, France, and staying there one night on his way to Montpellier. Not sure why, but it must be important. So you and Mr. Lombard will also be going to Cannes. I've made arrangements for your hotel room—the same place DiNetto is staying, as always. I'll e-mail the details within a couple hours. It's just over a three-hour drive from Portofino to Cannes. Any questions?"

"No, none that I can think of," she said. "But this will give us a shorter time in Montpellier."

"I was getting to that. Your return date will be extended by one day. We'll take care of everything on this end. Your new tickets will be held at the airport. You'll be on the same flight, same departure time, and you'll still leave from Paris, only it will be one day later than originally planned. You and Gaston will have your two nights in Montpellier." He cracked his knuckles.

"So then we're talking about an extra day of investigation," Claire said. "Very well. Time is winding down, and we want to accomplish our goal. It's within reach."

"I hope so, Ms. Caswell," Sergeant Massey said. He seemed edgy in a way she had never heard before. Claire could tell something was bothering him greatly. "But let me warn you again. You and Mr. Lombard must use extreme caution at every turn. Never let your guard down. Not for a second. You've been skating around some real trouble—you especially, Ms. Caswell. DiNetto knows you're still watching his every move. Your lives will continue to be in peril. Consider him extremely dangerous." He sighed. "I should probably be calling you home early, instead of extending your time, but I know you'd never agree. So, be extraordinarily careful. And call whenever it works for you—night or day. Never worry about the time on my end."

"Yes, I'll keep reporting in. Promise," Claire said. "We'll change disguises more frequently, so DiNetto will have to work harder to figure out which couple we are. Don't worry about us. We'll be fine. Oh, and we'll take care of extending the rental car."

There was a pause in conversation, and Claire heard the sergeant crack his knuckles several times in succession.

"Figure out what's in those boxes, Ms. Caswell," he said. "And the two of you get back here." He sounded disconcerted.

"Everything okay there, sergeant?" Claire finally asked.

He hung up.

21

IN HIS ROOM, DiNetto poured himself a double shot of AVIV vodka straight up. He dropped into a cushy armchair, sinking back into its comfort. He lifted his feet onto an ottoman. Sipping the unforgettable clear elixir, he let his mind drift.

Smoothest vodka in all the world, he thought. His lips curved into a cunning smile. That hint of sweetness. He sniggered. Only good people drank AVIV, he told himself. It was loaded with spirituality. Everyone would think he was good because he drank it. They wouldn't know the darkness that lurked in his soul. He allowed himself a sinister chuckle.

As much as he fought the direction of his thoughts, they darted back to his family, to his misfortune in birth, to his life of loneliness. He took a long gulp and nearly emptied the glass. He pondered how life had cheated him. How each member of his family had been ripped away from him. How he'd been left to fend for himself, the lone survivor of a group of five. An orphan in an adopted country. He thought about birthdays, holidays, and special occasions that came and passed, year after year, and how he would sit alone each time with vodka and wine as his only constant companions. The pangs of aloneness he had suffered after coming to America had been profound, and now they seemed a constant part of him, pounding in his head and heart.

Life was a doleful ride, he thought. Unexpectedly, a series of salty tears rolled down his cheeks in quick succession and into his mouth. In that instant, he was transported back to Italy—to the house he grew up in—to the day his tata announced they would all be leaving for America in two weeks. It was as if it had happened yesterday. He recalled the smells in the kitchen; the taste of his mamma's risotto, warm bread, and the thin slice of ham; his parents' faces, their skin so permeated with wrinkles at a young age and their eyes so sorrowful. He remembered the protests of his siblings, the hardness of the wooden table where he sat, and his mouth going dry. He relived the anger that had prompted him to storm outside into the cold, and the salty tears that had poured down his face. His expectation of fairness had vanished at that moment, never to return.

A low growl emanated from deep within him, and a guttural moan followed without his volition. He hadn't permitted himself to cry since that horrible day. Not really. Not until now. Not even when Carlo hung himself. Not even when his parents and little sister were taken in a dreadful car accident soon after they arrived in America. Not even at their shared funeral. But now, the floodgates opened, and he was unable to close them. For minutes, he sobbed with convulsive gasping, uncontrolled and unrestrained.

When at last the briny tears had emptied, he poured another shot of AVIV and drank it in a single gulp. He stared at its beautiful bottle. AVIV brought with it good luck, at least that was what its manufacturer said. The bottle contained one hundred hidden messages, and he was keeping a list of the ones he'd found so far. In Hebrew and English, the theme of AVIV was, "Pour with joy and toast from the bottom of your heart and may all your good wishes be fulfilled." His eyes were red and puffy. If only the contents really contained magic, he thought. If only good wishes in his life could be fulfilled. Maybe his pitiful soul could be rescued and somehow his life turned around.

The bottle continued to hold his rapt attention. He rotated it in his hands and read the fine print. He saw it contained water from the Sea of Galilee—the body of water where Jesus Christ performed some of His miracles. And he read that a company in France mixed sand from the Negev, a desert in Israel, into the glass when manufacturing the bottles that housed the magnificent transparent liquor. Even the seven ingredients seemed special. As the third shot kicked in, he mellowed considerably, and his memories, together with the pain they gripped so tightly, faded.

JIN WAS on a roll. Things were moving along nicely. He'd collected quite a bit of digital information about Cane Dougan and had started to develop the policeman's patterns of movement and his contacts—but he still needed more.

He jotted down the words he overheard Dougan say into the pay phone at the gay bar: "Unharmed. On to the next act. I'll keep you posted." Jin meditated on the curious words. Who was on the other end of the line? Why the covert call and the near riddle? Why a pay phone? Who or what was "unharmed"? And what did "on to the next act" mean?

Jin considered his options. Personal surveillance of the subject was out of the question, seeing as Jin didn't have a private investigator's license. Returning to the same bar in South Beach to pose as a patron was inadvisable. Dougan was bound to recognize him—the new guy in the bar who suddenly pops in all too often. Besides, it hadn't worked the first two times.

Early on in the case, Jin had thought about walking a friend's dog around the area where Dougan lived. Then he could observe any activity at his house when Dougan was off duty. After all, everyone notices the dog being walked, not the person walking the dog. But what would that gain? It would only prove Dougan's deceptive home life.

So he returned to cyberspying. It seemed his best and only real hope. The shutdown website where he had discovered Dougan's Sugarcane alias had given him some real leads. A few contact names had come up frequently. But he guessed many, if not all, were nicknames as well.

More importantly, he'd come upon an e-mail address for Dougan, using the nickname Sugarcane, in a gay chat room. It was time to zero in on that and discover what he could. Jin's goal was to use his computer to search Dougan's digital storage media to uncover legal evidence against him. Data recovery was the key. He needed to create a legal audit trail.

CLAIRE AND Guy changed clothes and left their room to walk around the pier. Claire scanned a handout about the area and a map she'd taken from the room, and she filled Guy in as they strolled. "It says Portofino is a tourist resort for the rich and famous on the Italian Riviera. Pastel-colored residences dot its half-moon-shaped seaside village, and it borders the transparent harbor waters." She pointed to an image in the brochure. "This place is gorgeous!"

"Not bad at all," Guy said.

"The brochure says Portofino is known for exquisite shopping, cafés, restaurants, and opulent hotels," Claire read on. "And diving, boating, and hiking." She pointed to the castle sitting high on the hill overlooking the village. "Tourists walk up the path to the castle. Reminds me of the castle in Porto Venere."

"Sounds like this place oozes with money," Guy said.

"And keep in mind, it's a stop on DiNetto's itinerary," Claire replied. She raised one eyebrow.

They strolled around the village streets and walked down to the water. The two had altered their disguises before leaving the hotel. Guy had selected a plum-and-white-striped polo shirt and blue jeans, and he tied a navy sweater loosely over his shoulders. Gradient silver metallic sunglasses and a mustache completed his look. Claire had pulled on her long dark wig with bangs and tied it back in a low ponytail. She dressed in a black short-sleeved shirt, black jeans, and a lightweight jacket and threw on chocolate-brown designer sunglasses. The two easily fit in with the tourists crowding the area. The sleuths even decided to alter their gaits to throw DiNetto a curve ball.

"We'll need to follow DiNetto when he leaves the hotel for dinner," Claire said. "We need to watch him closely to figure out why he's here and who he's meeting with. Aside from Milan, all his stops on the itinerary have been located alongside water. In fact, he's gone out of his way to drive to very specific locations on the water. And we know he met with someone on a yacht in Porto Venere in the dark of night."

"There are yachts here too," Guy said.

"Exactly," Claire said. "And we can watch them all from our hotel room. After dinner. When it's shadowy. That's when DiNetto will make his move."

"What's he doing on the private yachts? Selling drugs? Passing counterfeit money? Smuggling? Kidnapping?" Guy asked. "I wonder."

"It's the boxes. We've got to get a look inside those boxes," Claire said.

The investigators positioned themselves on a bench down the street, where they could see anyone and everyone exiting the hotel. They needed to follow DiNetto when he left the hotel. Guy sat guard while Claire ran to a nearby café and returned with two foamy cappuccinos. Doing the typical tourist thing, not wanting to attract attention, they sipped and talked, awaiting the departure of the target of their investigation. This was the part of private investigation that required a great amount of patience.

Time passed. Close to two hours.

As it was getting dark, DiNetto emerged from the hotel. He turned left and walked toward the waterfront. The sleuths paced fifty feet behind him, mixing with others walking the cobblestone streets of the area. On his stroll, DiNetto poked his head into various boutiques to greet the salespeople. It quickly became obvious that DiNetto knew Portofino well.

He meandered to the harbor and lingered around the bordering walkways. Then he selected an outdoor restaurant and spoke to the maître d'. He was led to a table for two on the edge of the water. Claire and Guy waited an appropriate amount of time and followed him in. They pointed to the area where they wished to sit—far out of DiNetto's line of vision—and followed the headwaiter to a rather secluded table. The moon provided some light in the darkness, and an occasional string of tiny white lights appeared here and there around the establishment. Also, a few strategically placed lanterns helped buffer the inkiness of night.

The setting was romantic, and not long after the two sleuths were seated, the investigators observed a young, attractive Italian lady joining DiNetto at his table. The slender female had dark hair and eyes, donned a low-cut dress, and wore spike heels. DiNetto got up when his guest arrived, kissed her on both cheeks, pulled a chair out for her, and immediately moved his chair alongside hers. The two cooed and flirted with each other.

Claire and Guy ordered spaghetti with tomato sauce for the first course and baked sea bass for two—accompanied by potato slices and black olives—for the second. The air felt cool and refreshing. They could hear the gentle lapping of the water against the pier as they dined, and they watched a stately long-legged heron perched atop a nearby boat bob in unison with the rhythm of the sea. The bird, so patient, waited to fill its long bill with a large fish.

Warm, fresh bread was delivered to their table, along with two glasses of red wine.

Claire looked up just in time to see a server lob leftover bread into the sea as he cleared a table near the water's edge. And she noticed a couple sitting at a spot adjacent to the eating area. The woman, quite pregnant, had a gleeful expression on her face, obviously amused by the waiter's actions.

Before long, a man sat down at the table directly next to them. The tables were in close proximity, with only inches separating them. The diner was alone, and he appeared to be in his midthirties. He spoke German when placing his order. The man frequently darted a glance over to the investigators, staring coldly. He even craned his neck slightly to hear their conversation. Claire and Guy were immediately aware of his attempt to eavesdrop, and each time one or the other sleuth looked over at him, he would quickly turn his head and direct his gaze straight ahead.

Claire looked around the entire setting, casually and quickly, directing her eyes not only on DiNetto but also on all other diners. If this man sitting next to them was a spy for DiNetto, she refused to let him see her specific interest in the Italian American. Just then, she saw the woman sitting with DiNetto get up and walk in the direction of the ladies' room. It was her chance. She excused herself, told Guy she'd be right back, and followed after her.

The bathroom was small, and its two stalls were occupied when Claire walked in. She stood next to DiNetto's dinner companion and waited. The sleuth looked at the woman and smiled.

"Enjoying the evening?" she asked.

"Very much so," the lady said, speaking broken English.

"It's our first time in Portofino," Claire said, "and I'm impressed."

"It is wonderful place for shopping," the woman said. She laughed. "The best of the best of the best."

Claire chuckled. "Anything special to look for?"

"Oh, it depends on your likes," the woman said. Her tone sounded somewhat mysterious.

"Give me a hint," Claire said. "I do like the best of the best . . . but at a good price, if you know what I mean."

The woman smiled slyly. "Oh, yes, I do—"

Just then, the door of a stall opened and a lady walked out.

The woman Claire was talking to made a hand gesture to her. "You go."

Claire thanked her and walked into the stall. When she came out moments later, the other stall was vacant and the woman was gone.

Darn, Claire thought. I needed a little more time.

Claire returned to the table and finished her meal. In her absence, Guy had ordered a slice of apple cake with a small scoop of vanilla ice cream to share. The waiter delivered it, together with two cups of espresso.

"When did he leave?" Claire asked, nodding to the empty table next to them.

"Just before you returned."

Claire filled Guy in on her conversation with DiNetto's companion. "I wish I could have had a few more seconds with her. She was about to tell me something." The female sleuth glanced over at DiNetto's table. The woman hadn't returned.

"She left the restaurant, Guy."

As Claire continued to look at DiNetto, he got up, turned, and seemed to stare directly at her. A chill ran down her spine. "He's looking right at me," she muttered under her breath without moving her lips. Suddenly, she began to laugh boisterously, using a tone Guy had never heard before—as if her dinner partner had just said something overpoweringly funny or as if she were affected by too much alcohol. Guy picked up on the hint and joined in with howling laughter. As she continued to act overly amused, her eyes followed DiNetto as he walked briskly from the restaurant.

"Something's in the air," Claire said once DiNetto was gone. "I can feel it. The man sitting next to us, the woman at DiNetto's table disappearing, DiNetto drilling his eyes into mine and then hurrying off." She stared straight ahead, deep in thought. "I think something will happen *tonight*. We're getting very close to discovering whatever it is he's planning, and it's making him mighty nervous."

22

THE SLEUTHS WALKED back to their room at the Splendido Mare. The first floor housed the lobby, check-in desk, several rooms, and a good-sized restaurant. That evening a female singer, accompanied by her pianist, performed a variety of songs to entertain the diners. Claire and Guy stood briefly on the sidelines listening to the talented professional.

When they returned to their room, the two kicked off their shoes. Cobblestone streets had proven hard on the feet, and they both complained about their blisters. They dropped onto the bed, happy to rest for a few minutes.

But Claire felt edgy, and her mind wouldn't allow her a break. She glanced at her watch, got up, and walked to the window on the waterfront side of the room. She slid her body between the window and the drapery. The space provided a secret place to peer out without being seen. Darkness was dominant, but the few scattered lights positioned around the pier mixed with the light of the moon and allowed her the opportunity to observe the scene once her eyes completely adjusted. She noticed little movement of any kind. There were the occasional tourists or locals wandering about, but most everyone was tucked safely away for the night. Claire stayed where she was for forty-five minutes, her eyes peeled to the harbor, continually scanning. It was amazing how the room window provided an absolutely perfect lookout for her sleuthing activities.

Guy woke and paced. "Anything interesting out there?"

Tunes from the singer pounded through the walls of their room, as if she stood right there performing. The noise irritated Guy.

"Not yet."

"You've been at this for a while," he said. "How much longer do you plan on standing there?"

"Until I see something."

Suddenly, her eyes were drawn to one end of the U-shaped walkway surrounding the water, to the place where three stately yachts were docked in a row. She noticed a form, and her eyes zeroed in. The light on a nearby post outlined a figure standing in the shadows. And then another. She couldn't make out who they were, but by their size and shape she determined both were men. The two moved furtively toward the middle boat, and then one man followed the other up the stairs to board the massive yacht. Claire squinted. Soon, a red light was visible inside the private boat.

"Come here, Guy. You need to watch with me. Something's going on out there."

Guy moved quickly. "What is it? What do you see?"

"Two people," Claire said. "Both men. They met at the pier and went aboard the middle yacht. If you look closely, you'll see a subtle red light inside. That light came on after they boarded. They moved strangely on the dock—secretively—as if they wanted to avoid notice or attention." She thought for a brief moment. "There's a clandestine meeting going on in that yacht, and we need to find out what it's about. One of the men could be DiNetto."

Guy's nostrils flared. "And just how do you propose we do that?"

"There's only one way. Hightail it over there and get close. Watch and listen."

"It's after one in the morning! Probably not real safe for us to walk down there by the water's edge. We have no way of protecting ourselves, should we need to. And what if the two walk out and see us? Not a good idea, Claire."

Claire was unwavering. "Stay put if you'd like. I'm going." She jumped out from behind the curtain, threw on a black cardigan sweater, tied a dark scarf around her head, grabbed the room key, and raced to the door. "Coming?"

Guy slammed his fist into a wall. "*Shit*, Claire. If I don't go, I'll worry about you. So you win. I guess I'm coming along." He pulled a black beret onto his head and chose his dark-colored jacket. "But we're not staying long."

Claire bolted from the room, and Guy followed closely behind.

The nighttime was downright cold. The smell of the sea filled Claire's nostrils, and her lips tasted the salt air. The only sound she heard was the gentle and repetitive lapping of the water. No other humans were in sight. Visibility was limited due to the darkness, and walking atop warped wooden boards without the help of sunlight was anything but easy. An acute sense of danger possessed her, but she pushed on. In the worst way, the sleuth wanted to be back in the room, cuddled up next to Guy, warm, cozy, and asleep. But this was a golden opportunity for detective work—one simply too good to pass up.

The two investigators moved cautiously, Claire in front of Guy, making their way along the seemingly endless rough-planked walkway. They placed one foot in front of the other, moving with deliberate steps, hoping they wouldn't be seen or heard.

Things were going smoothly until Guy's toe caught a buckled slat of wood. He tripped and went flying through the air. He landed directly on Claire, and the two fell hard onto the walkway with a loud thud. Guy immediately grabbed Claire, and together they rolled to the side of the wooden passageway opposite the water. Despite the pain they both felt from the jarring fall, they remained perfectly still, afraid to breathe or move, hoping the darkness would hide them.

"Are you all right?" Guy whispered so faintly Claire could barely make out his words.

She murmured an assent. But in truth, her entire body hurt. The full force of his weight had crashed down on her and almost knocked her wind out. The palms of her hands had scraped against the wooden planks, and they both throbbed with intense pain. But her hands had taken the brunt of the fall and stopped her face from hitting and skidding on the wood. She imagined her hands were probably covered with blood. And her ribs felt crushed. She wanted to cry, but she held back.

"How about you?" she quietly asked Guy.

But he didn't have time to answer. All at once, the sleuths heard two male figures, standing only feet away, talking softly.

"I know I heard something," the one man said.

"Maybe it was something in the water," the other said. "Or a boat bobbing and hitting a wave. I see nothing out here. Nothing at all."

"Perhaps you're right," the first man said. "I am a bit keyed up."

"Let's return to the boat," the other said. "We have more business to attend to."

The investigators heard two sets of footsteps returning to the yacht. When they were satisfied the coast was clear, they stood up.

Claire rubbed her hands together and confirmed they were bleeding. She wiped them gently on her jeans.

"We need to make our way over to the yacht," she said softly. "Follow me."

Guy tried to catch her—to stop her—but she was gone. He wanted to talk some sense into her, to convince her to retreat to their hotel room, to bring the night's investigative chapter to a premature end. To shower and fall into bed. But he realized that was not going to happen.

He trailed behind the woman who was braver than just about anyone he had ever known.

Soon they neared the yacht.

Claire turned to him and indicated with her hand that she was going up the stairs and that he shouldn't follow. He shook his head from side to side, but she crept up the stairs, anyway. Reluctantly, he walked to the other side of the wooden walkway and let the dark shadows of the night blanket him.

Once at the top, Claire crouched low and pulled herself toward the doorway. It was slightly ajar, enough that she could hear most all of the conversation between the two men. One of the voices belonged to DiNetto. The two men were arguing—both in English and Italian. Something about signing a contract. DiNetto seemed adamant about not doing so.

"If you don't sign, the deal is off," the other man snarled.

"Then the deal is off!" DiNetto said. "It's as simple as that."

"That's it? After all these long months of you courting me on this purchase, it's off because you're a bumptious jackass who refuses to sign a damn piece of paper?" the man said in utter disbelief.

"Watch what you say. I'm warning you," DiNetto growled. "Treat me with respect. And yes, it's as simple as that. The deal with you is off, my friend. Over and done. Many others are interested."

Claire could hear a chair being pushed back. She turned to dash away—but then the other man spoke.

"Wait a minute," he said. "Let me look in those boxes again."

In a brazen move, Claire moved her head ever-so slightly to allow herself a peek into the cabin. *Those boxes*, she thought, we have to find out what's in the boxes.

DiNetto's back was toward her, and she could see him opening two boxes and setting them down on a table in front of the other man. She caught a quick glimpse of the devilish grin on his face when he turned his head slightly.

"We need to make this transaction happen," the man said. "And quickly. I have the money, and you have the goods. We've agreed orally to all the terms, but I also want your signature on the bill of sale. I trust you, but I'm not a fool."

DiNetto bellowed, "Never! I do not do business that way. *Never in ink!*"

The other man scowled. "Then we are truly finished."

DiNetto began to walk out. But he turned around before stepping up to the yacht's doorway. "You seem to lack both intelligence and common sense. Apparently I miscalculated your value. Why would you let a deal like this slip through your fingers?" He paused. "I'll be traveling to Cannes tomorrow. If you wish to reach me, use my cell phone. If you decide to do business with me after all, you'll have to drive there for the transfer to be finalized. The clock is ticking, and time is running out."

Claire flew down the stairs and onto the dock. She motioned to Guy as she ran past him, and the two silently sprinted along the inky walkway, staying close to the shadowy side across from the water's edge. They made it back to their room without detection. When they walked inside, they kept the lights off. Their room was visible from the outside, and they didn't want to tip DiNetto that they'd just returned or were still awake—in case he saw them earlier and figured out which room they were in.

Once inside, Guy turned to hold Claire in his arms. "Tell me everything."

Claire relayed the conversation she overheard on the yacht.

"Did you get a glimpse into the boxes?" Guy asked.

Claire twisted her face into a grimace. "No! Once again, no!"

"Well, whatever DiNetto is into, we know there's a lot of money involved, and it's clear it involves the covert buying and selling of *something*."

"The secret is definitely in the boxes," Claire said.

In the dark, the two undressed and washed their injuries with soap and hot water before climbing into bed.

Claire exhaled deeply. "This feels *too* good."

Guy did not respond. She heard the quiet sound of his snoring. Exhaustion had taken him into the never-never land of his dreams. She pulled the covers up around him and then snuggled in next to him. Tomorrow morning, they would assess their injuries. For now, sleep was the best medicine.

JIN IKEDA'S resourceful side took over. Using sophisticated computer investigation programs and techniques—and with a sprinkle of pure dumb luck—he'd located and hacked into Dougan's e-mail history and cell phone records. He justified the hacking by telling himself anyone could do it if they only knew how.

There were many recent phone calls from an unlisted number with a Miami-Dade area code. He also found numerous e-mails between Sugarcane and someone identified only as the Anteater. Jin realized he'd need to uncover why Sugarcane and Anteater were communicating so frequently and cryptically.

In addition, reading a year's worth of Dougan's e-mails revealed a treasure trove of information. Jin uncovered clusters of e-mails from Sugarcane to the press over the last twelve months that divulged what appeared to be confidential police file information on open cases. Jin cross-checked the dates of the e-mails against Officer Figg's dates when information had been leaked to the press. He smiled.

"Bingo!" Jin crowed. He was victorious. Dougan was the mole. This was the evidence he needed to prove Dougan had leaked the critical confidential police information to the press.

And somehow the Anteater was connected to Dougan too. It seemed to be a separate matter from the press leaks. Now he just had to ferret out the identity of the Anteater.

CLAIRE AWOKE during the night. She crept out of bed, making certain not to disturb Guy, and made her way to the bathroom. Once inside, she shut the door and turned on the light. She examined her hands a bit more closely. Her palms were covered with abrasions. She touched her rib cage and cringed. "Ouch!" she breathed. Her shoulders hurt too, and so did her arms, and just about everything else. She opened the bathroom door, slipped out, stepped over to the bedroom area, and retrieved her backpack. She reached inside and located a bottle of aspirin. After popping two of the little white pills into her mouth, she drank the entire glass of water on her bedside table.

She returned to the bathroom, filled the basin with warm soapy water, and let her hands soak for some time. As she stood alone with her thoughts, she acknowledged it had been a tough night for the two investigators. She felt fortunate their injuries weren't more severe.

She took a long, hard look in the mirror and didn't like the face staring back. The image wore a look of utter exhaustion. This case had taken its toll from day one: the taxi accident in Milan, her scary train encounters, the bizarre incidents at the masquerade ball, her violent assault after DiNetto dumped her on the streets, and the aggressive attack by the skinheads. Now *this*—she and Guy both injured in a dreadful fall on the wooden walkway during tonight's escapade.

Her mind drifted back to a time when life had seemed simpler, when she'd smiled more and perhaps felt happier—a time prior to becoming a private investigator.

The life of a P.I. wasn't easy. Nor was it glamorous much of the time. It required constant courage, fearlessness, persistence, and perseverance. But then, it was the life she would choose again and again, and she knew it. Investigation was in her blood, and nothing else would satisfy those cravings within her to see justice done. Each case was different. Usually something appearing simple and straightforward at first glance quickly became anything but.

She forced a soft chuckle from her mouth. "Combat pay—that's what I deserve."

She patted her hands dry and returned to bed. She snuggled in next to Guy's velvety skin and instantly felt warmer. She closed her eyes. Tomorrow was another day, and considering how things had gone so far, it promised to be eventful. She nodded off.

23

Day nine
Portofino to Cannes, France

MORNING ARRIVED TOO early. Prolonged, dull pain radiated from every muscle in Claire's slender body as she tried to pull herself up from the bed. She glanced at her wounded hands. At least they looked better than they had a few hours earlier. She swallowed two more aspirins and drank another full glass of water. She yearned to sleep a couple extra hours to give her weary body more time to heal, but the investigators had an itinerary to follow. Today they had a three-and-a-quarter-hour drive ahead of them. They were off to Cannes.

Claire looked over at Guy. He was sleeping hard. She picked

up the phone and ordered room service. Then she jumped into a hot shower and stood under the welcoming spray for many long minutes. At the end, she turned the dial to cold and allowed the cooling water to beat down on the small of her back. She needed a jump-start today, and, as always, the trick worked. After toweling off, she washed her face, brushed her teeth, and combed styling gel through her hair. Claire dried her hair, then applied tasteful makeup, ending with a splash of coral lipstick. She felt human again.

There was a knock on the door. Claire threw on the hotel-provided white terry robe and walked to the door.

"Breakfast is served, *signora*," the room service employee said. He entered the room and placed a tray filled with plates covered with metal domes—to ensure warm food—on the coffee table.

The aroma of the food wafted past Claire. "Mmm, smells divine." She reached into her backpack and pulled out a bill to tip the young man.

He thanked her and exited the room, pulling the door shut behind him.

Claire walked over to Guy, leaned down, and kissed him on both cheeks. "Good morning, my dear. Breakfast is here. You'd better get up, or I might eat it all."

One of his eyes opened. Then the other. "Is it really morning?"

Claire smiled down at him. "It is. And we need to get going soon. We're driving to Cannes today." She walked over to the table and poured herself a cup of steaming, freshly brewed coffee. She took a prolonged taste and let the hot beverage trickle down her throat.

Claire was all too aware the time remaining to solve the case was rapidly dwindling. They were about to enter the final leg of the mission. Italy and Switzerland were behind them. Only France lay ahead. She so badly wanted to present Sergeant Massey with a neatly tied-up package at the end of this challenge—to provide evidence that exposed every detail of Anthony DiNetto's top-secret scam. Evidence that would lock him away. After all, the reputation of Caswell & Lombard, Private Investigation was on the line.

She watched Guy grimace as he moved to get out of bed and tried to stand.

"Are you in pain too?" Claire asked.

He shook his head up and down. "Yeah. I have to admit, I've felt better. How are your hands—and every other part of you?"

"Okay. A hot shower helps," she said. "And a little food in your tummy."

Guy walked to the sofa adjacent to the coffee table and fell down into it. Claire passed him a plate of eggs, chicken sausage, and toast with jelly. She poured him a cup of coffee and slid a grapefruit juice his way. Then she sat down next to him and started to eat her breakfast. The food's taste was even better than its aroma. The day would ask a lot of them, and neither was in great condition after last night's nocturnal caper.

Claire finished her meal and began to ready herself for the day. She pulled on her short red wig, clipped on dangle earrings, put on a pair of tortoise-shell glasses, and dressed in long jeans and an emerald-green blouse she hadn't worn before. She tied a paisley scarf around her neck and slipped on lightweight platform shoes to alter her height. Guy looked her over and had to admit he barely recognized her. But somehow DiNetto always did.

Guy poured himself another cup of coffee. "I need a few minutes to enjoy this." He sat back and took the extra time to ease into the morning.

Claire walked to the window near the water and looked outside. The sun was out in all its glory, illuminating the extraordinary Italian Riviera. Portofino was a special place, she thought. Just then, she spotted DiNetto walking along the opposite side of the walkway—across the water from where the yachts were docked. He had a distinctive walk, and it was easy to pick him out of a crowd. His bearing exuded power and self-assurance. And after watching him for days, she could spot him anywhere. Her eyes followed him as he walked into a waterfront restaurant to eat breakfast.

"We've got some time," she said. "I'm going into DiNetto's room to take a look inside those boxes."

"*What*? *Are you crazy*?" Guy fumed. "It's much too risky. And how would you gain access, anyway?"

The look of determination in Claire's eyes couldn't be mistaken. "You leave that to me," she said. "Be my lookout. If you see DiNetto walking back this way, call my cell phone and let it ring twice. Then hang up. I'll know it's you and leave his room pronto." She pulled off her earrings and glasses and set both on the table. She changed into flat shoes and grabbed her cell phone and room key. "I'll be back as soon as I can."

Guy stepped in front of her to block her way. He gently cupped her face in his hands and demanded her eyes fall only on his. "I know I can't change your mind, so be careful, Claire. Don't take chances—and make it quick."

The female investigator hurriedly left the room. She located the housekeeper's closet on the main floor and slipped inside. Three minutes later, she emerged dressed in a housekeeping uniform, with a pair of latex gloves tucked into one pocket. She looked around until she found an open door, walked inside, and saw a pleasant-appearing woman changing sheets on a bed.

Claire cleared her throat. "*Scusi*. I'm a new housekeeper here at the hotel, and I can't seem to find my passkey. Can you help me, please? Just for today?"

The woman looked her up and down. It was clear she spoke little English. She pretended she understood what Claire had said. "*Ho capito*," she said, nodding. But she continued to make the bed, not understanding at all.

Claire thought quickly, trying another tactic. "The list of rooms we need to clean—where is it?"

This time, the housekeeper seemed to understand some of Claire's words. "Cart," she said, pointing to the supply cart.

Claire walked over to the cart, found the list, and let her eyes scan the two sheets. She found DiNetto's room number with no trouble.

"I'll start two floors up," Claire told the housekeeper. She pointed toward the ceiling with her index finger. "About my passkey—I have misplaced it. Do you have an extra?" She pointed to the card hanging from the woman's waistband, then pointed to herself, shrugged her shoulders, and lifted her upturned hands into the air. She smiled sweetly, trying a second time to get a master key card to give her access to all rooms.

"*Certamente*," the woman said, again nodding. She understood now and handed Claire a spare passkey.

"Thank you," Claire said. "*Grazie.*" She walked slowly and confidently from the room. Once she was out of sight, she raced toward the staircase at the far end of the floor. Time was of the essence. She ran up the two flights of stairs and searched for his room. She found it without delay. DiNetto had placed the Do Not Disturb sign around the door handle. She pulled on the pair of latex gloves, removed the sign, and used the master passkey to enter his room. She pushed the door open and stepped inside. The door closed firmly behind her. She swallowed with difficulty, realizing there was no other way out should DiNetto unexpectedly return.

Claire's eyes darted quickly around the room. She noticed a clear, triangular bottle of AVIV vodka sitting on the bedside table and an empty glass next to it. She ran over to the chest, pulled open each drawer one by one, and searched desperately through the contents to find the boxes. They weren't there. She looked through the drawers in the two bedside tables. Not there either. She peeked inside DiNetto's luggage and checked under the bed. No boxes. She ran to the closet and peered inside. She pushed his hanging clothes to one side and looked up and down. Still no boxes. She carefully returned the hangers to their original positions.

The boxes have to be here, she told herself. DiNetto didn't have them in hand when she spotted him walking to breakfast, and he wasn't carrying his briefcase. *The briefcase*! Where is the briefcase, she wondered.

In a frantic state, she stopped cold and looked around the room. Where would he hide those boxes? Her cell phone rang twice. It was Guy warning her DiNetto was on his way back.

She could see no other potential hiding places. Maybe DiNetto left his briefcase at the hotel's front desk and placed the boxes in the hotel safe. Only seconds remained.

Suddenly, she spotted a bed pillow sitting on the desk chair. Its case looked rumpled and lumpy. Could it be, she asked herself. She sprinted to it, grabbed it in her hands, and looked inside. Two square corrugated cardboard boxes sat wedged inside. She slid them out, shaking. She opened the first box, and to her exasperation it was empty. Then she reached for the second, pulled it open, and it too was empty. They were only the outer boxes that the hinged wood laminate boxes fit into. There were no markings on the cardboard to hint at the inside contents. She returned the boxes to the case.

Time was up. Her adrenaline was pumping madly.

She raced to the door, stepped out, pulled it shut behind her, and remembered to replace the Do Not Disturb sign on the handle. She used her passkey to enter the room directly across the hall, and just as she moved inside, DiNetto appeared in the hallway. She prayed no one would be in the other room, and luck was on her side. She placed her ear to the inside of the door, and when she heard DiNetto's door shut behind him, she quickly fled the other room, ran to the end of the hall, and tore down the flights of stairs. She found the housekeeper's closet, disappeared inside, and moments later came out dressed in her own clothes. She sprinted to her room.

Guy was standing in the hallway holding the door open, waiting for her. A look of desperation was plastered on his face.

"That was foolish!" he said. "You're playing with fire!"

"*Way too close for my liking*," she admitted. "I'm still shaking."

She entered the room, Guy at her heels, and sat down on the bed.

"It was within reach," Claire said, clearly frustrated. "We were this close to learning the secret of the boxes." She held her thumb and forefinger up in front of her, showing only a small separation between them. "But when I opened the two corrugated boxes I found stuffed in a pillow case, they were clearly just protective cartons for the real boxes." Claire went on to explain how she had gained access to his room and searched high and low for the mysterious boxes.

"*Dammit!*" Guy said. He sat down next to her and slammed his fist into the mattress. "I was so hopeful this would be our chance."

"You and me both."

"Well, I will say this: your courage is off the charts, Claire. I'm not at all sure I could have done what you just did."

"Now we need to pack up and get out of here." She remained rattled.

"I studied the map," Guy said. "The entire drive ahead is basically through one long tunnel after another, all along the southern coastline of France. Looks like an exhausting stretch."

"What cities do we pass through today?" Claire asked.

"A string of them—Genoa, Monte Carlo in the Principality of Monaco, and Nice on our way to Cannes. We overnight there, then drive on to Montpellier the following day."

"Too bad we'll miss the scenic views along the waters of southern France," Claire said. "I thought at least we'd have those, but if we're inside dark tunnels the whole way . . . "

Guy dressed in a pink polo shirt and dark jeans. He put on black-framed sunglasses and combed his hair straight back, using styling gel to hold it in place. He pulled a couple strands down onto his forehead in an attempt to look suave. He inserted fake teeth—different than he'd used in another disguise—and tied a jacket around his waist.

Claire put her platform shoes back on, returned the clip-on dangle earrings to her ears, and donned a pair of burgundy sunglasses. She repositioned her red wig and added a wide headband.

The investigators stood in front of the room mirror and took a long and studied look.

"The disguises are good," Guy said. "Darn good. They all have been."

"Even clothing makes a huge difference, doesn't it?" Claire said. "The colors and whether it's loose or form-fitting."

The investigators packed the duffel, grabbed their backpacks, and left the room. They walked to the lobby, checked out, and continued on to the parking garage to collect their rental car.

As Guy drove out of the garage, DiNetto stepped directly in front of the BMW.

"Watch where you're going!" he screamed. "You could have killed me!" His eyes glazed, and his palms became sweaty. The rage within him made him dizzy, and his face turned bright red. As he glanced into the car, he looked from investigator to investigator and shook his fist.

Time froze.

Seconds passed like minutes.

Finally, Guy threw his hands up into the air and mouthed, "Sorry."

The look DiNetto gave them chilled the sleuths to their very cores.

He didn't appear to recognize them.

24

A CROWD OF tourists and locals spontaneously gathered around the entrance to the parking garage. Fuming, DiNetto stepped to the side, allowing the investigators to pass, but not before drilling his icy eyes right through theirs. The two acted as if there was nothing more to say or do, held their heads high, and tried to garner no further attention. Guy drove off in the direction of the road leading to the motorway.

"He *studied* us," Claire said. "His eyes bored right into ours."

"I noticed," Guy said.

Claire pulled off her wig, and using her fingers as a comb, she brought her own hair back into a low side ponytail. "We'll need to alter our disguises right away." She removed her earrings, glasses, and headband and threw a brightly colored striped sweater around her neck. "And we'll need to exchange our rental car again. It's too dangerous to stay in this one." She pulled out a tube of dark plum lipstick and applied it. Then she clipped a platinum curl to her ponytail.

"Agreed. And I was just getting used to this BMW," Guy said, attempting humor in a deadly serious situation.

But Claire didn't laugh. Her somber expression spoke volumes. She reached over and messed up Guy's hair as he drove. Then she carefully pulled off his glasses. "We need to solve this case and get back to the US." She reached into her backpack, pulled out a fake mustache and goatee, and pressed them onto his face. "There. This will do for now." She retrieved a bottle of spring water from her backpack and cracked it open. She took a long drink and then handed it to Guy. He readily chugged half the bottle.

The female investigator was deep in thought. That look of DiNetto's haunted her. It chilled her and left no doubts that he was capable of anything. The small voice within her raised an alarm: *DiNetto wants to kill you, Claire! And Guy! Beware! Beware!* The warning was direct and unmistakable.

"We need to wind this up and fly back home as soon as possible," Claire said. "It's not safe for us to stay in Europe much longer. DiNetto has it out for the two of us. He's planning to do us in."

Guy didn't question her instinct. He knew she was right. And quite frankly, he'd already come to the same conclusion.

Once he reached and merged onto the motorway, the investigators followed the GPS instructions, and Claire also watched the map. If all went well, the drive to Cannes would be uneventful.

Before long, the sky turned overcast again, and thick clouds assembled seemingly out of nowhere. At first, a gentle drizzle dotted the windshield, but soon a torrent of rain exploded onto the road. It was as if the sky had been collecting moisture for an extended period of time, could no longer contain its weight, then poured it out. Guy set the wipers to the highest setting, but they couldn't keep up. He spotted a gasoline station coming up just off the high-speed motorway, took the exit, and pulled into the establishment. Cars were lined up. He waited his turn. When it finally came, he pulled the rental vehicle under a covered area to refuel.

When the tank was full, he drove the car to the side of the property and parked. "We'll have to wait here until this lets up," he said. "It's making the driving close to impossible."

"It's strange how when we were close to the water in Portofino, the sun was shining brightly and the day was beautiful, with no rain in sight. And then we drive up the serpentine road on the steep hillside to reach the expressway, and *this* blows up almost immediately."

He nodded. "Yeah, it seems the weather changes very quickly here."

Finally, the rain eased, and Guy drove the rental car back onto the motorway. Within minutes, the traffic slowed, and soon the investigators noticed road signs indicating an upcoming detour. When they exited onto the detour, the arrows went in two directions. Not knowing which route to take, Guy drove right instead of left. Soon they found themselves impossibly lost and unable to find their way back to the main route. And to top it off, the GPS was no help at all. It had them going in circles.

Guy pursed his lips and stiffened his body. "I should have turned *left* at the detour. Now we'll have to go back. What a huge waste of time!"

"Well, we can't change it now. We'll have to go back the way we came and take the other road. Too bad it wasn't marked properly." She cracked the window open to let in some fresh air.

Guy exhaled loudly, turned the car around, and headed back to the detour exit.

Minutes later, he returned to the spot and turned onto the left path. The detour took close to forty minutes, and then, at last, he was able to once again enter the motorway.

"This whole thing with DiNetto," Guy said, "it seems to center around covert meetings with different men in each city on his itinerary. And I agree with you: the boxes—whatever they contain—are the crucial element of this whole thing. He seems to bring a couple along to each meeting."

Claire looked at him carefully, in total sync with his thought processes. "Exactly. And there's something else. As we've discussed, all these locations, with the exception of Milan, are very near water—a marina, a lake, or a sea. In each case, the water is covered with boats and pricey yachts. And it seems DiNetto is targeting the owners of the pricey yachts."

"So we can assume DiNetto is engaging with people who are very well-off," Guy said, shooting a glance her way. "People who have the means to pay DiNetto whatever he's asking for the goods he's selling."

The female investigator stared ahead as she spoke. "The boxes must contain something of great value. He may be selling whatever it is. Maybe to the highest bidder. What if he's showing the people he's meeting with a glimpse of the merchandise, then waiting to receive their best offers? It would make sense. It would also seem logical that the goods may be black-market counterfeits he's illegally trafficking. Or they could be the real thing he's selling off the grid for some reason." She pondered for a time.

"What do *you* think those boxes might contain?" Guy asked.

Claire furrowed her brow. "That is the question of the hour. Could be flawless diamonds . . . perfectly matched South Sea pearls . . . confidential government information on memory sticks. The possibilities are endless. Ask me tomorrow, and I'll come up with other potentials, I'm sure. Could be almost anything."

"We've got to find out." Guy's tone intensified. "It seems DiNetto might very well be collecting an elite circle of potential purchasers, possibly to drive up the price of whatever he's selling. This is getting more interesting by the minute. Seems he sets up a meeting in every port, doesn't it?"

Claire, consumed by her thoughts, didn't respond. Guy drove on in silence, knowing she needed to be left alone to think.

After a time, the investigators noticed signs indicating they were leaving Italy and entering France.

Driving through the seemingly endless dark tunnels almost all of the way, with heavy traffic continually swooshing past on both sides, made Guy weary.

When at last they drove into the city of Cannes, Guy pulled over, plugged in the address for the Hôtel Majestic Barrière on the GPS, and followed the directions right to its front doors. Similar to the other locations on DiNetto's itinerary, this hotel was directly across from the Mediterranean Sea. A driveway perpendicular to the street led up to the posh, imposing hotel.

The sleuths immediately noticed DiNetto's dark gray Ferrari parked near the entrance. Guy pulled over, signaled to a valet, and asked where the closest car rental agency was located. Upon obtaining directions, Guy followed the drive back out to the street to head in the direction of the business. It was time to exchange cars.

Just as Guy was pulling the BMW out onto the street, a car zooming into the drive careened toward the investigators, nearly out of control. The driver swerved dramatically and managed to pull his vehicle back to his side of the road just in time to avoid a collision. As Guy veered to the right to get out of the way, Claire managed a look at the other driver. She involuntarily shrieked.

Once Guy turned out onto the main street and was again on his way, Claire looked at him. A solemn expression owned her face. "The driver of that car was Officer Bubbiano from Milan."

"*What?*" Guy asked. "Are you sure?"

"I'm positive."

"Did he see us?"

"No way. He was concentrating on getting his car back into his lane."

"This keeps getting more and more intriguing, doesn't it?" Guy asked. "He could have killed us driving like that. He certainly seemed to be in a hurry."

"The question is, *why?*" Claire asked. "I say we return to the hotel, see if we can find out what's going on with Bubbiano, and then exchange our rental car. Otherwise, we might miss a shining opportunity."

Guy made a sharp U-turn and headed back to the hotel. He asked the valet to park the car at the end of the drive and informed him they'd be leaving shortly. The sleuths stepped inside and checked in. They were given an end room on the second floor with a view of the water from one side and a view of the front courtyard from the other. A bellman insisted on taking their duffel to the room, so Claire and Guy rode the elevator up with the employee. He walked with them to their room. Once inside, he explained the hotel's amenities and offered to bring them a bucket of ice. They kindly refused.

"Have a delightful stay in Cannes," the bellman said.

Guy tipped the man, and he departed. But no sooner had he left than another employee appeared, this one carrying a tray of goodies: fresh fruits; a dish of dried apricots, kiwi slices, and cranberries; a box of assorted white, milk, and dark chocolates; and a chilled bottle of Evian water. There were also bottles of Alain Milliat Nectar Framboise (raspberry nectar) and Jus Pomme Reinette (apple juice).

"Compliments of the hotel," the young employee said. He had a strong French accent.

"*Merci beaucoup,*" Claire said, ushering him quickly to the door and handing him a gratuity.

"Enjoy your time in France," the employee said.

Claire seemed preoccupied. She walked to far side of the room, and gave a quick glance out of the window facing the water. Across the street, along the water's edge, she noticed a full-sized merry-go-round. The revolving, colorful machine was filled with model horses, each one carrying a youngster around and around. Adults and other young people were gathered to watch. Claire couldn't see the faces of the kids on the ride, but for an instant she flashed back to times in her own childhood when she had ridden on a carousel. She recalled laughing, giggling, and feeling overcome with joy. She momentarily froze in the memory.

Then, suddenly, her eyes were drawn just beyond the merry-go-round to four men standing along the water's edge. She watched them for a moment.

"Guy, I see DiNetto, Bubbiano, and two other men standing by the water on the other side of the merry-go-round. Come look. I can identify DiNetto and Bubbiano by their postures and mannerisms."

"*Another* meeting?" he asked, glancing out the window. "What's Bubbiano's interest in all of this? I want to believe he's a man of the law, but that's getting harder and harder to do."

Claire continued to watch the foursome. DiNetto pulled two boxes from his briefcase, cracked them open, and held them to allow the two strangers to peer inside. Then Bubbiano pulled out two additional boxes and followed with the same routine. The men leaned in to examine the contents at a closer range. Moments later, DiNetto and Bubbiano closed the boxes and tucked them securely away.

"Okay, now I'm convinced DiNetto and Bubbiano have something they're trying to peddle," Claire said. "That has to be it, right?"

"A dirty cop? Great!" Guy said.

"That's how it looks, I'll have to agree. But sometimes things aren't as they appear." She continued to eye the men. "Perhaps there's another explanation."

"Or maybe not," he said.

"We'd better return our rental car and get something less conspicuous," Claire said. "Let's get out of here before DiNetto and Bubbiano return to the hotel."

Guy's brows signaled he was in deep thought. "I'll take care of it. You stay here and rest if you'd like."

"Are you sure?" she asked.

"Yeah. It's a better use of your time. But I do have one request before I leave. Can we order up some lunch? I'm starving. No, actually I'm past starving."

Minutes later, lunch was delivered to the room and vigorously consumed.

Then, within no time at all, Guy was on his way to the rental agency. Once there, he returned the blue BMW and rented a white Range Rover Sport. It was a noticeable change from the sports car and would do quite nicely.

Claire relished the time to catch up. She sat down on a fabric-covered chaise longue, pulled her notepad and pen from her backpack, and summarized what had happened since the last entry, including all investigative observations and thoughts.

She glanced at her watch.

"I'm going to check in with Massey," she said aloud. She pulled out her cell phone and called the Miami-Dade sergeant.

He answered.

"I've been waiting to hear from you," he said. "What's going on over there?" He yawned in the background. It was early.

Claire filled him in, making certain not to forget any details.

"Shit, Ms. Caswell," the sergeant said. "Excuse my French. No pun intended." He cracked his knuckles. "People have died for less."

"Tell me about it," she said. "I think we're entitled to battle pay." She chuckled softly.

"How close are you two to getting to the truth about DiNetto?"

"I'd say things are going to reach a climax soon," she said. "And we'll be there to watch."

"Well, your time will soon be up. Tomorrow you'll be in Montpellier—your final destination on the itinerary. If you don't figure it out quickly, I'm afraid the two of you will be returning home without answers. And it will all turn out to have been a grandiose waste of your time and the department's resources." His tone carried a distinct hint of fatalism and seemed suddenly abrasive.

"I said we're close to getting at the truth," she said firmly. "Don't give up on us yet."

"We'll see how good you really are, Ms. Caswell," the sergeant said. He inhaled and exhaled loudly. "You and the legendary Gaston Lombard."

Claire was surprised by his tone.

"We're doing our best, sir. It hasn't been an easy case. We've been through a war zone."

He cracked his knuckles again. "Yes, well, let's hope you return home with something I can act on."

"That's the plan," Claire said.

"Did I overestimate your abilities?" the sergeant asked.

His question stunned the female investigator. She paused momentarily.

"So I don't respond in a way I may regret, I respectfully decline to answer your question, sergeant." But then she continued, "You know the reputation of my firm. And frankly, I'm a bit insulted by your question. Especially in light of everything we've been through in this investigation."

"No offense intended," Massey said, letting out a sigh. "It's just . . . it's just that I have a lot going on here."

The call ended.

Claire let her head fall back on the chair. She furrowed her brow and rubbed her chin. What was the sergeant's problem? He seemed upset in a way he hadn't been before. He was tough. Nothing ever got to him. So what could it be? She closed her eyes and soon nodded off. When she awoke, two hours had passed, and Guy hadn't returned to the room.

She picked up her cell phone and called him. He answered after a short delay.

"Are you all right?" she asked. "It's been a long time since you left. I'm getting concerned."

"I'm fine. Had another stop to make. I'll be back soon."

"Okay. I'll be waiting."

When he walked into the room, he took one look at Claire and knew something was wrong. "Sorry it took longer than expected."

She didn't respond.

"What's going on?" he asked.

"Not sure," she said. "I had a strange call with Massey. Troublesome, really. I've never heard him question our abilities before . . . until today." She filled him in on the conversation.

"That's hard to stomach. Especially seeing as he sent us into a den of lions!" Guy fumed. "The nerve of that man!"

Neither spoke for a time.

"We should check in with Jin," Guy said at last.

Claire dialed the office in Miami Beach, and Jin answered.

"How is everything going, Jin?" Claire asked the new assistant.

"Everything is copacetic. Perfect. Ideal. Excellent. I think I was made for the job," he said. "All is well."

"That's good," Claire said slowly. "Have any problems come up, Jin?"

"No, Ms. Caswell. Everything is running flawlessly."

"Okay, then let's go over the phone messages."

Jin went through all the messages left for the investigators.

"So you don't have any questions, Jin?" the female investigator asked. "I'm amazed."

"No questions," he said. "None whatsoever. Everything is under control."

Claire hung up and turned to face Guy. "I'm concerned."

25

EVERY WAKING MOMENT Jin wasn't attending law school classes, he remained hard at work trying to wrap up the Dougan investigation. Officer Figg contacted Jin frequently to demand updates, and the student's nerves were frayed. He wanted to prove his capabilities to Claire Caswell and Gaston Lombard—and to the impatient new police officer who had hired the firm.

Jim followed the leads generated from his review of the chat rooms to the best of his ability. Maybe he'd find out something new about the Anteater, Dougan's frequent phone contact. Contributors to the chats almost exclusively used nicknames—humorous or familiar—so it was time consuming to track down their legal names. But one by one, he was doing just that. Once he identified each of them, he conducted background checks to see what he could discover.

He believed wholeheartedly in the technology of computer

forensics. He'd studied the field, felt confident in his knowledge, and hoped that with persistence he could accomplish his goal.

He was healing nicely from the beating he'd sustained in South Beach, but he promised himself he'd never again go out into the field to investigate. Clearly his forte was to forensically examine digital media—then identify, recover, analyze, preserve, and ultimately present the facts obtained. He'd also be called upon to give his opinions regarding the information he uncovered. This was his bailiwick—his sphere of expertise. It was where he felt comfortable. And where he excelled. This was where he would find the answers he needed.

After draining the flamingo mug of hot tea, he returned to the computer to continue his work.

DINETTO BELIEVED he was possibly going crazy. One minute he was convinced the American investigators were still tailing him, and the next he was certain he was just imagining it. He'd been warned early on about the sleuths and had watched for them to arrive in Milan. He had tried so hard to divert the sleuths from the beginning. To scare them into retreating by arranging for their taxi to be fired upon. To have them withdraw from the case due to fright. But things had gone terribly wrong. The driver had been shot in the head and killed. And the young man on the bicycle had been unfortunate collateral damage. This was not what DiNetto had intended. And the thought of what he had been forced to do to the incompetent sniper who'd botched the job . . . that haunted DiNetto too.

He winced. Why had his childhood been so devastating? Why had everything he loved been ripped away from him? Why was he continually forced to keep doing things he wasn't proud of? Why had money become his idol? Why did it direct and control all his moves? Money was the only thing that gave him any excitement in his adult life. And he continued to need more and more of it to satiate his wants and desires.

The police had been close to catching him in the past, but they never had. And that spurred him on. It encouraged him to expand his schemes—each time breaking the law a little more, getting even richer, and outsmarting the authorities to a greater degree. He felt unstoppable.

But was this what he really wanted from life? His mother, so sincere and devout, would be devastated if she were alive to hear what her son Antonio had become. He fought thoughts of his mother from his psyche—her touch, the smell of her perfume, her beautiful face, and her tender voice. And the gentle kisses she placed on his cheeks. Not a day had passed when she didn't tell him she loved him. She had even called him the apple of her eye. Suddenly, overwhelming sadness possessed him. He shook his head and blinked his eyes. He needed these thoughts to be gone. They were far too painful.

He poured AVIV into a glass and emptied it. "Better," he said aloud. Now, he felt *good*. For only good people drank that special vodka. He stared at the bottle and lost himself, as he often did, trying to find the one hundred hidden messages buried in the glass. He closed his eyes. Its distinct flavors played with his tongue. He felt addicted to the intoxicating beverage.

He opened his eyes and continued to gaze deeply at the triangular bottle with the Israeli blue bottom. He noticed the words "Celebrate Life" in several major languages of the world.

He filled a shot glass and emptied it.

"Hmm," he said. "I feel mellow, oh so mellow."

But then images of Claire Caswell and Gaston Lombard assailed his thoughts. In another lifetime, in another age, he would have pursued this Caswell woman—as he did most other women who crossed his path. Maybe even had a long relationship with her. She was beautiful and strong. Just what he liked in a woman. And there was something about her. What was it? Her eyes? Her lovely, translucent green eyes? They portrayed an authenticity he'd never seen before.

He couldn't even bring himself to set up further attacks on the female investigator. He felt a strange attraction to her. He wanted her for himself. But Gaston Lombard had corralled her. It was clear the two had a connection unlikely to be broken—even by an unparalleled ladies' man like him.

He smiled at the thought of wining-and-dining Claire Caswell. A look of contentment came over his face. He'd gladly give up all his worldly possessions in exchange for a real relationship with a woman he loved—a woman such as Claire who could share his life. Who could maybe even have his children, if he were a younger man. Someone to come home to. Someone who gave a damn if he lived or died.

What was he thinking? There was no chance of romance with this Caswell woman. She and Lombard were hunting him as if he were an escaped wild animal from a zoo. He'd have to end this potential threat to his freedom, regardless of his unexpected thoughts about the female sleuth. If she and Gaston Lombard kept snooping into his life, they'd certainly put the skids on his carefully executed plan, and that would never do.

He'd avoided taking care of the pair up to this point, but now it was time to give the matter serious consideration.

CLAIRE LOOKED at Guy as they readied for dinner.

"You make me happy," she said.

"What?" he asked, unsure of what he heard.

She smiled. "You make me happy."

Guy walked over, cupped her face in his hands, and kissed her lips. "You don't tell me that very often. I like it." He clutched her in his arms.

The closeness of the moment provided a fleeting, but necessary, respite in the investigation. Things had been intense since their arrival in Italy, and there had been little personal time for the two of them.

"When this is over, when we're home," Guy started, "watch out." He smiled suggestively.

"Thanks for the warning." She smiled sweetly.

The two dressed in disguises. Sometimes DiNetto seemed to know who they were in their disguises, and other times he seemed not to know. But they had to try to play it safe. Claire wore a white blouse with black jeans, put on the brunette wig, styled it in a bun, applied mocha frost lipstick, and wore pearl-white-rimmed glasses. Guy dressed all in black, pulled on his curly wig, tied it in a low ponytail, and made sure the fake mustache was secured between his nose and upper lip. He finished with a pair of wireless glasses.

"We need to go to the lobby and watch for DiNetto to leave for dinner. Then we'll follow him," Claire said.

The investigators rode the elevator down a floor and walked to the huge lobby just inside the hotel's entrance. They sat on comfortable chairs far away from the people standing at the check-in counter and concierge desk.

The duo observed the activity in the area while pretending to be a couple on vacation. They chatted and laughed to pass the time, always keeping their eyes peeled for DiNetto. An hour passed.

"I'm starving," Guy said.

"He should be coming down soon," Claire said. "Anytime, I suspect."

Close to another half an hour passed before DiNetto appeared. They heard his voice before they caught a glimpse of him. Dressed in flamboyant attire, he attracted the attention of everyone in the lobby. He strolled up to the concierge on duty and loudly asked for a recommendation for dinner. The hotel employee dropped what he was doing and quickly came to attention. He recommended a local restaurant just four blocks from the hotel, an easy walk. He first told DiNetto how to walk there, then pulled out a map and outlined the route using a highlighter.

Claire had crept up closer to the desk and with her back to the concierge craned her head to listen to the name of the restaurant and the directions.

"I'll call ahead and let them know you are on the way," the employee said. "Will that be *one* for dinner?"

"Make it *two*," DiNetto said. "And I'd like an outdoor table." He passed the concierge a tip.

"*Merci beaucoup!*" the employee said, shooting a quick glance at the size of his remuneration. "If I can assist you in any other way during your stay, please do not hesitate to ask."

DiNetto nodded. He walked outside, flagged a valet, and got into his Ferrari. Why walk when he could pull up in front of the restaurant in his impressive, mighty driving machine, where all eyes would be upon him when they heard the familiar sound of the famous car? He pulled his cell phone from his pocket and made two calls.

The investigators listened until the roar of the fine-tuned engine could no longer be heard, then set off on foot to find the establishment. They wanted to give DiNetto a running start in getting seated at a table.

Walking the several blocks to the restaurant was enjoyable. The evening weather was pleasant, and the two passed pedestrians who were strolling by the many boutiques to window-shop before or after dining at one of the nearby cafés. The atmosphere was relaxed, and the setting peaceful.

As the two approached the restaurant, they walked across to the opposite side of the street. They found a dark entryway of a business to hover in and looked across at the tables set up in front of the eating establishment. Their collective eyes searched the patrons one by one. Claire spotted DiNetto. He was dining with a woman close to half his age.

The sleuths discussed their tactic. They would have to bypass DiNetto to walk into the restaurant, and hopefully then they would be seated at an outside table with his back facing them. It might take some maneuvering on their parts, but it could be done. Claire and Guy walked toward the restaurant. They could see DiNetto and his female companion lean in close to each other, cooing and flirting. His behavior with the opposite sex was certainly predictable, Claire thought.

She tugged on Guy's arm, and they stopped. She turned and whispered, "Wait until I give the cue, and then we'll hightail it inside." She observed DiNetto and his guest keenly, and when the moment happened—when the two leaned over the table, closed their eyes, and kissed—Claire said, "Now!" The investigators briskly walked past the diners and into the restaurant's front doors.

"Well done!" she whispered.

A maître d' approached. "English?" he asked.

"Yes," Claire said, nodding.

"How may I help you this evening?"

"We'd like a table outside, if possible. One on that end." Through a window, she pointed to an empty table situated perfectly to suit their needs.

"Impossible, *madame*. Fully booked outdoors for this evening.

That table is reserved." He glanced at his reservation book. "Inside is fully booked as well." He paused to scrutinize the book a second time. "No, wait a moment. I apologize. I see we had one cancellation. Is indoors satisfactory?"

He was a no-nonsense maître d with a poker face and not prone to chatting.

"Yes, we'll take it," Guy piped in. He looked at Claire with pleading eyes.

"Yes, of course," she said, "that will be just fine. I do hope it's close to the window."

"Follow me," the employee said. He led them to a table close enough to the window to look outside. And to Claire's delight, she could easily spot DiNetto and his companion.

"*C'est parfait*," she said.

The maître d' turned his lips up ever-so slightly. "*S'il vous plaît profiter.*"

"*Merci beaucoup*," Claire said.

The sleuths ordered and waited for the entrées to arrive.

"DiNetto is certainly true to form," Claire said. "He acts the same regardless of which woman is sitting across from him at a table. The females are positively interchangeable."

"It really bothers me that the authorities labeled the death of the young woman at La Scala an *accident*. No investigation ever ensued, and it never will," Guy said. "Sometimes I worry that DiNetto will be able to continue on unchecked."

"Never say never," Claire said. "Even the best cons slip up. They get sloppy at covering their tracks."

After dinner, the sleuths waited for DiNetto to drive off in his Ferrari, then they walked back to the hotel.

Once in the room, they removed their disguises. Claire decided to soak in a warm tub. She was tired and needed to relax before bed.

After her bath, she wrapped her bare body in the fluffy terry robe the hotel provided. She stepped over to the desk and grabbed the maps of France. The next morning they would drive to Montpellier, the end of the road on DiNetto's itinerary. She took a look at the route that would bring them there.

Guy walked into the bathroom to take a long hot shower. The days had been grueling—nonstop, really—since the two had arrived in Europe, and Guy was feeling it in his body. The heat would help soothe his aching muscles.

Claire pulled the coverlet and top sheet down on her side of the bed and started to get in. But she stopped when she saw a smallish flat white box lying there. The attached note said, "For my lovely Claire."

She pulled the lid from the box. Inside was a velvet pouch. She pulled out its contents. It was a simple platinum bangle. Her eyes moistened. She slipped it onto the wrist of her left hand. It fit perfectly.

Just then she heard Guy turn off the shower. Two minutes later he walked from the bathroom, au naturel, and slid under the covers. "Happy, my darling?" he asked.

"*I love it!*" she said. She held her arm up for him to see.

"We're in France, and it seemed like the thing to do. I picked it up this afternoon when I went for the rental car. That's why it took me so long. I wanted you to have something special to keep as a reminder of our time here, even though this investigation has taken its toll in so many ways. It's my way of saying you make me happy too."

They embraced. And made love under the soft white sheets. They fell asleep, nuzzled tightly together.

26

BACK IN HIS room, DiNetto paced restlessly. He looked at his watch and made a call. Then he poured himself a shot of his choice vodka and drank it in a gulp. He set the empty glass on his bedside table and walked to the bathroom mirror. He took a long look at himself. He wasn't a bad-looking man. In fact, he was strikingly attractive. All women thought so. And he was wealthy—and soon to be wealthier yet. What more could he ask for?

As he continued to soak in his reflection, he murmured the stanza he recited so often—the one that expressed what his father, his tata, had taught him at a young age about the world:

Say it with diamonds,
Say it with mink,
But never ever say it with ink.

"*Never in ink!*" he repeated loudly. His tata would be proud he remembered. Little Antonio had always called his father Tata. His cousins living in southern Italy had called their father Tata, and he and his siblings always had too.

Tata had always instructed his children to do business only on a handshake. If a written signature was required, his tata would always walk away from the deal. Anthony strolled to the bar, poured himself another shot of the smooth vodka, and polished it off. He sauntered over to a window and gazed up at the stars as his mind raced. He was a good man at heart. Only good people drink AVIV, he again reminded himself. But as much as he tried to convince himself of his own goodness, he couldn't. He wasn't a good man. Not by any stretch of the imagination. He'd done terrible things.

Unexpectedly, the faces of the people he had killed or had set up to be killed floated before him, and he could not stop the flow of images. He bellowed, "*No!*"

He dropped onto the bed and closed his eyes. The images of his victims persisted. They held hands and paraded across his mind in a continuous circle, jeering and taunting him. He fell into broken sleep, haunted throughout the night by his dreadful acts. At one point he spotted his mother, and he called out to her, but she turned her head and walked away. "*No!*" he cried out silently. "*No!*" But the nightmares continued. He had made his bed, and now he had to lie in it.

Day ten
Cannes to Montpellier, France

CLAIRE AND Guy met the morning invigorated. While Guy was showering, she heard a gentle rapping at the door and stepped toward it, asking who was there.

"Delivery for Ms. Caswell," the voice on the other side of the door responded.

She peeked through the peephole and saw a young uniformed man she recognized as staff from the lobby. She opened the door.

The employee handed her a tiny box wrapped in silver paper and topped with a silver metallic bow. "This is for you, Ms. Caswell." He smiled from ear to ear.

"Who is it from?" she asked, eyeing the package carefully.

"Now, if I told you that, it would no longer be a surprise."

"One moment, please," she said. She ran to her backpack, reached inside, and returned to hand the young man a tip. "Thank you."

Guy remained in the shower, and Claire sat down on the bed and ripped open the package. What has Guy done now, she wondered.

The small box housed an even smaller one inside, covered in white satin. It looked like a ring box. She cracked opened the lid and was immediately at a loss for words. It was the most beautiful diamond solitaire ring she had ever seen. It glistened and sparkled as if lit from underneath. She pulled it from its container and held it with her right hand, staring at it in disbelief. Then she slipped it onto her left ring finger. Sunlight streaming through the windows caused the gem to twinkle and shimmer in a magnificent way. It was stunning. Set in a simple setting of white gold or platinum— she couldn't be sure which—it was an extraordinary piece. Claire searched for a note, but found none.

Her mind began to spin. It had to be from Guy, didn't it? But why a second gift? And why a diamond ring? Was he trying to push the marriage issue before she'd given him an answer?

She heard him finish in the shower. What should she do? She quickly returned the ring to its tiny box, placed it back in the delivery box, and shoved it into her backpack. She needed time to think. She couldn't answer him now. Not yet. She just hoped he wouldn't ask.

"How was your shower, hon?" she asked. "We need to get ready for the day."

"A hot shower cures many ailments, my dear," he said, grinning. "Just ask my formerly achy bones."

"Our time is running out, Guy," Claire said, pushing away thoughts of the ring. "We need to find out what DiNetto is carrying around in those boxes. Any suggestions?"

"I've been thinking about that a lot, especially in the shower. It's obviously the key to what DiNetto doesn't want discovered about his activities. I'm wondering if we should set a trap." The look in his eyes turned strangely serious.

"You're reading my mind," she told him. "I've got a plan. Here's what we need to do when we reach Montpellier."

THE SLEUTHS rode the elevator to the main floor. They consumed a quick breakfast, checked out, obtained their rental car from the on-duty valet, and started the drive to Montpellier. It was close to a three-hour drive, if all went well.

Claire had pulled her hair back into a high ponytail and placed an olive beret on her head. She wore dark sunglasses and a pale orchid lipstick. Guy had put on the straight light-colored wig, a cap, and a pair of gray sunglasses. He also tied a jacket around his waist.

The day's drive took them through more long man-made tunnels carved out of the rock bordering the natural coastline. Inside, the tunnels were dark, with vehicles speeding in both directions and traffic lights appearing from time to time to slow the traffic. The colored lights along the seemingly never-ending passageway momentarily brightened the otherwise underlit space. Cars sped past the investigators regardless of the speed Guy drove.

Out of the blue, Claire shared a random thought. "Isn't it odd that Ferraris are made in Italy, yet we haven't seen a single one—other than DiNetto's—on the streets the entire time we've been here? And he flew his over."

"Yeah. It is a bit strange, when you think of it," Guy said. "I guess there aren't too many people with that kind of money to put into an exotic car. Though we did see many at the plant. Wonder who's buying them."

"Well, we know DiNetto has money. The question is *where* and *how* he obtains it. Certainly not from his fake business in Miami."

"In my experience, when things don't add up—when someone is living far beyond his or her visible means—it almost always signals illegal activity of some sort," Guy said. "Often it's drug trafficking or some other nefarious activity."

Claire scrunched up her face and closed her eyes. "I don't think it's drugs with DiNetto. He doesn't seem the type, if there is a type. No, I think he's into something far more sophisticated. Something more glamorous. Maybe something smuggled."

"Interesting." He pondered her summation. "But what?"

"We don't know yet, but we'll find out," she declared with a look of confidence on her striking face. "And if DiNetto doesn't find a suitable buyer here in Europe, my guess is he'll bring the merchandise back to the US to sell."

"If that's the case, Sergeant Massey can have him followed, nab him in the act of selling stolen or smuggled items, and arrest him. He'll do some serious time," the former prosecutor said.

"Yeah," Claire said. "But we first need to ascertain what he's attempting to sell. Then we have to determine if the goods he's peddling are stolen, smuggled, or a sham. We need the whole story so the sergeant will have grounds to arrest the man making the sale and the person making the purchase."

As she spoke of the sergeant, their recent conversation echoed in her mind. His comments and tone seemed utterly peculiar, to say the least. He'd never spoken to her in that disparaging way before. Maybe he was just having a bad day. Or maybe another case was troubling him. It might have nothing to do with the work she and Guy were doing. Still, it nagged at her.

JIN CONTINUED his ferocious and tireless search to pin down Cane Dougan. He remained focused on one difficult question: Who was the Anteater? The nickname baffled him. During his research, he discovered an anteater was a mammal with a long, tapered snout. An animal with powerful front claws that feeds on ants and termites.

What an odd nickname, Jin thought. He delved further, looking for something more. He came across symbolism tied to the anteater and discovered that the creature was cautious by nature, worked best covertly, and sneaked quietly into ant nests to consume all its inhabitants before the small insects could even try to escape. The anteater knew stings from thousands of ants could spell his death, so speed became his protection.

Jin rehashed what he had just learned. Maybe, he reasoned, the Anteater is a man who sneaks up on unaware people, strikes, obtains whatever he's after, and flees the scene.

Hmm, Jin thought.

He needed to find the man or woman whose actions fit the symbolism of the animal. That way he could uncover the identity of the Anteater. Whoever hid behind that nickname regularly communicated with Dougan.

Digging even deeper into Dougan's e-mail records, Jin finally came across additional messages between Sugarcane and the Anteater—who still could not be traced to an actual name or individual. After reading the contents of the e-mails, even though most were cryptic, Jin was convinced something foul was going on. The language in some of the messages could easily indicate the Anteater was paying Dougan for certain information. If so, maybe there was a succession of questionable deposits into one of Dougan's bank accounts. Maybe even with a regular and recognizable pattern.

Would this information eventually turn into proof that Dougan wasn't just leaking case information to the press, but that he was also providing intelligence to a criminal? And therefore acting as an accessory to who-knows-what kinds of illegal behavior?

Figg had mentioned Dougan was angry because he had never been promoted. So the leaks to the press, Jin figured, were a bitter officer's way to get back at the department. But Jin still didn't know what information Dougan was sharing with the Anteater—or why.

Jin recalled Dougan's comments into the pay phone at the South Beach bar: "Unharmed. On to the next act. I'll keep you posted."

Finding the identity of the Anteater was crucial, and Jin felt sure he was zeroing in.

The assistant had more work to do.

27

THE FRAIL FIGURE of Franco Nef dropped into an ancient pine rocker stationed on one side of his workshop. Now in his mideighties, he felt the chair had been more loyal than any friend he'd ever had. He positioned his arms just so on its worn armrests and moved his body ever-so slightly to allow for a subtle rocking of the old seat with its high back and wooden legs. Both the man and the chair had been around for a long time, and now the older man's bones and the antique joints of the rocker competed to creak the loudest from years of wear.

Nef's mind spun wildly, and he needed some time alone with his thoughts. He wanted to ponder the creations he'd recently completed—to recollect each step he had performed along the seemingly endless and exacting way. He closed his glossy chestnut eyes and allowed his memory unrestrained freedom.

Performing meticulous movements, using a delicate touch,

he'd called upon great patience from deep within and allowed his fragile, nimble fingers to proceed with knowing skill, painstakingly breathing life into each work of art. All ten pieces. The tight latex gloves he had worn had given him better leverage, as sweat poured from his hands. The key to the arduous task had been to take it slow—not to rush. Rushing would never have allowed him to accomplish what he had undertaken. This exercise called for exceptional expertise, and he had been the perfect person to perform the task.

But now that his creations had left the workshop, he wondered if he'd done the right thing. He'd received enormous compensation for his work—a sum of money that would leave him wanting nothing for the rest of his life, however many years remained. Pangs of conscience plagued him in a way he never could have imagined or expected. As a man who had lived a life governed by high principles and scruples—until now, that is—his recent actions burned into his conscience as if his soul had been overexposed to the sun. He found himself trembling with anxiety.

Now that exorbitant amount of money seemed tainted, dirty. He decided to give it all away. He'd go out onto the streets, find needy candidates, and hand out envelopes stuffed with large bills until it was gone. Perhaps when the ill-gotten money was no longer in his possession, he might feel clean again. He wanted to feel clean again. And if the police came to question him, he'd sing like a canary. He wouldn't cover for what he'd done or what DiNetto had asked of him.

Why had he ever agreed to do it? Simply to prove that he could? That he was the best? That his skills surpassed everyone else's? He shook his head from side to side with disturbed persistence. Why, oh why, had he done it?

Unconsciously, he began to rock harder in the simple chair, and it strained to keep up with his movements. The old man's head fell to his hands, and he remembered the details of the endeavor. Taking in deep breaths, one after another, trying to calm his trembling, he recalled with full lucidity the day Anthony DiNetto had approached him. The formidable Anthony DiNetto—the man who yielded great power and respect—was a man no one said no to. When the request had come to him, the elderly man had initially felt honored to be the one selected in all of Neuchâtel to carry out a nearly impossible task. But now, after he'd accepted the challenge and completed the deed, why did he feel so stained? So ashamed?

He had used state-of-the-art instruments, tweaking here and adjusting there, striving for utter perfection. Only perfection would ever be acceptable.

"Be nimble. Make light movements!" he'd told himself over and over while working his magic. "This is possible."

He imagined the final pieces as he worked. This helped nudge him ever forward. Each one needed to be delicately formed and deceptively copied to mimic the real item. Assembling the parts rattled his nerves. Extreme care had to be taken, especially with the areas the buyers would be able to examine closely. The special tweezers he held between his fingers had quivered at times, requiring him to pause and to steady himself. Tiny pins had to be inserted, and surfaces polished equally. Quality, quality, *quality*! Only exactness would be tolerated. Visible flaws or defects would put an abrupt end to all of it.

The pressure had been great. And the older man often grew tired during the process. But in the end, the feat had been carried out flawlessly. He had worked on the originals so long ago and knew exactly how to replicate them now. He understood what needed to be created using dials, brass plates, radium paste, stainless steel, Plexiglas, and leather. More than anyone, he understood the cutting, the stamping, and the careful faking of the fading required to create replicas of the thin and graceful profiles with the sculpted curves—the most valuable, rare, and desirable of their kind. Replicas impossible to distinguish from the real thing.

His mind drifted as he focused on the 6154. He recalled that the originals had been created for the Egyptian Navy around 1954. They were attractive to look at, yet rugged in construction. Made as military tools, yet styled with the simplicity of Italian elegance. He believed only forty originals were ever made, with only ten or possibly twelve still known to be in existence. He secretly wondered if some of the other originals might still be somewhere in Italy, perhaps in antique shops, secondhand stores, flea markets, or even passed along to relatives of retired Egyptian naval officers. Set aside with no one realizing the object's true value.

He rocked in his antique chair, continuing to hold his head in his hands, hearing his own labored breathing, and weeping uncontrollably. He had accomplished the unthinkable for DiNetto. But now, like Lady Macbeth, he couldn't wash the blood from his hands.

ANTHONY DINETTO poured himself a shot of AVIV. He was drinking it more and more these days. Morning, afternoon, and evening. He inhaled the aroma of the pure liquid and took an unhurried swallow, savoring the smooth, velvety vodka as it oozed its way down his throat.

"Aah," he said aloud. "I am a good man. Only good people drink AVIV." He sipped the wondrous drink again. The flavors were subtle and delicious. He set the small glass down, let his head roll slowly onto the back of the chair, and shut his eyes. In no time, he heard a faint voice. Whose was it? As he concentrated, the utterance became clearer and closer. Eventually he recognized the sound of his mother's voice. She seemed to be visiting him more often these days—since he'd started drinking the magical vodka. Tears collected in his eyes and rolled slowly down and over his cheeks. He blinked them back as he struggled to hear her words. It was the familiarity of her voice that always got to him. It had been so long since he'd heard his mother speak. But as he listened this time, he didn't like her scolding words.

Antonio! Antonio! I am ashamed of you. You disgrace our family name. The voice paused. *There is still time to turn things around . . . but time is running out. Soon you will be hardened forever and unable to change your ways. Your tata and I taught you the right way to live. Why do you stray?* Her voice faded.

"Mamma, don't leave," he called. "Come back. I need you. I've always needed you. I've been so alone . . . "

But her voice didn't return.

DiNetto stayed in the chair for some time, saddened by her words, sheepish about his life, and unable to get up. He poured himself another shot of the clear liquid he now depended on to feel better each day. Why *had* he taken life's dark road? Why had he always chosen to walk on the shady side of the street when he could have chosen the sunny side? His mother had warned him time was running out. But her words were wrong. He knew full well time had already run its course. He'd passed the tipping point and was now irreversibly hardened. There was no way back. If hell were real, as his mother had always told him, he was surely destined to go there.

He finished the shot of AVIV. He'd masterminded many lucrative schemes in the past, but he was about to make his biggest score ever. He mulled over the endgame in his mind. Never leave behind a paper or electronic trail, he reminded himself.

He walked the few steps to a mirror and took a long look at himself while he spoke.

Say it with diamonds,
Say it with mink,
But never ever say it with ink.

"*Never in ink!*" he pronounced with obsessive enthusiasm. As he repeated his mantra, warm thoughts of his tata enveloped him.

28

CLAIRE'S MIND REFUSED to slow down. It was racing as fast as the cars zooming past them on the road to Montpellier. She was stuck on the case's most urgent question: What did the boxes contain? The answer held the key to DiNetto's secretive activities. The unanswered question plagued her. The soft voice within her—the one she always heeded—nudged her with an urgency she'd never before experienced, telling her to discover the secret soon, or it might be too late. She wanted to solve this case in the worst way. Not only did she want to bring a criminal to justice, but she also wanted Miami-Dade's Sergeant Massey to know his department could depend on the Caswell & Lombard firm to get this and any other job done whenever their services might be required.

She closed her eyes and imagined various items that would fit into the boxes. She had thought about this so often since she had first observed DiNetto holding them. The objects inside couldn't be very large, and the boxes appeared easy to carry, so she assumed the contents weren't heavy. When DiNetto opened the boxes to various people to show whatever they held, did that mean the items were all identical, or all different? And why was DiNetto racing between Italy, Switzerland, and France to display the items to various people along the way? What was the significance of these three countries in his scheme? The potential buyers appeared to be extremely wealthy. Was DiNetto selling stolen property? Planning a sale to the highest bidder on the black market? Selling to collectors? So many unanswered questions remained.

The investigators had taken note of the name of the yacht in the Portofino harbor where DiNetto had shown the goods to a man while Claire eavesdropped. Guy had researched the yacht, only to find out a corporation owned it, which led to another corporation, and yet another. It was impossible to determine the name of an actual individual.

Claire wished she'd found answers when she'd donned a housekeeping uniform and sneaked into DiNetto's room to search for the boxes. If only. If only he'd left the boxes' contents behind that day—her daring escapade would have paid off royally. But fate hadn't been on her side. If only she could have seen what was in the boxes when she'd boarded the yacht in Portofino the night of the secret meeting. But no such luck. So much of the success— or failure—of investigative work seemed to boil down to chance rather than action. And they hadn't had a lot of luck since arriving in Europe.

She reminded herself they hadn't been shot or otherwise seriously injured in the taxi incident. But others had. She shuddered and thought carefully about that. Yes, she and Guy had come out of the incident alive. And all other attacks on her had been thwarted as well.

She paused to feel gratitude. She and Guy had been protected all along.

DINETTO SAT in his room, pondering his life. He was having trouble getting going this particular day. He was mourning the reality that he had no special person to share things with. No one to attend special events with. No one to depend on. No one to forge a life with. No one who cared whether he lived or died. The issue hadn't plagued him before, but suddenly he was obsessed.

He closed his eyes and thought about Claire Caswell. Why could he not get this woman out of his mind? He had painstakingly selected the perfect gift for her and had it delivered to her room with no note attached. She'd never realize it was from him. But by the virtue of the act, he somehow felt good inside. If things were different, if Gaston Lombard weren't in the picture, perhaps he would seriously pursue a real relationship with the lady.

He daydreamed about all the things the two of them could do together, if only she'd give him a chance. He could prove himself. Money was no object now, and soon it would never concern him again. The two of them could travel the world. They could do anything Claire desired. He pictured her face. So pure. Almost childlike. Yet mature. And driven.

Reality arrived to jolt his thoughts. Not in this lifetime, he reminded himself. But he could dream, couldn't he? Just thinking about the possibility warmed his soul.

He poured himself a shot of the oh-so-soothing vodka. If only he'd lived a different kind of life—one he could be proud of today— things might be different. He exhaled deeply and felt the unbearable weight of his choices. There was no turning back. No chance of reversing his earlier decisions. He could only push forward.

Perhaps once he reached Montpellier, he'd take some time to look for another gift for the female investigator. He pondered. Yes, that was exactly what he'd do.

He laughed. The investigators thought they were so clever in their many disguises. But he had hotel employees watching them at every location. The pair had trailed him since first arriving in Italy ten days ago, so he knew they'd follow him to Montpellier. They must wonder how he always figured out their disguises, he mused. He had tried to scare them off, but nothing had worked. Their persistence was remarkable. Unshakable. How could he hate Claire Caswell for trying to ruin him, yet feel strangely attracted to her? It made no sense.

CLAIRE DIRECTED all her mental energy into concocting their next plan of action. It would take some time to put it all together and pull it off. But it was doable. And right about now, it seemed to be the only move that might work.

"We'll need to come up with a name. A background. A history. And a look," Claire said.

"I've got ideas for that," Guy said.

As the sleuths wheeled their way to Montpellier, they honed in on the fine details.

DINETTO PULLED himself together, checked out of the Hôtel Majestic Barrière, and left on his drive to Montpellier, a gem of southern France. He loved driving his Ferrari. The smell of the leather intoxicated him. And he delighted in the way it responded when he touched the gas pedal—leaving other cars behind in only a second or two. He never tired of hearing the sound of its mighty engine. Other drivers on the road gawked when the Ferrari passed, craning their necks to see the spectacular Italian vehicle with the famous *Cavallino Rampante*—the "prancing horse"—symbol on its spectacular exterior. Sometimes they'd flash DiNetto a thumbs-up as he flew past—usually traveling around eighty miles per hour. Just driving this car that exuded speed, wealth, and luxury made him feel special and important. It was definitely a vehicle made for him, and he manned the wheel with unrestrained gusto.

The three-hour drive west passed in no time. He arrived at the Domaine de Verchant, checked in, then decided to stroll its grounds.

A sense of great frustration permeated his being. He had assumed it would be easy to move the goods, but his failure to close the deal quickly annoyed him greatly. He'd fronted a substantial sum to make the scam happen. He'd even borrowed some capital from a lower-level partner, that officious clown who'd wanted him to sign an agreement about how they'd share the profits.

DiNetto, after all his hard work, wanted to reap the fruits of his master plan. And he was growing tired of waiting. Over the last week, he'd approached several prospective purchasers known to dabble in scarce and rare commodities. And while certain individuals had expressed interest and had promised to quietly spread the word to a handful of other collectors, not a single one had closed the deal. It would take the perfect buyer. He knew that all too well. Money was tighter than it used to be, and the buy had to be right. The transaction had to be discreet and stay a secret forever. He knew someone would make the purchase. He just needed to exercise his patience. But frankly, he'd never been a patient man.

He walked back to his car, got in, and drove the short distance to a quaint upscale specialty women's shop in Montpellier.

"What can you show me in mink?" he asked.

"We have many extraordinary items, *monsieur*," the owner said. "I will be happy to show you."

AS GUY drove, the investigators created the persona of a fictional man—an eccentric wealthy American living the life of an indulged hermit in southern France. He led a solitary life, one mostly devoid of friends or even acquaintances. Their plan required Guy to shave his head, wear a jaw insert, don clear-plastic eyeglass frames with tinted lenses, dress in expensive but casual clothing, and act like a loner. They had to create a name for their recluse, and after some debate they settled on Alexander Rudy Cotton, who preferred to be called Rudy.

Guy planned to post a handful of vague entries on Google mentioning sightings of the mysterious, seemingly off-the-grid Mr. Cotton. If DiNetto checked out potential buyers of his goods, the postings would create both intrigue and possibility.

DINETTO LOOKED over his several options. He wanted something that wasn't over-the-top, but he wanted it special enough to fuel Claire's fancy and curiosity. He knew it when he saw it.

"I'll take this one," he told the shop's owner, pointing to his selection. "Will you wrap it, please?"

"Of course, *monsieur*. It's a lovely piece. She is a lucky woman." The owner disappeared into a back room and reappeared a short time later, carrying a gift box wrapped in pale pink paper and tied with a delicate ivory lace ribbon. She placed it into a pale pink shopping bag with handles.

DiNetto paid for his purchase. As he stepped from the boutique, he smiled. He'd give anything to see Claire's face when she opened the second gift. But he knew that wasn't possible. Nevertheless, it warmed him to think he was giving a gift of mink—as a follow-up to an exquisite diamond ring—to the woman he'd never have.

CLAIRE AND Guy arrived in Montpellier and followed the map to the Domaine de Verchant. It had been a large, elegant French country house with a neighboring winery before it was converted into a hotel and spa. Much of the original château, constructed of old stone, remained both outside and in. The place was enchanting. Several other different-sized buildings, all with similar exteriors, shared the highly manicured grounds.

The two were given Room 10, which had been dubbed the Nur Mahal Room. They walked up the wide stone steps that led to their deluxe terrace room on the upper floor and stepped in. To their amazement, it was decorated with contemporary decor, an unexpected surprise after viewing the château's exterior. The space was inviting with its wood floors, black leather furniture, heavy black-and-magenta-swirled draperies, stark-white bed linens, very small but functional bathroom, and spacious walkout sundeck with chaise lounges. From the open-air platform, the sleuths could view the entire grounds. A stem of fresh white orchids sitting in a simple black vase decorated the living room coffee table, along with an assortment of nuts and other snacks.

They quickly unpacked and decided to walk around the area. Then they drove to the nearby shops and purchased some clothing to outfit Rudy Cotton. Two hours later, they emerged from the boutiques carrying several shopping bags. They drove back to the hotel and created hermit-like Rudy. Minutes later, Claire eyed their creation from top to bottom, nodding in admiration.

Mr. Cotton, with his smooth-shaven head, stood tall in white linen jeans, a loose-fitting matching jacket, a taupe pima cotton tee, a paisley scarf around his neck, and clear plastic eyeglass frames with tinted brown lenses. Claire was thankful she had packed so many pairs of glasses with the other disguise items. They'd so often been the perfect finishing touch. And the concealer had blended in so well that his scars were invisible.

"Remember," Claire said, "you need to be extremely laid-back. Don't be overly excitable about anything. And act as if you might possibly be interested in his product—but only if the price is right. You know the drill. Act a little offbeat, a bit quirky. Make him work for the deal."

"Piece of cake," Guy said.

The investigators ordered room service for dinner. From this point on, they couldn't be seen together. Claire agreed to stay at the hotel while Guy went out to find DiNetto and pose as an interested buyer. If DiNetto spotted her in the background, he'd certainly put two and two together and figure out the soft-spoken Rudy was none other than Gaston Lombard in yet another disguise. And that would never do.

"Keep your cell phone handy," Claire said. "I'm a phone call away. Keep me posted. I'll be sitting here in suspense." She kissed his cheeks. "And be careful. Take no chances. Get out fast if you need to."

Guy winked. "I'm good. Keep your fingers crossed that I can plant some seeds tonight. That's my plan."

He left the room and took the long flight of distressed white stone steps leading to the ground-floor check-in desk. He walked outside and set off in the direction of the dining area and bar. Coolness tinged the evening air, and darkness encapsulated the inviting glow of the restaurant. Offset contemporary umbrellas covered the tables, sporadic lighting provided soft illumination, and ground lights lit the stone exteriors of the buildings dramatically. Glancing around the property, Guy noticed three sizable glowing orbs of color sitting in the darkness, placed at what appeared to be random locations within the manicured grounds. Two radiated a soft orange glow, and the third emitted warm green. They seemed ultramodern in style and strangely out of place near the old-château-turned-hotel, but they contributed an air of intrigue.

Guy took in a deep breath and became Rudy Cotton. He walked up to the bar and sat down on a stool at the far end.

"Grey Goose on the rocks," he told the bartender.

As Guy nursed his drink, he stared at the glass and sat quietly in wait. After a time, DiNetto appeared and sat three seats away. He handed the bartender a full bottle of AVIV to hold behind the bar for his use only, and he ordered a double shot neat. Only two patrons were at the bar that evening—Guy and DiNetto. Soon Guy felt DiNetto's eyes drill into him. He didn't react.

"What are you drinking over there?" DiNetto asked.

Guy looked up at DiNetto. "Grey Goose," he said, using a deep voice.

"Have you ever tried AVIV?"

"No."

"Bartender, bring my friend here a taste of AVIV. You'll like it," DiNetto said. "It's smooth. Goes down easy."

Guy nodded slightly and thanked DiNetto. He took a sip.

DiNetto moved over to the stool next to Guy.

"I'm Anthony DiNetto." He extended his hand.

"Alexander Cotton. But I go by Rudy."

"You look American, Rudy," DiNetto probed.

Guy looked down. "I am. Originally," he muttered under his breath. He turned his body away from DiNetto.

Though it was clear Rudy didn't want to converse, DiNetto wasn't deterred. As always, he was compelled to boast. DiNetto prattled on about his life in Miami as he watched Rudy sip his drink.

"You look like a man of means, Rudy," DiNetto said. "If you'll excuse me, I'll return shortly. Save my seat."

DiNetto walked to the stairwell and pulled out his smartphone. Soon he would know more about the quiet Rudy Cotton.

29

JIN DOWNED THE tall latte he'd picked up on his drive to the office. There was no time for lunch. He furrowed his brow and dug in his heels. The investigators would be back in Miami in a couple days, and he was desperate to tell them he'd wrapped up a case on his own, put a criminal away, and brought income to the firm.

He'd gleaned lots of information through long hours of researching all he could about Cane Dougan—but he had to know more. He needed evidence: hard, irrefutable evidence of all his wrongdoings. Facts the Miami-Dade police officer could neither challenge nor deny. Facts that would put the supposed "officer of the law" behind bars—and not just for the serious press leaks, but also for the potentially dangerous help for which, Jin strongly suspected, the Anteater was paying Dougan. Nothing bothered the law student more than someone violating authority after being entrusted to safeguard the public.

Jin reviewed his notes again. First the big picture. Then the details, one by one. There had to be something to turn this case in his favor. He probed deeper.

Hours passed. He needed a strong lead. He nudged himself to look at the facts he'd gathered from a different angle.

After finding what he suddenly realized was a bank reference in Dougan's e-mails to the Anteater, Jin hacked into the police officer's banking records. He discovered evidence of substantial deposits wired into Dougan's account from Magnifico Notte Music Production, Inc., which had a downtown Miami address. What had Dougan done to earn these payments?

He researched the only individual name he found associated with Magnifico Notte Music Production, Inc. Its president was Anthony DiNetto. Jin racked his brain, wondering where he'd seen that name before. He shuffled wildly through the papers on Claire's desk and found it on her calendar. She'd recorded "Anthony DiNetto case— Europe" and blocked out the days she and Guy would be in Europe. Maybe the Dougan-DiNetto connection factored into the case the two investigators were on in Europe. The stunned look on his face gave way to a look of determination. He worked harder.

He hacked back into Dougan's cell phone records. He dug further and recovered deleted text messages between the two men. Nothing is ever truly erased, Jin reminded himself, smiling. Certain texts from Dougan to DiNetto started with "Anteater" as the salutation. One even said, "You're truly an anteater—hitting those who don't expect you and devouring them." Finally, hard evidence of the Anteater's identity: Anthony DiNetto.

But Jin's next discovery startled and concerned him greatly. He found texts from Dougan informing DiNetto of private information Sergeant Massey kept in a log on his desk. Dougan admitted to looking at it when Massey went to lunch each day. And the information dealt specifically with Claire Caswell and Gaston Lombard! The sergeant had summarized each phone call from Claire regarding the DiNetto investigation, and Dougan had passed along all that information to DiNetto.

It was mind-boggling!

Now Dougan's words into the pay phone in the Miami Beach bar made sense: "Unharmed. On to the next act. I'll keep you posted." He was referring to one or both of the investigators emerging unscathed from a dangerous situation DiNetto had planned.

He picked up his phone and dialed Claire's cell number. No answer. He tried Guy's cell number. No answer. He sent an urgent text to both numbers, asking for return calls ASAP. He had to warn them. DiNetto knew every move they were making. He knew about the disguises. He knew everything—and they were in danger.

He called Officer Figg and informed him of his findings. "You were correct! Cane Dougan is the mole. Have him arrested. We have all the evidence we need. He leaked confidential police information that compromised open criminal investigations. And perhaps more urgently, he interfered with a private investigation sponsored by the Miami-Dade Police Department. It's putting the lives of Claire Caswell and Gaston Lombard in dire jeopardy as we speak. Tell Sergeant Massey immediately. I'll call him too."

Jin hung up and called Massey. Within minutes, Dougan was arrested, cuffed, and hauled to a jail cell. Before officers took him away, however, Massey told him off.

"You're the worst," Massey growled. "Nothing but a spineless, good-for-nothing traitor."

"Yeah?" Dougan replied. "You deserved those press leaks. You never promoted me all these years. It was a real pleasure to tarnish the great Sergeant Massey's spotless reputation," he sneered. "And feeding DiNetto information? He blackmailed me at first. Swore he'd go public with a personal matter of mine. I had to go along with him. But yeah, then he paid me for the information. So after a while, I didn't mind doing it. I actually enjoyed it."

Massey wanted to punch him in the face, but he held back. "Tell it to the jury."

Jin kept calling and texting Claire and Guy. Where were they? It was critical he reach them. Sergeant Massey, alarmed at Jin's findings, also tried in vain to contact the investigators.

Day eleven
Montpellier

CLAIRE SURVEYED Guy with watchful eyes as they sipped their coffee while the morning sunlight poured into their room. She hadn't mentioned the diamond ring, and she knew he wouldn't mention it either. She figured he must be on shaky ground—being so brazen as to send her the most beautiful diamond ring she'd ever seen, despite her past reluctance to accept his marriage proposals. She knew he'd wait for her to make the next move—to give him an answer to his implied question. But she needed time to think. Opening the tiny box and seeing the magnificent ring had sparked feelings within her she didn't know were there. But was she finally ready to say yes?

Guy looked up at her and into her eyes, and she smiled at him. He'd been exceedingly patient with her—so tolerant of her constant delays—without becoming annoyed. It spoke volumes about his character. But now he'd actually gone out and purchased a magnificent engagement ring. The stakes had risen suddenly and considerably. Somewhere deep inside, she knew this would be his final attempt to persuade her to marry him. She also knew she didn't have much time left to make her decision.

Just then a tap sounded at the hotel room door.

Claire yelled out, "Who is it?"

"Your friendly hotel staff with a parcel for Ms. Caswell."

Claire looked through the peephole, opened the door, and accepted the package. She reached into her robe pocket, pulled out a tip, thrust it toward the young man, and thanked him.

He grinned and thanked her back. "Someone thinks you are *très spéciale!*" He winked.

"Guy, you shouldn't have," Claire said when he noticed her walking his way with the parcel. "Really." She ripped it open.

The white mink muff was flawless, and she slipped her hands inside its open ends. Her eyes danced with excitement and she smiled widely.

"It's beautiful! But what's the occasion?" She looked at him with searching eyes, hoping he'd explain what was prompting these expensive gifts.

At that moment, Claire noticed that Guy looked bewildered. He didn't answer.

"This is so lovely, but it's not necessary," Claire said, studying him and then the luxurious mink muff.

"That is not from me, Claire. But seeing your reaction, I wish it were! You must have another admirer." A glum expression overtook his face.

"You're kidding, right? This is *not* from you? Who else would it be from?"

"It's not from me, Claire," he repeated. "Isn't there a card?"

She searched the box, but didn't find one. She shook her head slowly from side to side. Suddenly, it occurred to her that if the mink muff wasn't from Guy, perhaps the diamond ring wasn't either. But no, she argued with herself. The ring had to be from the man she loved and who loved her. Didn't it? She had never even considered it might be from someone else. But should she mention it to him now, just in case? Not yet. First she needed to be clear about what was going on.

"I need some fresh air," Guy said.

He put on the curly wig and walked down to the lobby.

He asked around and located the staff person who'd delivered the package to their room. "Sir, who gave you the parcel to bring to our room minutes ago? The package for Claire Caswell."

Redness took over the employee's face. "I am sworn to secrecy, *monsieur*. I am not allowed to say. My apologies."

"It is quite important that we know. Please make an exception and tell me."

"*Non, s'il vous plaît, monsieur.* I cannot do that, or I will surely lose my job."

Guy stared directly into the young man's eyes. "I hope you'll reconsider. It's a matter of great importance."

The young man shook his head again, looking regretful.

As Guy walked away, he knew the employee would never reveal the information. How strange that someone would send Claire a mink muff. What was the purpose? One thing was sure. Someone else sending Claire a gift of this nature didn't sit well with him.

Claire knew Guy was disturbed by the gift. And truthfully, so was she.

When he returned to the room after a long walk, he asked her one question. "Any idea who sent this muff to you?"

"No. None whatsoever." Then she pondered, letting her investigator mind whirl. "Maybe DiNetto is behind this. Maybe he wants to get to you. Have you considered that possibility?"

"Well, if that was the motivation, it worked," he said.

"You know I only love you," Claire said. She kissed him. She still couldn't bring herself to ask him about the diamond ring.

DINETTO WAS filled with angst. He paced the floor of his hotel room, deep in thought. He was a man accustomed to getting whatever he wanted, whenever he wanted it. And for some reason, this Claire Caswell kept haunting him. She represented everything he could never have in a woman: beauty, brains, and stability. It had always been easy for him to pick up an attractive but empty-headed young woman at a bar—a willing and ultimately meaningless sex partner. But now he wanted more. He wanted something real. Someone with whom to enjoy the process of life, and someone he would love to grow old with. Someone he could trust explicitly. He was rapidly becoming consumed by this new urge.

He'd carefully picked out and sent the investigator two anonymous gifts, but he wasn't able to see her face when she opened either. He grimaced. He actually hurt deep inside. This was something he had never experienced before, and he was unsure how to handle it.

He walked to the mirror and looked at himself, as he so often did. He wasn't unattractive, he reminded himself. He dressed elegantly and wore fancy jewelry. And he smelled of expensive cologne—but he reeked of money. He was certainly a "catch" in the eyes of most females. But he wasn't interested in other women. For some reason, he was stuck on Claire Caswell. Her face wouldn't leave him. He had locked in on it when he saw her at the masquerade ball. Those green eyes even the mask couldn't hide. Despite the fact she was an investigator hot on his trail, he saw an alluring innocence glowing in her eyes, and they had captured him totally.

He cleared his throat and spoke with purpose.

Say it with diamonds,
Say it with mink,
But never ever say it with ink.

He smiled and vowed, *"Never in ink!"* as he met his own eyes squarely in the reflective surface. "Diamonds and mink, but *never in ink."*

He imagined Claire Caswell opening the diminutive box containing the radiant diamond ring. And then the second gift—the mink muff. He thought her eyes must have glistened brilliantly at the sight of each. And certainly she would have assumed her dashing inamorato, Gaston Lombard, had sent both items to prove his undying love. But soon, very soon, she'd discover her Mr. Lombard hadn't been the sender. She'd realize someone else was enraptured by her essence. It would certainly get her thinking. And it would bother Lombard endlessly. Exactly what DiNetto wanted in both instances. It might even cause an argument between the two lovebirds—a rift that would serve his purposes nicely. Then he could make his move.

"One day soon perhaps. One day soon," he muttered.

He glanced at his wristwatch. His meeting was coming up quickly, and he needed to get a move on. He grabbed two boxes, placed them in a bag, and locked his room. He passed through the lobby in such a hurry that he didn't notice Claire Caswell sitting there.

GUY LOMBARD, aka Rudy Cotton, trailed behind DiNetto in full disguise. The investigator was about to raise the ante.

As DiNetto marched quickly down the street, Guy wondered why the man hadn't jumped into his flashy Ferrari to drive to his destination. He soon found out. DiNetto met a man at a quaint street-side café only two blocks from the hotel. The men shook hands, then disappeared inside for a short time before reappearing, each holding a cup of coffee. They sat down on metal chairs placed next to a sidewalk table. Keeping out of sight but within earshot, Guy watched the interaction with interest from across the street.

The two men shared an animated conversation, and before long DiNetto set two boxes on the table in front of the other man.

"Take a look at these. I have more than the two," DiNetto said. "I have ten."

The man opened each box and peered inside. He gasped. After what seemed an inordinately long amount of time, Guy observed the man nodding slowly.

"Exquisite," he said. "Divine, actually." Extreme surprise radiated from his expression. Guy couldn't hear the man's words, but his face revealed everything.

"Where did you find these?" the man asked DiNetto.

DiNetto ignored the question. "Interested or not? I'll make you an offer you can't turn down. I'm selling the ten as a package deal— or there is no deal. One price for the lot." DiNetto's frosty eyes bore deeply into the other man's. "Others are bidding too. Do not hesitate. Give me your best price. One bid only."

"I will think it over and get back to you by tomorrow morning," the man said. "It's a definite possibility. These will no doubt turn one day for a great profit, especially ten together."

"I'm telling you, others are interested. Don't delay your decision."

"I will need some authenticity documentation on these, of course," the man said.

"Of course," DiNetto echoed. "I have all of that and will deliver it at the time of sale."

The men shook hands and departed, each setting off in a different direction. Guy crossed the street and fell in a comfortable distance behind DiNetto. After a few minutes of shadowing him, Guy spoke out loudly. It was time to make a calculated and bold move.

"Mr. DiNetto, is that you?" As Guy approached, he said, "We met at the hotel bar yesterday. I'm out partaking in my daily walk, and I thought that was you up ahead."

DiNetto turned, stopped in his tracks, and waited for Rudy Cotton to catch up to him.

"*Ciao*, Mr. Rudy," DiNetto said. "Or should I say *bonjour,* as we are in France."

"*Bonjour,* Mr. DiNetto—and *ciao,*" Guy said. "Happy to see you again."

"You are? Why?" DiNetto asked.

The two men talked as they walked.

"I've been thinking about our meeting. You too seem like a man of means," Guy began. "I'm wondering if destiny brought us together. You see, I have a sizable annuity that just reached its term, and I have money to invest. I'm a private person. I like to be left alone for the most part, as you probably guessed. I tend to avoid people, so I'm afraid I'm a bit out of touch with my investment advisors in the US." He paused. "I thought you could probably recommend a proper investment. I have been known to take risks for substantial growth, and I like diversity."

DiNetto thought quickly. While he had a handful of potential purchasers in the wings for what he was selling, he didn't yet have a confirmed buyer who'd come up with the cash. "Funny you should ask," DiNetto said. "I do have something to show you."

He had checked out this Alexander Rudy Cotton and discovered he was an extremely wealthy man—heir to a robust family fortune. Rich. Eccentric. And a loner, as Rudy described himself. A man from the US who lived alone in the south of France. The perfect target to bring his scheme to conclusion.

"How about we have some dinner tonight, Rudy? And wine. I'll show you what I have in mind. You might be interested," DiNetto said. "I'd like to know you better. I don't give out my investment advice to just anyone." He chuckled.

"Great. How about eight o'clock tonight in the outdoor restaurant at our hotel?"

"Eight it is. I look forward to seeing you then."

Their rooms at the château were located on different levels, and that made it easy for Guy to make his way back to his and Claire's room without DiNetto observing him.

Claire was anxiously awaiting Guy's return.

He quickly filled her in on what had transpired and his dinner plan.

"Tonight's the night. We'll know what's in those boxes tonight," he said.

"Finally," Claire said.

She warned him to be particularly cautious that evening and assured him she'd be watching from the shadows. "When the time is right—after it gets dark and after you've had a head start discussing the investment with DiNetto—I'll hide near the green florescent orb. That way, I can observe the two of you," she said. "I'll stay out of sight, but you'll know I'm there."

THE TWO took a nap, showered, and dressed for the evening. This was the big night. The one they'd been waiting for. They would solve the mystery of the contents of the boxes at last—and conclusively figure out DiNetto's grandiose scheme. It was tonight . . . or never. Tomorrow they were driving north to Paris and catching a flight home.

Guy looked into the mirror. He was surprised at just how different he actually looked. It was his best disguise yet. The shaved head was a big part of it, but it was the combination of all the elements. He hardly even recognized himself. He'd fallen effortlessly into the role of wealthy recluse Rudy Cotton, talking in a low tone whenever he became him.

"I'm rather enjoying this disguise," he said. "It's easy to be someone else."

"Never be overconfident," Claire told him. "That's when you can slip up. Things can always go wrong."

She glanced at her cell phone. It was dead. So was Guy's. They'd forgotten to charge them the night before. She plugged both in.

30

CLAIRE FELT STRESSED. Was she throwing Guy to the wolves? Usually they pursued criminals together. But tonight Guy would operate solo. And that worried her. He was tough—and capable through and through. There was no doubt about that. But DiNetto was a different kind of criminal. He was ruthless, manipulative, clever, and astute. He'd been around the block and back again many times over, and he couldn't be underestimated. He was a man who could and would buy any type of assistance he needed. On top of that, she believed he was a cold-blooded killer responsible for a number of deaths.

She thought about the young woman in the mink wrap, who met with an early death at La Scala. If Claire were a betting woman, she'd put her money on DiNetto having given the woman the mink wrap—and a deadly push.

Instantly, her jaw dropped and she froze. Mink. DiNetto

did send her the mink muff! It had to be him. How strange, she thought. She wondered about his motive. What did mink represent to DiNetto? And what about the diamond ring? Did he send her that too? She couldn't be sure. Not yet. While she still hoped upon hope Guy had sent the gorgeous ring, she didn't know with certainty at this point. The possibility that it might have come from DiNetto sickened her.

Her thoughts returned to Guy. She looked at her watch. He'd be meeting DiNetto just about now. Soon it would be time to slip outside and inconspicuously make her way toward the green globe light to lie in wait. She'd be ready if Guy needed her. She waited another ten minutes, grabbed her binoculars, and left the room.

From her hiding place, she could see the two men sitting at a table not far away from other diners. At first, it appeared they were making small talk. Then DiNetto stood.

"I want to go elsewhere for dinner," he announced. "There are too many ears nearby."

"We could do that," Guy said. "Although I must admit, I'm partial to the food here. That's the main reason I live here."

His subtle prodding to stay did not prove persuasive.

"No! We're leaving! We'll take my car."

Looking though the binoculars, Claire deduced what was happening. And she didn't like it. This would mean Guy would be alone with DiNetto wherever he decided to take him. She watched the situation with growing angst, unable to think of a way to help. She didn't dare follow behind in the white Range Rover, as it would be too obvious and put Guy in greater danger.

Guy trailed behind DiNetto as they made their way to his car in the distant outdoor parking lot. Claire observed Guy turn around twice and glance in her direction. She had a healthy fear of DiNetto and what he was capable of, should he discover the true identity of

Rudy Cotton. She quickly moved to the eating area, where she could better see the private parking lot, and her eyes trailed the two men as they walked to DiNetto's Ferrari. Guy got into the passenger seat. DiNetto walked a few steps away from the car, pulled out his cell phone, and made a short call before getting in behind the wheel.

The roar of the vehicle's mighty engine drew all diners' eyes toward the famous Italian automobile as DiNetto drove it from the grounds and it disappeared into the night.

Claire sat down and ordered a light dinner. She wouldn't breathe easy again until Guy walked back into the room. And she knew she could be in for a long wait. She glanced at her watch.

DiNetto turned onto the main road and drove for quite a distance before he pulled into a lot adjacent to a small French restaurant. There were only three other cars in the lot.

"We'll eat here," he announced, maintaining the control. "It's never crowded."

"Looks like an excellent choice," Guy said, using an unusually bold voice for Rudy.

"I have a surprise for you, Rudy," DiNetto said. "Come along."

The men entered the restaurant, were seated at a quiet table with four chairs, and began to peruse the menus.

Before long, two women dressed provocatively and wearing heavy makeup approached the table. The scent of cheap perfume filled the air.

"Hello," the auburn-haired woman said in an alluring voice. "Are we late?" She sat down next to DiNetto.

"No. Actually, you're right on time." He looked over at Guy. "Rudy, these ladies are my surprise for you! I'd like you to meet Gigi." The woman sitting next to DiNetto extended her hand toward Guy. The two shook hands.

"Pleased to make your acquaintance, Rudy," she said.

"And this is her friend, Josie," DiNetto said. The woman with a head full of short black curls thrust her hand toward Guy.

"You are kind of cute," she giggled. She slid into the chair next to him.

"Let's order, ladies. Then we'll get on with other things," DiNetto commanded.

A server appeared, and DiNetto ordered two bottles of expensive red wine for the table. All four ordered salads and entrées.

Guy knew what DiNetto had planned—and he wanted out.

"Can we speak alone?" Guy asked DiNetto. "Now, please!"

The men excused themselves and walked outside.

"What the hell's going on?" Guy yelled. "This was to be a business dinner tonight to discuss investments. I told you, I don't like being around people much, and I meant what I said. Now you bring *them* to me?"

"Relax, Rudy. It's okay. You enjoy this evening, and then tomorrow we'll talk business."

Shit, Guy thought. How do I get out of this? He quickly decided on a plan.

"I'm not going to repeat myself, DiNetto," he fumed. "I'm not interested in some floozy whore. If that's your preference, so be it. It's not mine. And furthermore, I resent you attempting to force your preferences on me. You've got some nerve! Either the ladies go, or I do! The choice is yours. What will it be?"

"Chill out, Rudy. You certainly ruined my plans for the evening. But no worries. We'll just have dinner together, and then the ladies will leave. Think you can handle that?"

"Very well," Guy said. "But I don't much care for it. I told you, I'm a private person. You need to honor that."

"By the way, you passed the test," DiNetto said, suddenly looking strangely relieved.

"*What* test?" Guy asked.

"If you'd wanted more than just a handshake with those women, I never would have done business with you."

They returned to the table, dined, then DiNetto waved the women off.

"Now," he said, "let's get on with it."

For a time, the two men discussed investments. Seeing as both were amply schooled in the area, the conversation carried on smoothly.

"What are you interested in at this time?" DiNetto asked.

"I'm not sure," Guy said. "I'm open, I guess. Something different. Something I haven't delved into before. An investment that will excite me."

"Then I think I have just the thing for you." He paused. "But I can't show you until tomorrow morning. This isn't the place to bring out the merchandise." He raised an eyebrow. "I can assure you, it's an intriguing prospect, though."

"You're going to keep me in suspense another day?" Guy asked. "I'd like to know now."

"I'll show you tomorrow morning. Tomorrow is soon enough. Then you can make your decision in the daylight. We will meet at 8:45 sharp, just outside the front entrance. We'll walk, stop for coffee, and then you'll see the goods."

"This seems very mysterious. You've definitely piqued my curiosity."

DiNetto drove back to the hotel and shook hands with Guy.

AS GUY stepped into the room, he breathed a heavy sigh of relief.

"What a night, Claire," he said. He drew her into his strong arms and held on tightly. He placed a long kiss on her waiting lips.

"I was really worried about you. Glad you're okay. Tell me what happened."

They slipped under the covers, but didn't talk right away.

Day twelve
Montpellier to Paris, France

MORNING ARRIVED. The investigators dressed at the break of dawn for their final day in France, then packed the duffel. They faced a six-and-three-quarter-hour drive to Paris's Charles de Gaulle Airport to catch the overnight flight to Miami, departing at 8:25 p.m. Considering the requirement to arrive at least two hours before an international flight, they had to depart the hotel no later than 11:30 a.m.—preferably by 11:00 to allow a little extra time. They had a lot to accomplish in a short time. It was now or never.

Guy was meeting DiNetto for an early breakfast and to see the goods. The investigators could barely wait.

"I'll call Massey while you're meeting with DiNetto," Claire said. "I need to fill him in."

Guy kissed her.

"Don't keep me waiting too long," she said. "I need to know what's in those boxes!"

"We'll know shortly." He disappeared through the doorway.

As planned, DiNetto was standing just outside the front doorway carrying a tote when Guy arrived.

The men greeted each other and started to walk.

DiNetto glanced around. He hadn't spotted the investigators lately, and that both puzzled him and made him nervous. What were the two Americans up to?

Guy adjusted the jaw insert with his tongue. While it did the trick to totally change his appearance, it was uncomfortable. He worried it might dislodge and pop out.

The two arrived at the coffee shop where DiNetto had met the man the day before. They went inside, ordered coffees, and carried the beverages to an outdoor table.

Petite cinnamon rolls were delivered on the house.

The men drank the java and sampled the warm-from-the-oven pastries.

"Doesn't get any better than this. I love these early mornings," DiNetto said. He inhaled the fresh air and looked around, absorbing the beautiful day.

"That's why I live here most of the time," Guy said. "*C'est très magnifique!*"

Guy was grateful Claire had taught him a few key French words and phrases. It strengthened his Rudy persona.

"Do you miss your family in the States?" DiNetto asked.

"No," Guy said decisively. "They only like me for my money. I don't miss them at all."

"Does it get lonely? Always being by yourself?" DiNetto asked.

"You seem very curious about my life," Guy said. "No. I'd rather spend time with myself than anyone else I know. Most other people aren't as interesting."

"Spoken like a genuine recluse," DiNetto said. "Personally, I like to be around others . . . mainly beautiful women." He chuckled.

"Well, to each his own. Now, are you going to show me this potential investment opportunity of yours or not? Seems like you enjoy keeping me on pins and needles."

"Okay, Rudy. Now that I have a French coffee under my belt, I'm ready to do business."

"Show me what you have."

DiNetto reached into the bag and pulled out a box. He set it before Guy.

"Take a look, Rudy Cotton."

He was getting his first good look at one of DiNetto's mysterious boxes. The box itself was a substantial object, beautifully crafted out of a light-colored lacquered wood. Guy grasped the cover and pulled it open. Immediately, he saw a silver plaque bearing the words "Officine Panerai" against a deep-brown velvet lining.

He told himself not to act overly excited, but he couldn't help but gawk. "May I hold it?" he asked. "What is it . . . exactly?"

"Yes, of course you can hold it. After you examine it, I'll tell you the specifics."

Guy spent several minutes looking at the piece, clearly vintage in nature.

"I'm guessing there's quite a story behind this," Guy said, a look of undeniable concentration written over his face.

"You can't possibly imagine."

Guy was clearly intrigued, but again tried not to overtly show it. "Tell me. I want to hear all about it. What's its value?" He glanced at his watch.

DiNetto smiled coyly. "Slow down. We have all the time in the world to talk. Let's not rush. I think we can do business, Mr. Cotton, but there's one catch."

DiNetto watched Guy's expressions, and for a moment, something about him seemed familiar.

31

DINETTO HAD GUY'S full attention.

"This is a vintage Panerai 6154. It's a watch that combines Italian design with Swiss technology. Panerai is famous for making watches for the Regia Marina, the Italian Royal Navy. These watches have a strong connection to the sea. Giovanni Panerai opened his first store and workshop in Florence in 1860. This is what is known: *only forty of this model were ever produced*," DiNetto emphasized. "Of the forty, only ten—or, more recently, twelve—are known to be in existence today, according to the world of watch collectors. In fact, collectors worldwide consider this watch to be among the most valuable and desirable of all the vintage Panerai models."

Astonishment etched Guy's face.

DiNetto pointed to the item. "Its long, thick leather strap was made to fit over a diving suit, and the watch is capable of long submersion in seawater. The original Officine Panerai company created and made this particular watch specifically for the Egyptian Navy. Probably in 1954. Hence its other name—Egiziano Piccolo, or 'the Little Egyptian.'

"This beauty is very large—forty-seven millimeters in diameter. Its case is thin—cushion style—but rugged. It was designed as a military tool, but with Italian influence. The case is made of stainless steel, and the domed crystal is made from Plexiglas. It has a screw-down crown that makes it water resistant. The case was ordered from Rolex, but possibly another manufacturer produced it and fitted it with a seventeen-jewel Rolex 618 movement." DiNetto paused. "Am I giving you too much information?"

"No," Guy said. "I'm fascinated. You said it's called the Little Egyptian. Did Panerai also make a larger version?"

"Very astute, Rudy. Yes, Panerai later produced a model 2/56 for the Egyptian Navy that was sixty millimeters. It was known as the Egiziano Grosso."

"Okay. Go on. Go on," Guy said.

"Panerai supplied the dials of the Little Egyptian, and most of them were actually marked 'Radiomir Panerai.' The leather straps had a large trapezoidal buckle stamped 'GPF Mod Dep.' Radium paste was applied to the brass-plated dials, and numerals and dial markings were then cut out of an upper plate set atop the radium. They call it a sandwich dial."

DiNetto could see that Rudy Cotton was hooked and couldn't hide it.

"There's an interesting fact you should know about this watch," DiNetto continued. "Extreme fading has occurred to the dials of these watches over the many years. While they were originally black, the strong radioactivity of the Radiomir material in the sandwich dial bleached out the black and turned many of the dials a light shade of brown. Also the radium in the hands created bleached concentric circles around the dial. Look right here." He pointed them out. "That's how you know it's authentic."

"You weren't kidding about the tale connected to these watches. I see why they're highly collectible," Guy said.

"You should underscore the word *highly* when you put it with the word *collectible* in this case," DiNetto said. "Are you ready for this? Twenty years ago, this watch would have been worth approximately fifteen hundred dollars—because the primary value was in the Rolex movement. However, a couple years ago, a vintage 6154 Panerai sold in New York for a thumping $326,500 at a Christie's auction!"

Guy looked dazed. "I knew they had to be valuable, but I couldn't have guessed—"

"Well, there's more. Ten of these extremely rare watches were recently discovered in a secret hiding place. They'd been hidden away by relatives of a man once involved with the Egyptian Navy. Full documentation—a complete record of ownership—was also found for each individual watch."

DiNetto paused and stared into Guy's eyes. "*This is one of those ten watches.* It is an unbelievable find, Rudy! They've never been worn, but their dials and hands have aged due to the radioactive decay I told you about."

"I'm interested," Guy said.

"Well, you and a handful of others, I'm afraid. I was hired to sell these watches as a single lot to a collector who can appreciate them. It's a condition of purchase coming directly from the sellers. Those who found this collection—still not publicly believed to exist—have asked me to locate a proper collector to purchase all ten as a set. I've been tasked with locating someone who will hold this precious collection close to his or her heart. This is a top-secret opportunity, Rudy, and must remain that way forever. It can never, under any circumstances, be discussed with anyone.

"I'm known to wear the latest and most expensive Panerai watches. That's why the owners contacted me, and I agreed to sell the collection on their behalf. They researched who has a love of Panerai watches and also has connections with heavy-hitter collectors. Apparently my name came up frequently, and the sellers contacted me in Miami. And I agreed to do it."

DiNetto raised his brows. "It's a heavy burden. I won't let this collection go to just anyone with money to burn. I want the purchaser to relish and enjoy with gusto these rare, priceless pieces. To hold them in a safe place, away from the prying eyes of the rest of the world, to be quietly maintained . . . until some day when they are again sold under the radar as a lot to another honorable purchaser who will agree to secret them away and keep them secure. That's a vital part of the terms of purchase—"

"What are you asking for the collection?" Guy cut in, acting unable to be put off any longer.

"Calculate the value of the ten pieces—keeping in mind what one recently brought at the Christie's auction—and then give me your best offer. You'll have only one chance to tell me your best price. Select others will also be doing the same. I'll make my decision based on the top offer. Fair enough?"

"All is fair in love, war, and the purchase of a rare lot of priceless vintage Panerai watches," Guy said. "I want these in my portfolio, but I'll have to check them out first. I am a born skeptic, if nothing else." He grinned.

"But of course. I'll give you the name of a man who worked on these original pieces in the mid-1950s. He is in his eighties now and has authenticated all ten of these watches for me. His name is Franco Nef, and he still lives in Neuchâtel, where the watches were produced. You can contact him directly to verify." DiNetto wrote the name and contact number for Mr. Nef and handed it to Guy.

The men shook hands.

They walked back to the hotel and parted company. Guy arranged to meet DiNetto in an hour with his decision.

CLAIRE ANXIOUSLY paced from one corner of the room to another, awaiting Guy's return. When he finally walked in, she couldn't contain her exuberance. "Tell me everything! I can't wait another minute!"

"*Rare watches*—the likes of which I've never seen before! There are ten of them. Timepieces so rare and over-the-top expensive that only the wealthiest of the wealthy could ever own them. I held one in my hand, and I didn't want to give it back. For those few moments, I felt like royalty. The quality exceeds anything in my wildest imaginings, and the story that goes with them is remarkable."

He quickly summarized DiNetto's history of the watches.

"So what's the scam?" Claire asked. "DiNetto's covertly showing exquisite vintage watches to prospective wealthy buyers. Are they the real thing? Fakes? Knockoffs? What?"

"According to DiNetto, they're real. Recently discovered in a secret cache. And he's been engaged to sell undercover to a worthy buyer who will keep the purchase quiet so the recently discovered find remains safe."

"Something doesn't sound right to me," Claire said. "Let's call the number DiNetto gave you and talk to the man who supposedly made some of the original forty watches and verified that these ten are part of those. We may learn a lot." She looked at her wristwatch. "We're running out of time."

GUY USED the room phone and placed it on speaker mode. Together, the two investigators questioned Mr. Nef. When the call ended, they had the information they needed.

"Just as I suspected," Claire said.

The sleuths brainstormed.

Claire walked to the window, held back the swirl-patterned drapery, and peered outside. "Let's go over the plan. You'll meet up with DiNetto in a few minutes and give him a high number." She turned her head around and looked at Guy. "You'll have to persuade him to sell the watches to *you*." She hesitated and scanned the grounds again. "Make him an offer. Double their value. If the lot is worth over three million dollars, offer him over six million. Indicate you want the collection at any price."

"He can't turn away from that offer," Guy said.

"Precisely."

"I'll be ready."

"DiNetto is set to return to the States today. Tell him you're traveling back today as well, to transact some other business. You'll need to make sure the transaction ties itself up back in Miami— that payment is transferred in the US." She turned her gaze to him, eyeing him for a reaction, but he didn't flinch. "That way, the fraud will occur in Miami-Dade County and within Sergeant Massey's jurisdiction. He wants to make the collar—he's put so much time into this case. And he made me promise we'd be on the plane this evening, no matter what. So time is short."

"We'll be ready to leave at eleven, or close to it," Guy said. "You have my word. Leave it to me." His face looked agonized. The pressure of the approaching climax of their investigation suddenly fell squarely and weightily on his shoulders.

"*This is unbelievable!*" Claire suddenly blurted as she glanced outside. "Guess who just sauntered up to DiNetto and is standing by his Ferrari in the parking lot? And the two of them are engaging in serious conversation, if I'm reading their body language correctly."

Guy dashed to the window, stood directly behind Claire, and looked out. "I wouldn't believe it if I wasn't seeing this with my own eyes. Dammit, Claire—here he is again! *Why*? What is the bloody connection between them?"

"Not sure, but it's about time we find out," she said. "Do you think Bubbiano will recognize you in your latest disguise, *Rudy*?"

"Not a chance." He turned and looked into the mirror above the dresser. "I'm beginning to actually like this getup. It's a whole new me." He grinned his famous grin. "Actually, I think I've half convinced myself I'm Rudy Cotton."

"Well, don't get too used to it," Claire said. "I'd like the real Guy to come back permanently as soon as this is over." She forced a smile. "Play with Bubbiano a bit before you submit your offer. See if you can't lure him into a bidding war for the pieces—that is, if it turns out he's one of the interested buyers. Assess his credibility. That might tell us if he's a bona fide buyer, in on the scam with DiNetto, or a cop going after a scam artist." She continued to watch the scene as it unfolded before her eyes. "Remember, Bubbiano had up-close-and-personal contact with DiNetto in Milan, then followed him to Neuchâtel, showed up in Cannes, and now we see him talking to DiNetto in Montpellier. For all we know, he may have been in Porto Venere and Portofino, but we just didn't see him. He probably was. We know he rented the masquerade ball costume we believe DiNetto wore that evening. I don't believe in coincidences. We need to figure out his role in this thing in a hurry."

"I agree," Guy said. "And in Cannes, we witnessed Bubbiano and DiNetto together showing boxes to the two men they met."

"I haven't forgotten that either."

Claire stared straight ahead for several minutes. "Be careful,

Guy. DiNetto is in the final lap of his race. He planned things carefully all along the way. He's put in lots of time and energy." The look in her eyes became deadly serious. "He could become dangerous if an obstacle blocks his path to the finish line."

"I'll watch my back," Guy said.

"Please use *extreme* caution." The expression on her face sent chills ricocheting throughout his body. "You'll have to make up a story about your financial situation to tell DiNetto. Maybe say you need to return to the US to make certain the money is immediately available from the annuity. Tell him you can pay him upon arriving in the States—maybe even at the Miami International Airport. Yeah, tell him your trustees will meet you at the airport when you land. That's believable. Say the trustees will accept only a signature in person for a transfer of this magnitude, or something to that effect. Sergeant Massey will be at the airport gate, in the background, as you and DiNetto step from the plane. He'll witness the transaction—the exchange of money for the goods purchased. Then his officers will storm in and nab him. And collect the watches from his checked luggage."

"DiNetto is still operating under the assumption he's selling the collection to an unsuspecting buyer—*me*—in the hopes I'll never become the wiser," Guy said. "That I'll never learn the truth. And if the truth were to come out at some point, no doubt DiNetto would simply deny he knew anything about it. He'll swear he thought the watches were the real things. What DiNetto doesn't know is that we're on to him. We know the truth."

Guy paused to catch his breath, then continued, "We have a key witness—Franco Nef—who has agreed to expose the entire scam from start to finish. A man who participated in the con, but now wishes to clear his guilty conscience."

"What about Bubbiano? Which side is he on?" Claire asked.

32

CLAIRE HAD BEEN lying low since Guy took on his latest disguise. DiNetto's seeing the two investigators together would definitely have blown Guy's cover—and hers. She was restless and anxious to resolve the case. And they were close now. Soon she and Guy would drive to Paris and board the plane that would take them home. What could possibly go wrong? But just when she started to feel hopeful it would all go smoothly, the little voice inside her warned: *You have no idea what is coming, Claire Caswell. Be vigilant! Be wary!*

IT WAS time for Guy to rendezvous with DiNetto. He walked down the wide, primitive stone steps leading from the room, overly aware with each step what would soon be expected of him. His mind was on high alert. He stepped outside and walked toward the bar, but didn't spot DiNetto sitting there. Glancing at his watch, he sat down on a stool and ordered a Perrier with lime. As he sipped the cool beverage, he reviewed exactly what he had to accomplish. He was grateful for a few moments to do just that. Deep in thought, he suddenly became aware that someone had sat down next to him. When he looked up, he expected to see DiNetto. Instead, it was Officer Bubbiano.

"I am to show you the watches a final time, Mr. Cotton," Bubbiano said in a low tone. Guy noticed several boxes sitting in a large canvas bag at his feet. "Let's move over to a more private table. Shall we?"

It appeared Bubbiano didn't recognize Guy Lombard in his Rudy Cotton disguise.

"Yes, we shall," Guy said.

A LIGHT rapping on the hotel room door summoned Claire. She walked to the door and said, "Guy? Is that you?" She assumed he had returned for some reason.

She heard a muffled, "Uh-huh."

She opened the door a couple inches to peer out, and just as she did, DiNetto jammed his shoe into the opening and forced his way in. In a flash, he locked the door behind him and turned to face Claire.

"Ms. Caswell, I've come to see you," he said. "Just you and me." He wore a wolfish look.

As he viewed her up close, he realized she was even more beautiful than he'd thought—her eyes greener and more translucent, and her skin smoother.

He stepped closer to her, and she stepped back.

"I'll scream!" she warned boldly. "You need to leave this room at once!"

"If you scream, my dear Claire Caswell, your precious Gaston Lombard—or should I say, your precious *Rudy Cotton*—will be killed. It's as simple as that." His tone left no room to misinterpret his message. As she looked at him, he took on a gravely sinister demeanor, and at once she knew his intent.

"Did you really think you'd fool me with that newest disguise? I'll admit this one was better than the others, and it did fool me for quite a while. But in the end, I saw through it. There was something in his expressions that finally tipped me off."

A look of despair appeared on her face.

"Now I think it's time we got to know each other better. Don't you agree, Claire?" He moved in even closer. "I've dreamed of this moment. And I've waited a long time. Don't disappoint me."

He lunged toward her, grabbing her waist with one large hand and covering her mouth with the other. He threw her down onto the bed and landed on top of her with all his weight.

She gasped for air and struggled violently.

"Get off of me!" she screamed, but her voice was nearly inaudible, muffled by his oversized palm.

He removed his hand from her mouth and thrust his lips onto hers. She moved slightly away from him and bit down on his lower lip with all her strength, immediately drawing blood.

Despite the pain, DiNetto remained eerily calm, single-mindedly intent on his goal. He raised his head up an inch and wiped away the steady stream of blood flowing from his lip.

"That wasn't nice, Ms. Caswell," he said. "I'm afraid you'll have to pay for what you've done. And just think, you haven't even properly thanked me for the gifts I sent you."

She was filled with disgust and nearly overwhelming fear. "You sent the ring and the mink muff? You *no-good*—" She wiggled madly to get free from his weight holding her down. "You revolt me!" But her words were only muffled grunts. She continued to struggle as all color drained from her face. She saw no way out.

"So feisty," he whispered. "I love it. Gaston Lombard could never buy you a ring of that quality! You need to be with me. Only I am worthy of your love."

She could feel his breath on her face.

"Get off of me!" she desperately tried to blurt out. "You're delusional! I want nothing to do with you!"

DiNetto caught the gist.

"Then you know the consequences, Ms. Caswell." Using one hand, he reached into his pants pocket and pulled out his cell phone. As he did, Claire saw a tiny flash as something else fell out. It was the faux diamond she had placed on her lower lip at the masquerade ball—the diamond the jester had ripped from her. So it had been DiNetto!

He pushed a button on his phone and said, "Do it!"

He looked into Claire's eyes. "The choice was yours."

Her eyes showed torment. She screamed a stifled, "*No!*"

DiNetto immediately pressed his hand even harder over her mouth.

With his other hand, he unzipped his pants.

ALL OF a sudden, the door swung wide open as Guy and Officer Bubbiano burst in and charged toward the bed.

Claire looked up with tear-filled eyes as Bubbiano and Guy yanked DiNetto off of her. Bubbiano drew a fist back with the intent of laying it squarely on DiNetto's face.

"Allow me," Guy said. "This needs to come from me."

He spun DiNetto around viciously and punched him squarely in the face with such force that his jaw cracked. "*You son of a bitch!*"

Guy roared. "You place a hand on her ever again, and it will be the last move you ever make. *Capisci?*"

Bubbiano pulled DiNetto's arms to his back and slapped hand-cuffs firmly around his wrists, making certain they were on extra tight. DiNetto's lip continued to bleed, and the left side of his face started to swell. He crumpled to the ground.

Guy rushed to Claire, helping her gently from the bed. "Are you okay?"

"Yes," she said, trying to steady her shaking voice. "I'll be all right—thankfully." She looked at Guy and then at Officer Bubbiano. "You came just in time. But how?"

"I must apologize for everything you have been through since coming to Europe, Ms. Caswell," Bubbiano said. "I have kept my eyes on you and Mr. Lombard the best I could, but sometimes I lost track of you for a time. My force and I, personally, have been after this thug for a long time." He nodded toward DiNetto. "I have already filled Mr. Lombard in. We will transport him back to Italy to stand trial for multiple murders and one of the most elaborate counterfeiting schemes Italy has ever seen. We know all about it and have evidence to support each murder connected to him."

He looked at the investigators gratefully. "Thank you both for helping bring this case to a head. Catching DiNetto red-handed, holding the evidence in this watch scam, was the last thing we needed to nail his coffin shut.

"Just think—DiNetto hired a hit man to shoot at your taxi and scare you off when you first arrived in Milan. But instead, the taxi driver lost his life, and so did the bicyclist. Then DiNetto murdered the hit man as payment for his sloppy work. And the young woman in the theater, she probably never realized he had drugged her wine at dinner. Poor thing was probably in the wrong place at the wrong time and heard something she should not have. These murders and the horrific things he did to the two of you—especially to you, Claire—were all connected to his scam to sell the counterfeit Panerai watches. He had to get you off his trail."

Bubbiano shook his head. "He will pay for it tenfold." He looked off into the distance as if reliving his work on the case. "We've tailed him for months, tapped his phone, and have built a strong case. Lots of investigative work behind the scenes.

"I'll let Sergeant Massey know we have him. He knew DiNetto was up to something nefarious; he just did not know how bad it was. We have been working together on this case for some time. Sergeant Massey and I go way back."

"Oh, we weren't made aware of that," Claire said with some surprise.

Bubbiano smiled slightly. "I mustn't keep you any longer. Safe travels today. I hope the next time you come to Europe it will be under different circumstances. It really is a wonderful place to visit."

"Oh, there's one more thing," Claire said. She ran to retrieve her backpack, reached in, and pulled out a small box. Then she picked up a larger box on a chair. "These belong to DiNetto. I don't want the diamond ring or the mink muff." She handed Bubbiano both items. Guy glanced her way quizzically, and she knew she'd soon be explaining the gift of the diamond ring to him.

Bubbiano took the items from Claire, then pulled DiNetto to his feet and led him from the room, manhandling him roughly.

As soon as the door closed, Guy pulled Claire into his arms. "Time to go home, Claire. You've been through a lot on this case." He kissed her gently on the cheek and on her lips, and he held her tightly.

She wept.

After a couple minutes, she suddenly broke free.

"Something is bothering me," she said. "How would Bubbiano

know the woman who fell from the box at La Scala had been drugged at dinner? An autopsy wasn't conducted. He couldn't have known that unless—"

She hurried to the window. Bubbiano and DiNetto were nearly out of sight when she spotted them. But as she looked out, to her shock, she saw Bubbiano walking next to DiNetto arm in arm. The two men were laughing, and DiNetto's wrists were no longer cuffed.

"Guy, we've been had!" The look on her face said without words the horror she felt.

She grabbed her cell, now fully recharged, and turned it on. Suddenly, she saw urgent texts and calls from Jin and also Sergeant Massey. Guy turned his phone on and saw similar messages. She quickly dialed Massey's cell number and let him know what had just transpired. "They're getting away," she said, "as we speak! We need to do something fast."

Instantly, a plan hatched.

"I'll contact the Italian border police and the Milan police department to inform them of the situation," Massey said. "We have the evidence they need now. They'll apprehend them when they cross the Italian border. When I'm done making those calls, I'll call you back. Hang tight."

Claire and Guy simultaneously glanced at their watches.

"We have to leave in twenty minutes," Guy said, "or we'll never make it to Paris on time for our flight."

They discussed the fates of Bubbiano and DiNetto as they waited for Massey's call. They knew the pair was racing back to Milan in DiNetto's Ferrari. When the fancy Italian sports car crossed the border into Italy, they also knew police cars would swarm in and pull it over. Both Bubbiano and DiNetto would be placed under arrest on the spot. Separate trials would be held in the matter, unless the men confessed to the crimes. Either way, lengthy sentences in an

Italian prison would result for both men. In all probability, Franco Nef, the watch counterfeiter, would testify for the prosecution in the trial and return all money earned. In recognition of his cooperation, he would receive a light sentence in Switzerland for his part in the scheme, or possibly just probation. Sergeant Massey's force would seize DiNetto's unprotected assets in Miami Beach, and the felon's bank accounts in the US would be frozen.

"They'll both be tried for the murders and the counterfeit watch scheme. Neither will see the light of day again," Guy said.

Claire's cell rang. It was Massey.

"Everything's been arranged. They'll be picked up and then jailed pending trial or resolution. I'm not surprised Bubbiano is involved," he said. "I tried to use him as our European liaison throughout our investigation of DiNetto, but he seemed to be dragging his feet the entire time. He professed cooperation, but it was never forthcoming. I had notified Milan's chief of police of my observations and hunches regarding Bubbiano, and the force's higher-ups have been quietly investigating him. I couldn't say anything to you earlier. I couldn't let you do anything to tip Bubbiano that his actions were under scrutiny. It might have blown the whole investigation. Since we spoke earlier, I did some checking. Bubbiano and DiNetto were childhood friends in Turin. Looks like they planned the Panerai scheme together. Both expected to be on easy street as soon as an unwitting buyer could be found.

"My other sources at the Milan police department, higher up than Bubbiano, had tapped Bubbiano's cell phone. They suspected he was dirty. They just told me he and DiNetto had secured a man in the US willing to buy the lot at a price well surpassing three million dollars. It would have happened in a couple days. They concocted the elaborate story of the recent find of the ten watches, then paid one of the original watchmakers to create the counterfeits. Quite a plan, I'd say. Bubbiano and DiNetto—once he arrived in Italy—have been under surveillance by the Milan police department for the last ten days. They have plenty to put them away: surveillance tapes, photographs, phone recordings, forensic evidence, et cetera, et cetera.

"Oh, and there was a dirty cop on my force for some time too. Important information kept leaking to the press. Confidential information was being betrayed, and felony cases were put in jeopardy. Several were lost because of the breaches. My reputation was on the line. I tried to handle it in-house, but to no avail. Then, unbeknownst to me, one of my new officers, Figg, hired your firm to ferret out the culprit.

"Your new assistant, Jin Ikeda, did an outstanding job. He discovered that the department's leaky faucet was Officer Cane Dougan. And you'll never believe this—Dougan was also feeding DiNetto whatever he could glean from my handwritten log about your investigation in Europe. At first DiNetto blackmailed Dougan to get the information, but then he just paid the greedy worm. Anyway, the upshot is that Dougan was on DiNetto's payroll willingly. Jin found written proof of it all. That's why he's been trying desperately to reach you. He believed you two were in considerable danger."

"No wonder DiNetto always seemed to know our comings and goings," Claire said. "And our disguises. But Jin never actually mentioned he was *investigating* a new case."

"You should know that Dougan's been arrested and is sitting in jail, thanks to your new associate." He paused. "Say, when do the two of you need to leave for Paris to make your flight?"

Claire looked at her watch. "Now," she said. "I'll call you when we're back. And I have some chocolate bars from Neuchâtel to drop off for you!"

"Oh, one more thing," the sergeant said. "Good work! I know I was a little rough on you that one time we talked, but . . . "

"I understand," Claire said graciously. "You've been under considerable stress. We look forward to seeing you when we return."

The sleuths quickly gathered their belongings without a minute to spare.

"All's well that ends well," Guy said, exhibiting his famous grin. He locked the room door behind them.

"Wait until I fill you in on what Jin did for a new client," Claire said. "You won't believe it!"

On the drive to Paris, Claire and Guy called Jin and listened to his version of the tale. Frantic at first, he calmed down slightly when he heard DiNetto would soon be arrested.

"You did a great job, Jin," Guy told him. "We want to hear every detail when we get home."

Claire was deep in thought. She closed her eyes and imagined how the diamond ring had looked and felt on her finger. Even though it hadn't been from Guy, she knew he'd buy her one—if she'd only say yes to his question. She remained torn.

The sleuths arrived at the airport in Paris just in time. They dropped off the rental car, checked in, ate a snack, and boarded the plane at the appointed time. They both fell asleep shortly after takeoff and remained that way until they landed in Miami—Claire resting her head on Guy's shoulder, Guy holding Claire's hand, and both utterly exhausted from the case that had taken them to Europe.

Claire received two texts from Massey on the flight home, but she didn't see them until they landed. The first read: "When the Ferrari crossed the border into Italy, unmarked cars zoomed in and arrested Bubbiano and DiNetto on the spot. The ten fake watches were seized, along with the forged records of ownership and authentication, and the Ferrari was confiscated, as it was used in the commitment of a crime." She shook her head and smiled when she read the second: "Also, I was just promoted. It's **Captain** Massey now, thanks to the two of you."

SITTING IN jail, humiliated beyond measure, DiNetto daydreamed about pouring himself a tall shot of AVIV. If the smooth vodka could trickle down his throat, and warm his inner being, he'd feel good about himself again. It may not happen for a long time, but he would wait. AVIV was worth the wait.

He closed his eyes. Claire Caswell had gotten under his skin, and she, together with the apparently omnipresent Gaston Lombard, had been his demise. He wouldn't forget they had taken him down. Where he was going, he'd have a lot of time to think about things— and to devise his revenge. He took in a deep breath and exhaled slowly. He loved and hated that woman.

LIKE THE phoenix, he would rise again. Another cycle was coming down the road. As he let his head rest on the concrete wall of the holding cell, he boldly recited the familiar stanza—his only family legacy:

Say it with diamonds,
Say it with mink,
But never ever say it with ink.

Never in ink!

Cast but a glance at riches, and they are gone,
for they will surely sprout wings
and fly off to the sky like an eagle.

Proverbs 23:5

My gratitude to Gary Friedell for his expert view

into the world of Panerai watches

and for his reference to

Vintage Panerai: The References

by Ralf Ehlers and Volker Wiegmann (2009).